Praise for Alex Beecroft's
Under the Hill: Bomber's Moon

"Beecroft's writing dazzles, brimming with lush descriptions of worldly and otherworldly landscapes, taut conflict, and two finely drawn romantic leads...readers will delight in every moment of their adventure."

~ *Publishers Weekly*

"This is quite simply a perfect story—no slow moments, no 'meh' characters, gorgeous writing, a complex and coherent plot.... Fantasy fans absolutely must pick up this book—and if you're not a fantasy fan, I urge you to get it anyway—you won't be disappointed."

~ *Reviews by Jessewave*

Look for these titles by
Alex Beecroft

Now Available:

Captain's Surrender
Shining in the Sun

Under the Hill
Bomber's Moon
Dogfighters

Under the Hill: Bomber's Moon

Alex Beecroft

SAMHAIN
PUBLISHING

Samhain Publishing, Ltd.
11821 Mason Montgomery Road, 4B
Cincinnati, OH 45249
www.samhainpublishing.com

Under the Hill: Bomber's Moon
Copyright © 2013 by Alex Beecroft
Print ISBN: 978-1-60928-942-3
Digital ISBN: 978-1-60928-724-5

Editing by Anne Scott
Cover by Lyn Taylor

First Samhain Publishing, Ltd. electronic publication: April 2012
First Samhain Publishing, Ltd. print publication: March 2013

Dedication

To all those readers who loved the historicals but are taking a chance on me being able to write something a bit different. Thank you!

Chapter One

Ben bolted out of sleep, halfway to his feet before he realised he was awake. What was that noise? Something was wrong—he could feel it pressing under his breastbone. He thought he'd dreamed of a subterranean groan, felt again the rush of sticky re-breathed air and then the smoke. God! The smoke, pouring through the shattered windows of the train…

But this was his bedroom. Look, there—the alarm clock cast a faint green light on the claret duvet and gold silk coverlet, familiar as closed velvet curtains and his suit trousers hanging on the back of the bathroom door. 3:14 a.m.

His breathing calmed slowly. Was that what had woken him? Just another flashback? Or could there be an intruder downstairs?

Tiptoeing to the wardrobe, he eased open the mirrored door, slipped on his dressing gown and belted it, picking up the cricket bat that nestled among his shoes. The closing door showed him his determined scowl—not very convincing on a face that looked as nervous and skinny as a whippet's. Licking his lips, weapon raised, he seized the handle of his bedroom door, eased it down.

And the sound came again. All the doors in the house fluttered against their frames, the ground beneath him groaned, tiles on the roof above shifting with a ceramic clatter. A crash in the bathroom as the toothbrush holder fell into the sink. He jumped, crying out in revulsion when the floor shuddered and the carpet rippled beneath his bare feet as if stuffed with snakes.

Earthquake! An earthquake in Bakewell? Home of well dressing and famous for pudding? The sheer ludicrousness of the idea flashed through his mind even as he raced down the stairs. You... What did you do in an earthquake? Stand under a door lintel, wasn't it?

As he reached the living room, it happened again. He clutched at the back of the sofa while the entire house raised itself into the air and fell jarringly down with an impact that threw him against the wall. Bricks moving beneath his fingers, he pulled himself along the still-drying wallpaper into the hall, flung open the front door.

There was blackness outside—the streetlamps all guttered out—and silence, a silence so profound that the pressure began again inside his throat. It was so much like being buried underground. As he strained his ears for something friendly—a barking dog, a car alarm—a wind drove up from the Wye, filling his ears with whispering.

No stars shone above. But in the neighbour's windows, he could see something silver reflected, something that moved with liquid grace.

No way!

The curve of a horse's neck traced in quicksilver reflected in a driving mirror. A stamping hoof—drawn out of lines of living frost and spider web—splashed in a puddle. Drops spattered cold over his bare ankles.

Coming up from the river, across the bridge, up the sleeping suburban street they rode, knights and ladies. Glimmering, insubstantial shreds of banners floated above them like icy mist. Harps in their hands, hawks on their fists, and now he could hear the music; it was faint, far away, *wrong* as the feeling that had driven him out of bed. Alien and beautiful as the moons of Saturn.

"No way!"

He clapped both hands over his mouth, but it was too late. The words were out, full of blood and earth and inappropriate, human coarseness. Their heads turned. He caught a glimpse of armour, shadows and silver, as one of the knights reined in his horse, glided close, bending down.

The creature smelled of cool night air. Its inky gaze raked over Ben from head to toe, like being gently stroked with the leaves of nettles, a million tiny electric shocks. His skin crawled with the prickle of it, ecstatic and unbearable, and he gasped, held on the point of a pin between violent denial and begging it to do more.

Long platinum hair slid forward over a face drawn in strokes of starlight. "Which eye do you see me with?"

"I..." croaked Ben, his mouth desiccated, his lungs labouring. "What? I..."

Something in the garden—something huge, covered in spikes, lifted up the house, foundations and all, and shook it like a child's toy.

"Fuck!"

Terror goaded him into action. Lurching back into the hall, Ben slammed the door, locked it, shot the bolts top and bottom, fumbled the chain into its slide and reached for the phone. Nine-nine-nine got him a brisk, polite young woman saying "What service please?"

Outside, crystalline laughter tinkled in the starless night. The walls flexed like a sheet of rubber. "Police please! I..." *...think I'm being attacked by fairies.*

And everything went quiet. Down the street a burglar alarm brayed into the night. He opened the door a crack to see the streetlamps shining vulgar yellow-orange over a score of double-parked cars. There was, of course, no evidence the creatures he'd seen had ever been there at all. He took a deep breath, decided against setting himself up for a charge of wasting police time, and let it out in surrender. "Never mind."

"Yes? Was it corporeal, would you say, or etheric?"

Ben rubbed his fingertips over the rough paper and vivid blue ink of the advert in the Yellow Pages. Whatever he had expected from a man who helmed an outfit called The Matlock and District Paranormal Investigation and Defence Agency—MPA for short—this clipped, military baritone was not it.

He'd phoned up in the sheer need to talk to someone who wouldn't think he was a loony. Hoping, perhaps, for a nice old lady who would invite him round to the shop for a stress-relieving chat about accidental exposure to hallucinogens, and what he could best do to realign his chakras. He didn't expect to be going over the incident like a mission debriefing with a man whose voice sounded as if it came accompanied by a huge handlebar moustache and a nasty attitude towards what he would undoubtedly call "arse-bandits".

"Um, ethereal, I suppose. I don't know, I didn't..." Perhaps he should have tried to touch? They'd *looked* as substantial as wisps of mist, but what if they were really solid, capable of fading in and out of the visual range of the human eye? "I'll, um, next time I'll do tests."

"Put the kettle on. I'll be round in fifteen minutes."

Oh God! Supernatural attacks and suburban disapproval in the space of a single morning. *And* he was late for work. He tucked the phone into his shoulder and rearranged the keys hanging in the key cabinet into order of size. *Not* so that he

12

could more easily find them in the dark, just because it was more pleasing that way. What was he doing, phoning a random bunch of cranks like this anyway? It was a doctor he needed.

"Please, just forget it. I'll...I expect I was dreaming. I'm sorry to trouble you."

Putting the phone down Ben wandered into the kitchen. Groggy after a sleepless night, he wiped the table and put out cups and the sugar bowl, opened a packet of biscuits and slid a few onto a plate beside the milk jug. Bright summer sunshine poured into the room, glittering from the gold edges of his dinner service, displayed neatly on the pale oak dresser. The walls gleamed, buttercup yellow, and flecks of silver in the dark granite work surfaces pinged the eye with sparkles. He'd just poured water on the tea leaves and set the pot to steep when the half-expected rat-a-tat-tat came at the door.

Ben sighed. Mr. Matlock Paranormal was certainly living down to his expectations. Ignoring anything he didn't want to hear? Check. Too manly to use the doorbell? Check.

Straightening his tie, Ben took a deep breath, walked down the hall corridor and opened the door with a touch of defiance. His visitor stood half in the porch's shadow, half in sunshine, backlit by the strong summer light, and for a moment all Ben could process was tawny gold and earth colours. Then the man stepped forward into the shade—a tall fellow with sandy, spiky blond hair, an air of athleticism, and an open, confident face made quirky by a nose once broken, set slightly askew.

He held out his hand. "Wing Commander Gatrell. Call me Chris."

It was worse than Ben had imagined. Military *and* hot. A combination that spelled trouble at the best of times—and this was very much not the best of times.

"How d'you do." He made sure his handshake was firm and

brief. "And, well, what do you do, exactly?"

The Yellow Pages lay open beside the phone. Gatrell nodded at the advert without looking away from Ben. "We do exactly what it says. Investigate and defend against the paranormal."

"Who're you going to call: Dambusters?"

Gatrell gave him a startled, piercing look before forcing a chuckle that revealed the beginnings of laughter lines around his eyes. "I hear the Ghostbusters one twice a day on average, but that's new. Not bad." He shrugged off his tweed jacket and hung it up on a coat hook without asking, as if he were in his own home. "I should paint it on the car. Give me a hand in with the equipment."

Doesn't include "please" in his vocabulary, Ben thought, to distract himself from the sight of the man bending down to bring a Geiger counter and something that looked like a short-wave radio with extra tubes out of the boot of his shabby white Volvo. Suggesting he was a man whose fashion sense had been formed by the Famous Five books, the wing commander wore olive-drab moleskin trousers, his lighter green shirt tucked in and topped with a beige-and-russet knitted tank top.

"Take this." Gatrell dropped a grey scuffed device into Ben's hands. "As we're here, we'll do the outside first. Walk round the house, tell me if it beeps."

Ducking his head over the scanner, watching the needle tremble as he passed the yew arch his father had spent so much time clipping, Ben allowed himself a small smile. It was good, after a long night spent terrified to look out of the window, not to be alone any more. He knew himself well enough to realise that if he had really believed last night's incident was a mere hallucination, he *would* have called the doctor. The fact that he had not done so meant that, on some level, he believed what he had seen was real. He could bear a little contempt, surely, if it brought with it the flesh-and-blood company of another human being. Particularly one who just might know what to do next.

A noise disturbed his thoughts. In his hands the grey box vibrated, the needle flickered between red and black fast as a snake's tongue. As he approached the corner of the new extension, the machine's buzz became a beep and then a shriek.

"Aha." Gatrell appeared at his shoulder, checked the readings against his own and gave Ben a triumphant grin. "Inside, then."

Going indoors, they walked carefully together around each room, scanning the walls. Ben's apprehension returned as Gatrell's clear, observant gaze took in every detail of his life from the thousands of CDs to the sheet music, perfectly squared up, on its stand.

"You keep it nice."

Was it a compliment or a hidden jibe? Ben tightened his grip on the whatever-it-was meter and scowled. "I like neat. Don't expect me to apologise for not being slovenly."

Gatrell paused in front of the bookshelf full of gay fiction. As he browsed the titles, Ben waited for the inevitable recoil, waited for him to angrily demand the machine back, invent some spurious excuse to walk out the door, leaving Ben to fight the underworld alone. *Oh, here it comes.* He swallowed hard, bracing himself. But Gatrell just drew a sergeant-majorly fingertip over the top shelf, raised a sandy eyebrow at the complete lack of dust and said, "You'll make someone a lovely wife."

Fuck you! Ben thought, feeling more bitterly stabbed than the little jibe really merited. *Get out of my house.*

The retort, *Why, Wing Commander, I didn't know you were*

interested, formed in his mouth. Before he could say it, Gatrell had opened the door, gone through into the newly built living room, and Ben's anger and sarcasm were foiled. The moment during which he could say something without making it into a big issue passed in silence, leaving him fragile and resentful and looking for trouble.

As Ben came into the room, Gatrell opened the side panel of the bay window and leaned through, looking out at where Castle Road made a sudden swerve, just outside Ben's front garden. Closing the window, he turned round and brushed his hands on his trousers. "I believe you."

"What? What do you mean?"

"Was that a cup of tea I saw on the table?"

Bloody hell. Ben stopped himself from clasping his hands together and bowing like a genie. It was all too likely this man would fail to spot the irony in a mocking, *Yes, oh master.* Instead, he bit his tongue again and brought everything out of the kitchen on a tray. Pouring tea, he offered biscuits and tried not to notice that Gatrell's stiff upper lip meant that when he smiled his mouth actually turned down at the corners.

Once more, tea and biscuits dragged back civilization from the brink of chaos. Gatrell dipped the HobNob, gestured vaguely with it. "Eighty-nine percent of our calls are from lads who think it's fun to put on a Halloween costume and try to scare the life out of me." He engulfed the softening half of biscuit before it dropped, dunked the second with a shrug. "Up to and including coming at me with chainsaws. A further ten percent tend to be cases of drug abuse, drunkenness or merely nerves. You'll have to forgive me if I've become a bit jaded.

"However, we do come across something genuine once in a while, and I think this is one of those occasions. So—I believe you. Your house was attacked by..." he tilted his head to one side, sceptical, "...spirits, you said."

Ben rolled his eyes. "Fairies. It was attacked by fairies, all right."

Gatrell laughed, but Ben cut off his inevitable remark with "Don't! Just don't, okay? I know what it sounds like, and I can take a bloody good guess at what you're going to say next. So let's pretend we've done that part and move on, all right?"

The colour of the man's eyes was golden brown, flecked with green. They looked hard and old as nuggets of amber as he said, "Far be it from me to attempt to inject some levity into the situation. As a matter of fact, you're right. I know better than to laugh at these creatures. And how did they attack you?"

"There was something with them, like a giant. It kept lifting up the house, smashing it back down. I thought it was..."

Ben's tea slopped from his mug over his fingers. He looked down, surprised, and saw he was shaking. With both hands he eased the cup back onto the tray, stood, meaning to find kitchen roll to mop up the spill, and seized up as he had done last night under the gaze of the elven knight. Able to watch, to think, but not to move.

They had both trodden in dust from the front garden—pale grey footsteps tracked across the aubergine carpet. The sitting room's newly papered walls rose to a ceiling to which he had not yet managed to give a second coat of paint. His mandola on its stand in the corner stood serenely upright, its strings twinkling. Around the bowl of flowers that partially hid his parents' wedding photo, screening off the sight of them in traditional Indian dress, the sideboard was dry—the water hadn't slopped. Not a single petal had fallen.

Ben caught Gatrell looking at it, sceptically. He closed his eyes, breathed in through his nose—catching a lemony cologne with undertones of sandalwood, an earthy, bright smell that rustled something in the recesses of his mind. "I know... Things look too neat. I can't explain it. Everything shook. I thought—when I woke up I thought at first it was another bomb."

"A bomb?" Gatrell rose from his seat in a lithe movement and looked at Ben with those penetrating hazel eyes. His gaze was nothing like that of the elven knight—nothing like it at all, but Ben shivered nevertheless. "When was this?"

"I was in King's Cross station when it was bombed. I'd been at university in London, but I came back North soon after because I couldn't do it any more. The underground...I couldn't." Black tunnels barely large enough to fit the train within them. All those people, crushed up against him, all screaming, bewildering doors and darkness—arches that opened on flames and the slide, the faint ceramic sliding noise of keystones shifting, dirt trickling down like rain, boulders tipping above his head. His chest burnt with smoke as he tried to hold his breath, suffocating. Train tracks live with lethal voltage as they stumbled through the darkness. Up escalators that shuddered with each step. Thousands of feet of rock above him held up by willpower and the klaxons, everyone screaming and he was going to fall...

And my parents. Oh God, Mum. Dad. They came to visit me and... No!

"Whoa. Whoa."

Disorientated, Ben flailed between past and present. Then flames gave way to roses nodding over the window, Gatrell's face close enough for Ben to see the faded freckles over the bridge of his nose. Ben recognised that the man's arms were around him, holding him up, just as they loosened their grip. That sage-green shirt that looked so 1940s, looked like it belonged in a world of winceyette sheets and hot Bovril, was soft to the touch as he clutched it while he got his bearings.

"Flashback?"

"Yeah."

"Get them often?"

Reluctant to try walking all the way to the kitchen just yet, Ben mopped up the spilled tea with his clean handkerchief and clutched the damp fabric like a lifeline. "Not since I moved back up North. I thought they were over. I don't... I like to think I'm not going mad, but..."

Gatrell picked up the grey device Ben had left beside his cushion and ran a comforting thumb down its pitted surface. "You're not going mad," he said kindly. "If you were, we wouldn't have picked up anything on these."

"But the—"

"As for the flashbacks, I get them myself. Bloody nuisance, but nothing to be ashamed of. Right then. Our next move is, we relocate to the pub and I'll buy you a drink."

"I'm sorry?" Ben's distress escaped him in a quick flap of the hands. "I didn't call you so that we could socialize. All right, you believe me! I hoped you wouldn't. I hoped you'd tell me I was imagining it all. I'm really not happy at the thought that there's something...*legendary* out there coming to get me. But I fail to see how going down the pub is likely to help."

The upper lip straightened again as Gatrell oppressed another smile. But the expression passed quickly, turning into something grimmer. "Maybe I didn't make myself clear. Step one, get out of this house. Continue this conversation elsewhere." He passed the machine from one hand to another. "You saw the readings go off the scale. Something is still here, and whether it's residual energy or a more sentient presence, I'm not willing to risk leaving you here with it." The smirk lifted the corner of his mouth again—ironic, not at all comforting. "You see, I was trying to find a way of saying that which didn't

19

involve melodrama."

Ben gazed with disbelief at the device's dial, unreadable in the shadow of Gatrell's fingers. *Get out of the house?* It was that serious? The relief he'd felt at finding someone who believed him peeled away, revealed how very much more he had desperately wanted to be told he had dreamed it all.

Hair like cobweb under dew. If the creature's gaze left tracks of static electricity painted on his sensitised skin, what would the trailing slide of each strand of hair be like? Would its lips on his taste like lightning?

Imagining lightning hitting him in the mouth, Ben folded up his damp hanky and rose. Better foolish overreaction than that. "You could have just come out and said it. Would I need a bag?"

"Good idea."

"Just give me a moment, I'll go grab—"

Gatrell brushed his hands against his trousers. "I'll come with you."

"I think I can find the way upstairs by myself."

The smile fell from Gatrell's face and all the lines tightened. He straightened, parade-ground style. "Mr. Chaudhry, you seem to have got the impression I am playing at this. I'm not. You are under my protection. I will come with you."

The crawling sensation of having stuck his foot into a trap from which he could not withdraw took the containing cap off his panic and a "Fuck that!" escaped almost involuntarily.

"Unless you intend to tell me to leave?"

No! But there was the rub, because everything in Ben leapt in denial at the thought of being abandoned to face either a real threat or his own dreams alone. "Would you? I told you not to come, but you came. Would you go if I asked?"

Silence in the room. Ben's heart beat hard, the air rasping in his throat as it went down. Beneath the rolled-up cuffs of his sleeves, the sinews in Gatrell's arms stood out as his fingers twitched. They were, Ben noticed, fine hands, fine arms, it might almost be pleasant to be grabbed and shaken by them.

As Ben's lizard brain jerked itself back from the distraction, Gatrell too shook himself, shifted his weight and brought something out from the depths of his trouser pocket.

"No, I wouldn't. I've seen these things before. I wouldn't let anyone face them without backup." He reached out and dropped into Ben's hand an iron nail, its sharp point embedded in a wine-bottle cork. "Here, take this. Be as quick as you can."

The iron, warm in Ben's palm, felt anachronistic, hard to believe, like something out of the sixteenth century. It brought to mind history lessons, museum trips, witch trials and savagery—it was the kind of thing the superstitious had buried in the walls of their houses to drive off evil spirits. His mood seesawed back from anger to terror at the touch of it. But he wasn't going to let Gatrell see that, so he pocketed it, ran upstairs, took out a selection of folded underwear, paired socks, a change of shirt and tie, and packed an overnight bag.

Outside the window the sky shone deep sapphire, shading to indigo. No clouds moved across its gemlike expanse. As he dropped cufflinks into their leather case, the matching raps and rattles brought home to him how silent everything else was. No birds sang. The trees of the garden stood as if painted on a glass backdrop, waiting to shatter. He reached out a hand to straighten the bedcovers, and a voice like sliding water murmured in his head.

Ben recoiled from the sheet, clamped his hand around the nail. As if snapped off at the switch, the voice ceased. Ben's breath caught in his throat with an *ah* of shock. *God!* Picking up the bag, he clattered downstairs without zipping it closed, plunged into the living room. Chris was not there. *So much for his fine words. Bastard!* But racing out again, Ben found him kneeling in the hall, packing up the radio-with-tubes thingy, a frown between his brows and the corners of his mouth scored deep with suppressed emotion.

"Oh God, I'm so screwed." Ben skidded to a halt as soon as he felt the man's presence close about him like fortress walls. "It *is* still here. I just heard it. What the hell am I supposed to do?"

Chris looked up, his lean face bright from the light of the open door, expression open, hands on his knees. "I'm sorry, Ben," he said quietly. "I wish I knew."

Chapter Two

The fire was barely bright enough to show Flynn his own hand, and hers atop it, the needle-sharp fingernails making dimples in his skin. Beyond the hand, a rootlike wrist disappeared into a sleeve that smelled of sour earth. Wind brought a deeper scent out of the bowels of the cave— something cold, wet, almost metallic.

The fire burned moss—all smoulder and no heat. A trickle of white smoke wound into the air between Flynn and this thing whose pupil-free black eyes reflected the pale blur of his face. "If you want stronger," her voice slipped across the dark like the sound of falling dust, "you must pay more. Fifty years."

The touch on his skin felt frail and chill. Five encircling pinpricks, nothing more. But it was as hard to stand still and bear them as it would have been to endure the touch of five hypodermics loaded with disease. His breath smoked in the air and sweat trickled cold down his spine. "Ten."

"Do not try to be clever, sky-rider. If you wish what I give you to be worth fifty, you will give me fifty. If you give me more, it will be worth more. I, who was once a queen of Faerie, do not haggle like a common merchant at a horse fair. Fifty."

Fifty years! Flynn pulled his hand closer to his chest. His heart thudded strong in the cavern of his ribs—he could feel the strength in it, ardent and young, feel the sureness of his own body, swift and sturdy and free of pain.

His recoil brought her farther out of the dark, showed him the toothless sunken arsehole of her mouth, the yellow unsupported cheeks that seemed half-melted from her face. She moved tentatively, as though every step, every breath, took agonising effort—a shrunken, hunched thing in a rotting ball gown so overlarge on her he could have fitted his forearm between the knobs of her back and the fabric.

He'd come in, picking his way over the rubble without breaking a sweat, smooth skinned, handsome, fast and strong. He would hobble out a seventy-year-old. Was it worth it? Take the gamble on the off-chance the skipper would hear him—the even more unlikely hope he could do anything to help?

Those dark eyes were shiny as obsidian as she watched him with the patience of the rocks amongst which she dwelt. She was an honourable thing in her way, giving him time to understand the enormity of his decision, to freely consent, or not, as he pleased.

His final day in the real world came back to him with such clarity he could almost smell it—the air shimmering with the high-pitched kerosene smell of aviation fuel, the departing trundle of the bomb handlers in their tractor. White stars shone over the Lancaster. It was a cloudless night. Good weather for the bomb aimer, maybe, but also good weather for enemy fighters and anti-aircraft batteries down on the ground.

Well, he'd thought even then, if tonight was the night they bought it, thank God he and the skipper had seized the day first. Plugging himself into the intercom, he ran through his preflight checks, firing up the H2S magnetron. Squeezed into the wireless operator's station, Tolly pushed his helmet earpiece back from his ear to say, "Where were you yesterday? You missed a wonderful dance. You and the skipper find something more interesting to do?"

The creak of his chair beneath him and the rustle of logbooks and sextant as he leaned up to look out of the side of the cockpit and watch Skip come strolling, finally, up to the plane. The man looked good, even in regulation overalls and Mae West life jacket, carrying a packed lunch and his helmet in his hand. Brylcreem slicked back his hair and darkened the blond to a mousy tan, yet all that did was to emphasise the colour of his eyes and the startling, self-satisfied smile.

He walked with a smug gait, a saunter that seemed to have in it some of the hazy, lazy heat of midsummer, transparently well-shagged and happy. Stopping a moment just in front of the wing, he looked up, and the crook of his grin, the touch of fingers to his forehead in a jaunty half salute left Flynn feeling as though the outer layer of his skin had been removed—hot all over and uncomfortably exposed.

"We met some girls." Flynn gave Tolly his own version of the same satisfied smile and watched the answering leer with relief. "Munitions workers. Very good with their hands, and that's all I'm saying."

"Oho." Tolly clicked shut a switch on the radio and scratched the mix of razor rash and pimples at his throat. He grinned up at the skipper as he made his way past the mid gunner and clambered over the main strut. "Flynn tells me you had your joystick polished last night, Skip. Let's hear all the gory details."

The look on Skip's face! Priceless. He'd almost swallowed his tongue for a second before he added it all together and came back with a laugh and "A gentleman never tells."

Skip eased himself into his seat, his back to them and his oxygen mask raised to cover his face. Preflight checks and a clipboard handed back to the erks. Doors sealed and the engine noise building to a deep, rumbling throaty roar. A different kind of excitement gave a matching spinning bellow in Flynn's belly as he fastened his own straps and felt the gentle roll forward that presaged another long, tense night of tedium punctuated by chances to die.

"All right, lads, enough chitchat. Let's get down to work, shall we?"

Flynn couldn't tell any more how long ago it had been. Some period of time longer than a week, shorter than a year. There had been a light from above that he took to be a bogey and then nothing, none of the rolling and diving he expected, no sound of the gunners returning fire. Just light, followed by darkness, and when he woke he thought he must be dead, and in paradise.

Funny to think it now, when he was about to trade fifty years of his life for a chance to go home.

With his free arm, he hugged himself, his leather flying jacket creaking comfortably at the pressure, the sheepskin collar warm against his cheek. The last time that evening, before reporting for duty, he'd worn it as they made love, both of them loving the feel of the leather, the residual thrill of flight and glory, and risk. Even now a faint scent of the skipper hung about the lambswool like a ghost.

Seventy-three years old, and there wouldn't be any more of that even if he did get home. No more flying, no more fighting the Hun, and perhaps after three tours of ops he'd already done enough, but... Inside him all his buoyant thoughts, the hope that had kept him sane in this malignant world, seemed to draw together, wither into a black lead sphere and roll away.

You always bring me home.

I always will. As long as you give me a heading to steer for.

It was like jumping out of a plane—the long, sick moment before moving a foot, before descent became inevitable—and no one to shove him in the back and make the decision for him. "All right," he said, screwing his eyes closed, breathing in hard as he tried to fill himself with that ever more elusive smell. "Take it."

Augh! His eyes snapped open at the squirm about his wrist, the saw-edged slide of something hard and dirty into his flesh, and so he was in time to see her needle-pointed nails lengthen, slick out from her fingertips and drive through his skin, up the veins of his arm, parting the muscle, winding about the bone. *Augh! No. No no no!* He screamed, tried to wrench himself away, but it held him fast, the barbed tips of the nails sinking into the joint of his elbow.

Exquisite pain—the kind of pain that shredded reason and left him howling, nothing behind his eyes but the enormity of agony. Then it eased and he found himself human again, collapsed onto his knees, one arm curled about his head, the other still held in that obscene grasp. His breath came in chuffing sobs like the sound of a slowing train, tears on his cheeks that he hadn't known he was shedding.

The pain shifted, settled into a hot, itchy, infected burn as he watched her swallow his youth as a man might down a yard of ale. Big gulps of it, her form straightening with each swallow, her hair sprouting, her face tightening. She almost filled the dress by the time it stopped, a grandmotherly looking woman in her eighties with the dead black eyes of one of the fae and a smile of delight.

"Sure there's no more to give there, deary? Twenty more years and you would get my gratitude with it."

He coughed his way back to stillness, fighting the urge to weep. So he was seventy-three now? Maybe...maybe when he'd got hold of Skip they could think of a way to get it back. His lost fifty years, maybe... Laughter came from the same place as the tears. Maybe he could get a refund when the job was done.

Uncurling the arm that had been clamped for protection

around his head, he felt his face carefully, frowning when he couldn't feel any difference. He took his hand away from his chin and looked at it, puzzled. No. Nothing had changed. Bemused, he stood up—no protest from his knees, no weakness, his sight was as sharp as ever—and reached into one of the pockets of his overalls for his cigarette case.

The same face as ever stared out at him from its milled-steel surface—the face that had earned him his nickname, Flynn, from his resemblance to the actor. Not an extra line on it. And yet there she stood, younger by all the years he had failed to lose. "What? What just happened?"

Her nails were still buried in his arm. "My magic is in the sideways places," she said, with a motherly smile. "In the shadows of walls and the thresholds of worlds. You could give me fifty more and be unchanged."

The reprieve hit his system like a double shot of whisky, leaving him feeling giddy, expansive, well disposed to all the world and a little sorry for her, that after all that effort she'd only managed to achieve very old instead of ancient. "In that case," he said, "why not? It seems I've got it to spare."

There were teeth in her smile now, though they were brown. "Lie with me after and I will give you a dream."

He laughed. "No, I don't think I can go that far." Because even if he hadn't already been taken, he was not going to forget the nails in a hurry.

Outside the cave he took a deep breath of early-afternoon air, permeated with sunlight. Behind him, the landscape continued to rise in tumbled mounds of grey granite boulders, grown over by gorse and grass. Sheep grazed there and watched him from their slotted eyes with expressions of superiority.

A red-tailed kite swung across the deep blue of the sky, and he felt it watched him too, its head hunkered down between its shoulders.

Had he chosen to turn, he knew he would see the white ribbon of path snaking up into the hills, sun reflected in tinsel glints from the motionless figures of the watchers on every corner. Follow the path for a couple of days and one came to a stone lintel and two massive uprights carved with spirals—the doorway of the palace. Fingering the pouch the hag had given him, rough leather filled with dust, Flynn wondered if he should return there. If he did this in a basin in his own chamber, would Oonagh know? In one of the public fountains, at midday when they were all asleep—would she know?

Yes. Almost certainly, yes.

So he kept his back turned on the highlands and looked down the slope to where gorse gave way to silver birch, all gold-green leaves and white stems and flutter. Beyond that flirty edge of its skirt, the forest deepened, darkened, tangled up. When he was new here, and she still acknowledged his existence, Queen Oonagh had said there were monsters there. He had no doubt that she said nothing more than the literal truth.

But he walked down the slope, through bath-water-warm sunshine, butterflies pirouetting about him. Then under the first cool shadow, and on to the deep cold and quiet that made him think of the sea. It sounded like the sea too, as the wind *ssshed* amongst the leaves over his head and dappled stars of light danced like the butterflies around him.

Monsters or not, down at the bottom of the slope there should be a stream. Or a puddle, even, in the print of a deer's hoof or a wolf's forgotten paw.

The air smelled of moss and wet leaves, the hyacinth and honey scent of bluebells, and just as he thought this, the trees drew apart and he found himself bursting out into a glen carpeted with the flowers. The sun shone bright gold overhead, and the little bells nodded in a sapphire mist about his knees, and the scent of them was reeling sweet. He thought for a moment that they rang—a dim and tingling sound, brighter than brass, more mellow than silver—and he laughed again. This place, this prison, it had its charms.

"Oh!" On the other side of the clearing something uncurled from the long grass, startled and graceful as a fawn. He registered glittering horns, big dark eyes in a woman's face, bared breasts, bare *everything*, svelte and poised, before she clapped her hands to her mouth and he wrenched his gaze away, looked desperately down into the sea of flowers, feeling sick with embarrassment and arousal and shame.

"I beg your pardon, miss. I didn't realise anyone was here."

She moved, fluid and swift, with the sound of bells about her, running towards him. "Please." And she stopped an arm's length away. He could see bare feet, skin the tawny brown of a lion's mane, ankles encircled by golden anklets, and the central pendant of a gossamer-gauzy skirt pink as a peach.

Blinking, he fixed his gaze on her face, and his self-conscious monolog was interrupted by the realisation that she'd been crying. Cooled, instantly, Flynn looked around for the threat. "What is it? Are you hurt?"

"No." The long hands that strayed back to cover her mouth were covered with the spiralling shapes of tattooed flowers, her fingers and her wrists ringed with yet more gold. "Yes."

Looking up, he realised that her horns were actually a towering headdress. A crown of gold. Leaves and bells hung over her forehead and mingled with her long black hair, chiming as she moved.

"I'm not hurt. I'm kidnapped."

If he lowered his gaze cautiously past her chin, it was dazzled once more by the link on link of heavy gold collar, spangled with gems that covered her shoulders and her chest right down to the rise of those naked breasts.

"Not robbed, clearly," he said and was startled to hear himself say it out loud.

"Kidnapped isn't enough?" She sniffed and rubbed her eyes with the heels of her hands, so that she could glare at him. It didn't have the force it should have done, coming from those liquid dark eyes, but Flynn stepped farther back nevertheless.

"There are monsters out there," Queen Oonagh had said, and he believed her because she was one of them. Yet Oonagh looked like a spun-glass angel, her breathtaking beauty concealed beneath swinging cascades of pearl. Oonagh looked like whatever she wanted to look like, but it didn't take long acquaintance to discover the heart underneath was as soft as diamond.

"This world is like an insane sanatorium," he said. "How do I know you are what you seem?"

She tilted her head and took a step closer. That was all. But it arrested all his attention—something so perfect about it, the way she raised her foot and set it down again, the angle of her leg, the angle of her neck and the way her arms shifted, just slightly, to balance her, fingers spread like wing feathers. "What do I seem?"

All that jewellery—rings and bracelets and armlets and collar, skirt and anklets and earrings. She was as opulently bejewelled as the elf queen herself and held herself with as much nobility. He thought of the women of Fiji, and it occurred to him that she might, by her own standards, be fully dressed. In which case, all his ostentatious modesty and restraint would be going right over her head. "Like a princess," he said and would have groaned at the cheesy chat-up line if it had not been nothing less than the truth.

She smiled and made a gesture with her hands that even he could tell represented joy. "Oh, you see clearly! I am Sumala daughter of Chitrasen."

"How do you do." Flynn held out a hand instinctively to shake. Equally instinctively, he remembered his first and hardest-won lesson. In the land of Faerie, one should never give one's real name. "I'm Flynn the Navigator. I was kidnapped too, believe it or not. I'm not a monster in disguise... If you're wondering."

"You're a human." She laughed, the bells in her hair echoing the sound. "That is demon and god enough in one being. But I am lonely and I would rather spend time with a monster than with no one at all. Can you play music?"

"I can tinkle a little on the ivories." Since she had neither tried to rip off his head yet, nor—as far as he was aware— ensorcel him for nefarious purposes, Flynn risked a smile. "But as I don't actually have a piano on me, the question's a bit moot. In the meantime, I don't suppose you know where I might find a pool?"

The faintly dreamy hunger of her request for music sharpened into understanding and delight. She stamped her foot and set all her bells pealing. "You have a way of looking out! Perhaps even sending a message? I too have those who would rescue me if they only knew where I was. Come with me."

Out from the meadow, on the opposite side from which he had entered, a ribbon of trampled grass showed where a path wound farther into the forest. It dipped beneath tangled oak bows, and lobed oak leaves rustled on every side. Silently, through the breathing hiss of the foliage above, autumn leaves drifted down upon them like phoenix feathers, red, gold and umber. Yet the canopy itself never thinned, and all the trees stood arrayed in the shining new green of early summer.

Following Sumala, Flynn wondered again whether he had fallen in with some enchantress, some hag in a maiden's form. Perhaps even the same hag he had left rejuvenated in the hills, who had changed her appearance and come back to try again for that slap and tickle she'd asked for.

Sumala's hair rippled like silk down her back, the colour of sleep and the infinite night sky. He began watching her back— the slender shoulders, the flex of her spine, the sway of her round backside under that semi-transparent peach-coloured skirt.

It's been a couple of weeks, old son. I didn't think you were the kind of man who'd break your promises. Let alone this soon.

It's been months, Skipper.

In his head, the memory of his lover raised a sandy eyebrow and looked at him sceptically. He couldn't even remember if they'd promised to forsake all others along with the vow that *You're mine. You always will be.*

Besides, I'm just looking.

She's too good for you anyway. You'd see that if you looked properly.

Sometimes the voice of the imaginary skipper in his head was eerily nothing at all like his own. He shivered and looked up just in time to catch the inhuman grace of her movement as she leapt up from ground to boulder to bough of a fallen tree trunk as high above as the canopy of a spitfire. And sometimes, he thought ruefully as he tried to scramble up himself, slipping on lichen, his hands greened and his arms reminding him it had also been months since he'd suffered through a regular dose of physical exercise, it knew what it was talking about better than he did.

He slipped down a third time, lost his temper, backed away to a decent distance, then ran and vaulted for the top. A cheek full of splinters later, already raw hands rubbed to bleeding by jagged bark, he scrambled finally onto the faintly curved top of the trunk.

Sumala laughed, her hands—held in front of her mouth—not managing to shield the unrestrained amusement. Her eyes shone with laughter, and the giggles shook the many chains of her necklace and produced a shivering metallic echo. His face heated with humiliation and anger, but as he opened his mouth to tell her not to mock, she sobered and looked him directly in the eye.

A moment passed. Something he couldn't put a name to happened between them, and then he was shaking his head like a dog which has heaved itself out of a stream, trying to dislodge a persistent feeling of remorse. What had just...? It was as though he had been plunged in water, clean and deep. Or had it been only the innocence in her eyes, the kind of innocence powerful enough to lure and tame the unicorn.

And what on God's green earth was he thinking about now? He shook himself a second time, profoundly unsettled, unable to say why.

That was a little bizarre, Skip.

The craving for a cigarette swept over him. A cigarette and a warm corner of the hangar where he and Skip could lean together, his lover's rangy body companionably tucked against his as they talked in low voices, passing the roll-up from hand to hand, each one feeling the other's lips on the warm paper as he inhaled.

Isn't it all? Come on, Flynn. Give me some coordinates so I can bring you home while there's still a home to defend.

A wind blew in the treetops and whiffled through his hair.

He turned his face up into it and breathed in and out, a long fortifying sigh. When he opened his eyes again, he found Sumala kneeling very demurely two feet away from him. Between the two of them, a fist-sized hollow in the trunk cradled a tiny pool of rainwater, mirror smooth. Holly leaves trembled and glistened darkly overhead, allowing through only the occasional moving star of bright green light. The surface of the water and the sky were the same.

"May I look with you?" Sumala asked, "My father is powerful. If I can reach him, he may be able to help us both."

Flynn took the rough leather bag from his breast pocket, eased open the stiff thongs that held it closed. He was just about to hand it over when a thought burst upon him like ack-ack. What if this was Queen Oonagh in disguise? That would explain things all too well—the combination of sex and innocence specially chosen to arouse a man's protective side and lull him into slavering stupidity at the same time. Wouldn't that be a cruel trick, to allow him to find a way of making contact, to go through that whole appalling business with the nails, and then to snatch the hope for freedom away at the last moment? Oh yes. That would be a trick worthy of her.

But what if Sumala was telling the truth, and she too was imprisoned here against her will? If this was also her last chance to contact her loved ones, what kind of a cad would he be to say no?

Ah, what the hell? It was like an op, wasn't it? You didn't know when you started that you'd be coming back again. No reason not to start. "Here." He held out the pouch and let her dip her fingers in the top. "You go first."

As pixie dust, the stuff in the pouch was a disappointment—a fine grey dirt with larger reddish flecks and the occasional brown crackle of a disintegrating leaf. Sumala took a pinch, no more, and cast it on top of the little pool's mirror surface. "Dust of wisdom, dust of time, show me the nearest kin of mine."

The patter of dust broke up the pool's still reflection of the canopy of leaves. Ripples travelled outwards and broke on the rim of the hollow, and then it stilled once more and a light shone up out of it. Leaning forwards, Flynn saw the yellow flames of torches, as if in a mirror, and deeper in he made out the intricately curved and carved throne room of the palace under the hill.

Nacreous walls reflected the light. The throne in the centre of the room was bone coloured, and the queen on it as white and shining as pearl. *She's Oonagh's...daughter? Mother? Distant cousin?* Flynn's breath of betrayal hissed through his gritted teeth. He snatched back his outstretched hand and covered the open pouch with his other hand.

At the same time, Sumala gave a cry of delight, moving to his side and hugging him. "Oh!" she exclaimed. "Karshni! It's Karshni!" She beamed at him as though she'd found a long-lost treasure, scoffing at his suspicious look.

"No, not *her*, silly. Concentrate. See who she's looking at."

That appeared to be Bram, the Captain of the Guard, an elf with hair the colour of flames and eyes like witchfires.

"That's no better."

"No, in his hands. Ssssh."

In the captain's golden hands a sphere of light trembled. Within it, the altogether prosaic light of electric bulbs lit up the inside of a pub: dirty blue carpet and scuffed dark-wood bar, a man sitting reading a book amidst the empty plates and crumbs of what looked like enough food for a birthday feast.

"Crikey." It worked then, this magic. Far away, through two

different sets of viewers, as if at the wrong end of a telescope, he could see his own world. "Oh bloody hell." And he wanted it now. He hadn't imagined the pain of seeing it again, the curling inwards of a grasping, hungry homesickness like the closing of a bear trap.

"Sssh!"

"My queen." Bram's voice sounded tinny and flat, broadcast by the surface of the water. "I will return and put out both of his eyes, and there the matter is at an end."

"Don't be a fool. Look at him, my champion. Look at him more closely."

The water-bubble world expanded, the film of it scarcely visible now as a second layer of shimmer beneath the surface of the pool. Sumala squeaked again with excited recognition, and Bram gasped at the same time.

"You see it? What a blessed chance, if chance it was. I want him captured and brought here at once." Oonagh clapped her hands and the world-bubble popped, leaving shards and stars floating icy bright through the twilight of the chamber. "Quickly, now, for the threads are beginning to come together and I feel the picture form beneath my hands."

"What about the girl?"

"Hm." Oonagh tied a knot in one of her strings of jewels and unravelled it with a flick of the wrist. "You are right, we cannot let the girl run around free. She is forever to be found in the meadow of Narcissus. Have her brought here. I want her under lock and key."

Sumala grabbed Flynn's wrist, tried to haul him to his feet. "Quick! Rise. We must not be found." She was strong, with a dancer's long, lean muscles, and he swayed forward under the tugging, his shadow falling over the little puddle. At once it showed him nothing but himself.

The stab of loss made him wince. "Let go! I get my turn to look."

"She is coming for us!"

"She's coming for *you*," he said, annoyed at her assumption there was an "us". They'd only just met. He had his own concerns and no sort of responsibility for her. And that little view of home had been so keen a thrill, so heartbreaking. "Besides, the palace is two days' travel away. We have two days before anyone can get here. Time enough for me to look."

The dust felt gritty and greasy to his fingertips, as dirty as the hag's mouldy skirt. He had scattered it before turning his mind to the problem of poetry, so the incantation could have been improved upon, but he'd learned at least to be more specific than Sumala had been about who he wanted to see. "Into this pond I...these ashes flip. Put me in contact with my Skip."

It almost seemed the same pub. He was looking down on the skipper's bent head. Out of uniform and dishevelled, he sat with an untouched pint in front of him gazing at a flat silver box, like a cigarette case. Flynn bit his lip, forcing down the overwhelming rush of fondness: those ears, that sandy hair— what had he done to it, he looked like a hedgehog. The nape of his neck, his shoulders, his hands, turning the device around and over. *I'd forgotten how he fidgets.*

Flynn cleared his throat with a strangled, embarrassing sob. "Skip? Skipper, look up." He coughed, wiped the heel of his hand over his cheek. "For God's sake, look up."

Nothing. Skip's shoulders rose in an inaudible sigh as he put the box down and turned his attention to a stack of papers.

"Skipper?"

"He can't hear you." Sumala kicked the bark next to Flynn's knee. "Not across worlds. You're wasting time."

"But I can see him. So he could see me if he was looking?" Flynn fished out his cigarettes again, angled the case to catch the moving lights of the forest canopy and reflect them down into the pool. They danced over the table and the papers on it, and over the backs of the skipper's hands.

Come on, Skip. Look up. Look up, damn it!

And Skip did, his eyes almost green in the smoke and gloom of the dimly lit room. Flynn recoiled, shocked. They'd been the oldest members of the squadron at twenty-two and twenty-three years of age. Grand old men, they'd joked, still with puppy fat padding their cheeks. That was gone now. Skip's face was the face of a man ten, maybe fifteen years older than Flynn remembered, lean and weathered, a little worse for wear, with the beginnings of crow's feet around his eyes.

"What...?"

Skip rose from his seat, mouth agape, all shock and confusion like he'd just been punched. It was possible to read his lips, across two universes: "Flynn...? Flynn, is that you?"

And all the lights went out as something blocked off the sun above him, thrust metal claws through the treetops. Boughs shattered and fell. The down draught of air was like standing beneath an autogiro. Flynn's ears popped as the wing beat changed and the air streamed upwards past him. Sumala yanked hard on the collar of his jacket, trying to get him to move. Her hair and skirt pulled upwards into that turbulence like flags.

Damning them all, Flynn looked back down for a last glimpse just as she got her foot into the angle of his bent knee, simultaneously levering him up and shoving him in the shoulder, hard. He lurched sideways, and the mossy, slippery bark of the huge trunk slid beneath his legs. He made the mistake of trying to stand and his boots skated on the damp wood as if on ice, pushing out from beneath him. A scrabble and a curse later, punk bark came off in his hands as he grabbed to steady himself, and he fell sideways, outspread like a starfish, straight to the forest floor.

Made up of wood so rotten it was all fibres and air, the ground beneath was soft as a mattress, carpeted with the white stars of wood anemones and the purple heart-shaped flowers of violet. He hit it with the reflexes trained into him while preparing for bailout, rolled, and was on his feet again in seconds.

It was just fast enough to let him know he was too late. Something black and feathered had punctured the canopy of the trees. Beams of bright sunshine swept across the forest floor as rhythmically as a searchlight while the great wings lifted and lowered. The talons of the thing closed about the fallen tree, spanning it easily in their huge grasp. Its eagle-like head bowed down, its mad gold eye taller than Sumala. Its metal-shod beak might have snapped her up whole, but all her concentration was aimed at the elf riding the great beast, wickedly gleaming silver spear levelled at her heart.

Rather than run, Sumala had grasped the spear about the socket and stood straining to hold the head away from her heart. A cold gleam ran along the blade, but Sumala looked more furious than afraid.

"I am a hostage here, not a prisoner. You can ask me to come and I will come, but I *won't* be treated like a slave."

The elf above her, not Bram, but one of the palace guard, slipped the butt end of her spear into a socket on her saddle. She spoke a few quiet words to her mount and smiled very sweetly. The eagle shrugged its powerful wings, and the thrust powered the spear tip forwards until it just touched the central ruby on Sumala's necklace. She jerked as though electrocuted.

Her knees buckled and she slipped off the tree trunk. With a cracking, whooshing blast of air, the eagle pounced and clawed her out of the air as she fell.

Flynn dived for cover, rolling under the spiky curtain of a holly tree's shade. But the elf knight spared him not a glance, any more than she might have paid attention to the work of the worms in the soil. With four powerful, lung-blasting wing beats, the eagle rose into the sky, Sumala visible only as a glimmer of gold in one curved claw. Sunlight touched the black feathers with glints of blued steel and made its rider shine like silver as she turned in a great sweep and flew off, back towards the palace under the hill.

Flynn unclenched his fist and looked at the pouch still held tight within. Some grains had spilled on his palm and stuck there in the sweat. He brushed them back inside and tied it tight. Now he could look properly. Now he could concentrate on his own rescuer, on finding out what the hell had happened to Skip to make him look like that. Skip had seen him, no doubt about it; he only had to get back in contact and they could plot together a way of getting him home.

She wasn't his responsibility, after all. They'd barely met. And she'd pulled that thing on him—the thing with the eyes. God knew what she'd already done to him. She could look after herself.

Damn and blast it. He combed the dirt and leaves out of his hair, brushed himself down, and set off on the long walk back to the hill. Because, with all of these things, she was still a friendless girl who needed help and you couldn't, you just couldn't, turn your back on such things.

Chapter Three

Chris watched Ben Chaudhry brush the crumbs and dust from the Red Lion's velvet settle. He did it with a neatness and thoroughness that appealed to Chris in these days of general lax standards and mediocrity. The young man seemed self-possessed and calm, reserved, unruffled.

But he'd have to be an unusually thorough idiot to be genuinely undisturbed by a brush with the Good People, so Chris gathered that what he was watching was an admirable performance of putting on a brave face.

That faltered a little as Ben slid in behind the artfully aged dark wooden table, placed his bag between his feet and lowered his head into his hands.

"Here. Get this down you." Chris slid a pint of Dutch courage towards him, put down his own beer and the couple of packets of peanuts he had tucked into his pocket, and looked about for a seat.

"What am I going to do?"

Dragging over a plush-topped stool, Chris sat and concentrated on cutting open the foil packet of nuts with his penknife while he wondered what to reply. A familiar ache groaned in Chris's belly like the twinge of an old war wound. Yes, exactly like that. He thought of saying, *Panic. Abandon all hope that your life will ever be your own again.*

Chris poured himself a handful of peanuts and chewed on them in an attempt to disguise the long, pessimistic pause. Ben had eyes like mirrors of obsidian, and Chris knew just from glancing up that he wasn't fooling the boy one bit.

But not every case is the worst case. Let's rule out the easy answers first.

"Here's what I think has happened," he said. "You've built your new extension out into a Faerie Rade. That's..." *...a path between worlds. The only way they have of travelling from one dimension to the next, from one reality to another.* No, best not to go into his multiple-universe theory at this point.

"That's a traditional processional route. Very important to them. A path they've been using for untold thousands of years. You've planted a pile of bricks in the middle of it and painted it magnolia—"

"Grape, actually."

Chris looked up, met a bland look. With that lack of expression, the boy could have been a statue, or a still from one of those Bollywood films—the young hero, the questing prince. And that was not an appropriate thought to entertain about a client.

"I'm quite happy to say I don't know the difference. But, if you can tear your sensibilities from interior decorating for a moment, I have a sledgehammer in the van. The plan is to get some protection, go back, knock down the corner of the extension so as to free up the rade, leave them some bowls of milk and honey by way of apology, and Bob's your uncle."

Ben's blank expression became blanker for a moment, like a man trying not to show he's just bitten into a lemon, and Chris kicked himself internally yet again. Ben seemed to bring out his worst side—a side he wasn't too happy to discover he had. It was despicable of him to needle this young man who'd come to him for help, and who probably got this sort of thing on such a regular basis for being gay and Indian (and how did that work, anyway? Were they more accepting or less?) that he'd learned to shut it all off behind that frozen face.

Ben looked away, surveying the cheerful room, the mahogany bar that propped up a dozen tourists. The blackboard on the wall said *Welcome* in big blue letters. Outside the door, under the blossoming hanging baskets, families with children were eating ice creams. Chris could tell when Ben set it behind him, moved on, by a tiny lessening of tension and a sigh.

"I can't afford to have my life disrupted like this. The bank's been extremely understanding, but I've already had so much sick leave, I feel like the world's worst employee. And I have a business plan, an investment plan, a mortgage on fixed terms for five years. Things I have to do to keep on track for my retirement..."

Chris snorted. A tidy mind to go with the tidy habits, and the assumption they all seemed to make these days—that they would live to grow old. Chris himself hadn't been able to believe that one since he was a child. *"How* old are you? Twenty-five? And you're worried about your retirement fund?"

Chris leaned forward, both his hands on the table and all his weight on them, just as Ben cursed beneath his breath, shook his head and tried to stand. Between them, the table lurched. The beer glasses plummeted towards the floor. Chris's glass hit, bounced off the carpet, spraying beer over his ankles. He caught Ben's glass mid-fall, placed it back on the table with a strange feeling of satisfaction. He'd deserved that, no doubt about it.

Leaning down, he poured a small stream of brown liquid from the cuffs of his trousers, pleased as he might have been if he'd got fresh with a girl and she'd thrown her drink in his face. Not that that was ever likely to happen. But if it had, it would show character, and he liked character.

No! The tendency of his thoughts distressed him. He stamped them down hurriedly. "Mr. Chaudhry, you're a man who needs to be in control of things, I can see that. But the fact is you're not in control of this. Complaining about it does as much good as complaining about being on a crashing train. We must appease them now, or you stand to lose a great deal more than a mortgage. Maybe your life. Maybe something worse."

"You're trying to frighten me."

"Damn right I am. Scared is the correct response to these things. If you're not scared, you're not thinking straight."

"And you'd know all about straight," Ben snapped. Standing, he hoisted his bag onto his shoulder, cheekbones like razors and his mouth like a blade. Spirit was one thing, but Chris recognised that he'd pushed too far—that his charge was about to go AWOL. Now all he could do was apologise or hand things over to someone else. Someone who wouldn't jam his boot in his mouth every time he spoke.

Or she, as the case might be. He fished out the mobile phone Stan had made him carry and looked at it in suspicion. Sleek, silver and thin as an After Eight mint, it looked more like something dreamed up for Buck Rodgers on Saturn than a decent appliance to him, but at least Stan had fixed it so that he only had to hit two of the tiny buttons to get through to Grace.

"Hullo?" There seemed a note of strain in her voice, but he could hear a baby caterwauling near her, so that explained that.

"Hello, Grace? It's Chris. Can you get over to the Red Lion ASAP? I've got a lad here who needs protection, and if I'm not much mistaken, he's about to run out on me. Could be a matter of life or death."

Ben paused behind the table, allowed his bag to touch the

tabletop, taken aback.

Grace's sigh was all but drowned out by the crying. A racket of metal sounded like a saucepan falling on a tiled floor. "Chris Gatrell, have you been insulting your clients again?"

Did he always do this? Surely not. He'd thought it had been particularly acute with Ben because the young man was so calm and poised and perfect he made Chris feel inadequate. Besides, he didn't think that Grace was getting the point. "No," he said. "No, I've been perfectly polite. So we can expect you in...?"

He looked at his watch—ten to twelve—just as a muffled clunk and the sound of Grace shouting something indistinct to an onlooker on her end of the line segued into her saying, "I can't come at all, Chris."

"Oh." He didn't know what else to do; he couldn't let Ben leave and walk outside where *they* could do whatever it was they intended to do to him. He reached out and took hold of the straps of Ben's bag, the one that, he knew, contained Ben's phone and laptop and electronic personal-organiser-come-nanny. He didn't think Ben was narked enough to walk away from several thousand pounds worth of stuff, not when he got over his annoyance and remembered for himself what could be waiting out there.

Sure enough, Ben glared at him, then picked up the empty beer glasses and headed over to the bar to refill them, and Chris lowered himself to pleading. "I really need you to give this young man the full works as regards protection, Grace. There are some powerful entities showing an interest in him. And he's... Well, I admit we haven't exactly hit it off."

"I *can't*. I'm all the way down in Devon at my sister's baby's christening. I told you this on Monday, Chris. I won't be back until the weekend. You'll have to deal with it until then. You don't have to be offensive. You can be nice if you try. Why not try it?"

"I..." *...don't even know I'm doing it until too late.* No, that was too much to admit, even to the padre. And beside the point too. "I can't leave him alone until he has some defences. And I can't expect him to kip down with me or one of the other team members until the weekend."

As he swivelled slightly in his chair to keep an eye on Ben, the barmaid pinched her lip between her teeth and said, in a whisper that carried as well as a shout, "You know the wing commander well?" Very up to the minute in 70s retro-chic, her blouse rioted with big pink and orange roses. But her hair was a snake's nest of white dreadlocks, and he could have put his index finger through the holes in her ears, stretched as they were over flesh tunnels of amethyst.

"I only met him this morning." Fortunately Ben did not look over his shoulder and catch Chris eavesdropping. "He seems...interesting."

Chris eased forward on his seat so he could hear the conversation better. That was one thing wartime intelligence did for you—gave you an appreciation of hearing the other side talk when they thought you weren't listening.

Grace made a tutting noise through the gap in her teeth. "You could ask Phyllis to put him up for a couple of days. She—"

"I wouldn't dream of asking a respectable woman to take in a young man she doesn't know. Besides which, the client won't take it. I'm telling you he's this close to walking off."

Over at the bar, the barmaid laughed and shot him a small, pitying glance. He dropped his gaze to the phone before she caught him staring, looked up again to hear her tell Ben, "Oh aye, he is that. Can't be blamed of course, but..."

"But?"

"I don't like to carry tales, but he was medically discharged from the RAF, in the nineties. Grounds of insanity. He has a little group of UFO watchers who meet up in here once a month. Potty, of course, but they're a harmless bunch. We watch out for him, poor man, but we don't encourage the customers to take too much notice of his stories. All right, sir? I thought I'd better warn you."

Chris quickly moved his seat closer to the table and turned his back on the bar with a feeling of vindication. "And the barmaid's just told him we're all lunatics. When's the soonest you *can* get back?"

He could almost hear her shaking her head, a Doppler effect at the other end of the phone. She breathed in hard, let it out soft. "I can't miss the christening or the party after. But I'll get the last train up and I'll be at your door first thing in the morning. Will that do?"

"You'll get your reward in heaven, Padre."

She laughed. "You know I was thinking of a box of chocolates as a down payment."

"You'll get that too."

"So easily bought." She snorted and rang off as Ben returned.

"So that's it." Ben swept the empty peanut packet off the table, dried off the surface with a bar towel, scrubbing at a spot of gravy that had congealed in the corner. He took the detritus to the bar, came back and grabbed his bag. He looked hopeful, rejuvenated, full of new zest. "You're mad. So am I, of course. Barking mad. I saw something that wasn't there, and I phoned the local loonies and got you. I imagine you really are trying to help and thank you for that, but I think I'll just go home and phone my therapist."

A rambler, coming out of the toilets behind their table swung his backpack in a great arc to try to get it back on his shoulders. The side of it collided with Chris, knocking him backwards for a moment. Ben took the chance to draw his own bag out from under Chris's hands and make a break for the door.

Chris scrambled to his feet, pushed the hiker aside and launched himself after.

The door stood open, framing a rectangle of blazing gold, green and silver as the summer sunshine outside made the grassy peaks and grey stones of Bakewell glisten. Lazy blurs of engines and colour idled by as cars drifted slowly through the tourist throng.

"Ben, don't!" Chris caught him by the arm as he was about to step from the doorway into the light, hauled him physically back into the snug of the pub. They were evenly matched—Ben perhaps had the advantage of youth, but Chris was the one trained to apply leverage in unarmed combat. He tightened his grip, settled his weight and stopped Ben in his tracks. Ben cursed and pulled at his arm, trying to break the grip just as the barmaid got between Chris and the door.

"Shame on you, sir! And when I was just telling this gentleman..."

She had stones in her ears—stones with holes in the centre of them. He looked through them automatically and saw *them*. He saw them, for the first time since the fireball, the crash. For the first time since that insane time he'd tried so hard to forget, he saw them. They were still there. They were everywhere!

Chris's grip slackened. A wave of cold pressure and fire swept over him beneath the skin. He could feel his lips and his fingers go cold and white, his mouth dry, his eyes bulge. Ben pulled his arm away, rubbing it, but his flight had stopped. He looked in Chris's face as if he could see what Chris was seeing from the reflection in his eyes. His mask of confidence flickered for a second, and there was terror under it.

That glimpse of someone else's need snapped Chris out of his own panic. He lunged forward, grabbed Ben by the shoulders and turned him to face the door. "Look. Look!"

"I don't want to." Ben shook his head frantically. "I don't…I don't want to see. I don't want it to be real."

Chris would have said the same thing, if he could. His heart went out to the boy. But there was no time for all of that. "Don't be a coward, Mr. Chaudhry," he said. "Look."

Ben's shoulders stiffened under his touch. He pried his eyelids open, winched his head up and confronted the open door. Nothing for a moment, only a street and a grey terrace of shops and houses on the other side of the road, and Chris had time to entertain a terror that they'd gone into hiding, they'd shown themselves to deliberately make him look more of a madman than he already did—and that they would now hide, and Ben would see nothing after all.

But the flint dressing of the walls shouldn't move like that, surely? Shouldn't spin and drift like particles in Brownian motion? "Is it really doing that?" Ben whispered, leaning back now against Chris's hands as if he needed them to hold him up. "Is it swirling, or am I just going to faint?"

"I see it too."

The rest of the world stood still as always. Only the nodules of flint in the walls of Barclay's bank across the road stretched themselves, unfurled into ugly little hunched creatures with long fingers, opened whiteless eyes, blue as sapphires, and looked straight at Ben.

"Ah!" Ben yelped, staggering back out of the sunlight of the door into the dim, stale smoke and spilled-beer refuge of the pub. Chris caught him and steadied him, and eased him down onto a seat in the centre of a circle of disapproving gazes.

The barmaid gave a sniff and tossed her wormlike hair just as Chris knotted his fingers together to still their trembling. "How about a cup of coffee, love?"

She glared at him and looked down with something like betrayal at Ben. "You might have told me you were another one o'them. At this rate we might as well call ourselves the Space Invader's Arms." But she disappeared for a moment and the slosh of a percolator later returned with a cup of coffee and an individually wrapped packet of burnt caramel biscuits.

One coffee. Chris watched Ben sip it, hands cradling the bowl of the cup, hunched over it as if for warmth, and he wished he'd had the presence of mind to ask for one for himself. Or whisky. Whisky would be good.

Ha. Well, he could worry about his own reaction later. He couldn't afford to lose it while he was still in the pilot's seat of this conversation. He grabbed a chair, sat down next to Ben and waited for Ben to recover. It wasn't until Ben reached out and stilled his hand by force that he realised he'd been repeatedly brushing ash off his knees—ash from the burning cockpit. Imaginary ash. He'd been covered in it, black and greasy with the burning fat of the flight engineer who'd gone up like a candle when the first incendiary struck.

When he looked down now, Ben's long, slim hand curled reassuringly over his own. The nap of his trousers changed colour depending on which way it was stroked, and his repeated brushing had left it in stripes of green like a well-mowed lawn. The fruit machine twittered to itself in the corner. Sunlight lay on the floor like a solid block of heat. And over in the games room, the jukebox clattered as it flicked through its library of CDs.

"I saw you see them," Ben said at last, raising his head with an expression that pleaded for reassurance.

In response, Chris pulled himself as tightly together as he could manage and smiled. "She has no idea I use her ears for surveillance devices. Stone with a hole in it, you see. Very useful. Normally I can't see the buggers at all. I'm not sighted like you are."

"It's hard to believe, in here. Even now..." Ben pushed at a cigarette burn in the blue-and-pink-floral carpet with his toe. "It's all too normal. I saw them. I know you saw them, but I can't... I still can't bring myself to finally accept it."

"That's partly my fault." Chris reached out and touched him lightly on the arm. The pressed and laundered linen suit looked so clean it would repel even imaginary ash. "She's right, the barmaid. Normally we work out of the church hall, but once a month we're double-booked with the ladies' flower club, so we meet here instead. 'We' being Matlock Paranormal.

"I brought you here because this is a safe place. Grace, that's our priest, she did the full blessing, protection, whatnot. They can't get in here. It's..." Chris smiled, as reassuringly as he could. The expression Ben gave him in return—hesitant, brave, ever so slightly warm—tugged something inside him, maybe groin, maybe higher. Hoping it didn't show, he retreated swiftly into business. "It's a fortress of the mundane. Has the disadvantage of making you complaisant, mind you. Makes it all that much harder to believe. We haven't worked out a get-around for that one yet. Have to rely on your mental toughness, Mr. Chaudhry."

"Speaking of which." Ben got up, took his coffee cup back to the bar and returned to the blue settle. Sliding into the corner, against the wall, he put the table between himself and the world. "Are you insane?"

Chris shrugged. It was a complicated question and rather, he thought, beside the point. When faced with paranormal threat, what's better—the sane man who doesn't believe you or the madman who can help? "Are you?"

"I see fairies. Yes, I probably am. But that wasn't the question."

Sighing, Chris returned to his seat. Perhaps intrusive personal questions did come with the job. Perhaps Grace was right, and he should roll back the defences a little in the name of establishing some kind of trust.

"Well then. I was a pilot. Stationed at Downham Market." The fen country. The endless skies had seemed bright to him, the flatness of the land bracing, masculine—a landscape with nothing to hide, everything on it visible for miles and miles. Afterwards it gave him the creeps, being so exposed, and he'd retreated up here, to the hills, where there were more chances to hide.

"Did regular night flights over Germany. Fourth of August we pick up an unidentified bogey. Turns out to be a classic UFO." *Light on his face. Light in the corner of his eye...*

Chris gathered himself. Decided to make this fast and short. He'd open up about something else, if necessary. This—this wasn't fit to be touched.

"They shot me down. *Us* down. They shot *us* down. Seven of us in the plane. I was the only one who got out alive."

"God! I'm sorry!"

"No..." Chris gulped a mouthful of beer, and another, feeling his dried throat moisten, washing away the taste of roast pork. Wiping his condensation-wet hands over his face, he tried to wash that clean too, scrub away the thick coat of ash. "No, it's fine. I woke up in hospital some time later. My memories of what had happened in the intervening period, well, they made

53

no sense—typical abductee stuff, except with elves."

He was able to smile now, albeit bitterly. "'Shot down by UFO' didn't go down well with the higher-ups, but...well, there was some stuff they couldn't ignore. All very awkward and embarrassing. The upshot of it was they gave me a pension but officially discharged me as insane. So here I am, trying to protect the world from things I can't even see, with a curate, a geek and a twitcher on staff. Could use a man with the Sight, if you ever fancied leaving the day job."

Ben pulled his suit jacket close about him, sinking his chin into the collar like a tortoise retreating into its shell. He had not let go of Chris's wrist, and the touch felt heavier than it should, as though the fingers were made of warm gold. Chris believed he should pull away but made no move to do so.

The waitress passed, carrying bowls of ice cream with chocolate sauce and fan wafers, a wash of vanilla scent fell cool over the table.

"I feel...cheated," Ben said quietly, still hiding his face as if the confession embarrassed him, as if he offered a vulnerability in fair exchange, having seen too much of Chris's pain. "I'm a proper Indian seer, but even the spirits I see are British. My parents would be proud. It seems I've completely naturalised."

And wasn't that a minefield? Chris hauled in his scattered wits, tried to recompose himself enough to pick his way gently through. Trouble was, he didn't do subtle, didn't fully understand what was "PC" and what wasn't, couldn't be sure he wouldn't open his mouth and put his foot in it. *Mate, I appreciate you opening the subject up. Trusting me. I'm not sure I'm worthy of it.*

In the end he chickened out and just shrugged. "Stands to reason you'd see British fae in Britain. They're a conservative lot. Fight over their territories like nests of ants and don't mingle. Grace tells me the Sidhe in her own part of the world are different again. And the same—treacherous little bastards. Just like people all over are different and the same. And speaking of Grace, we have a problem there."

Ben gave a huff of amusement through his nose. Cynical amusement, perhaps, as if to say, *I see what you did there, shutting the conversation down before it could start.* But he yielded to the turn and said, "What about Grace?"

Over in the snooker room, someone put Paul Oakenfold's "Southern Sun" on the jukebox and turned it up loud. The stuffy summer room filled up with drowsy music, like the whining of insect wings.

Chris drew an arrow in the nap of his trousers, smoothed it out again, looking down. It seemed there were no safer waters in this relationship—he merely floundered from one tricky subject to another. "I'm afraid you won't like this."

"I haven't liked anything you've said so far. Why break the habit now?"

That was better than a vulnerability Chris didn't know how to deal with. He beamed as normal service was resumed, and Ben caught the smile and echoed it.

"It so happens that Grace is in Devon today, all dressed up in her Sunday best for a christening. She finds herself disinclined to skip the reception and rush back in the middle of the night, when as she so truly observes 'I can deal with it my bloody self.'"

"So you expect me to sit here all day long and wait? What exactly can they do to me if I choose to go out and face them? Will they rip me limb from limb? Eat my brains?"

"The question is more, 'What can't they do to you?' And my answer to that is 'I don't know. Do you really want to find out?' There are limits to their power—they don't come up well against the church, for example. But on their own territory they are unstoppable, coldly intelligent and devastatingly cruel. Whatever they did, it wouldn't be quick or clean. You don't want to test them, Ben. I mean it."

He stopped himself. Browbeating the man was not going to help. Ben too was clever, subtle. He knew himself that he couldn't go up against these things alone—or he wouldn't have called for help. He was just pushing, testing, finding out what he could trust and what would crumble under him.

"I'm afraid this does indeed mean that you're stuck here for the evening. And when they throw us out at last orders, you'll have to spend the night at my house."

"Your house?" Ben pressed his fingers to his eyes. His voice fuzzied at the edges with cynicism and weariness. "Not the church?"

"I don't have the key to the church."

"Why does this suddenly sound like a bad chat-up line?"

It sounded like that to Chris too, and he knew it wasn't. He refused to let his mind go there. Or, at least, to let it go any further than it had already drifted.

"I'm flattered to know you're thinking of me that way, Ben." He gave the sentence the most dismissive turn he could manage, thumbed open his phone. "I'll get the others to come over, you can pick which one of us you want to kip down with. Sound fair enough? If you really don't trust us, draft in a friend to come with you, guard your virtue."

Ben's Adam's apple bobbed as he swallowed a retort. It must have tasted bitter, if the hardness of his mouth was any indication. "I don't need a chaperone, Mr. Gatrell. Your attitude is quite off-putting enough. I just..."

He fell silent and Chris answered for him. "You've just had your life turned upside down, and you're looking for a good
56

excuse why it isn't as bad as all that."

The understanding startled a small smile out of the young man. It was like the touching of a match to the wick of a candle; it lit up everything about him, made Chris want to draw close and warm himself at the glow. "Can't say I asked to be involved in all this either. But what was it that film said about not choosing the time we live in, but having to do the best we can with what we're given?"

Probably a good idea to leave now, before he wrecked the fragile moment of peace. Or, worse, gave Ben cause to suspect that if he baited his requests with that smile, Chris would be hard-pressed not to give him anything at all that he asked for.

Pulling a pebble with a water-bored hole in the centre of it from his pocket, Chris opened the door, checked the street outside. "At any rate, you should stay here today. Let me take a recce to the library, get you some books. Grace'll be back tomorrow morning, then we can get you sorted out and independent again. In the meantime, next time you're tempted to run your internal conspiracy loop, try remembering that you phoned me."

Chapter Four

Ben pushed the remnants of his steak and kidney pie away and picked up *A Complete Guide to Faeries and Magical Beings*, the most accessible of the books Chris had brought him. The cover mocked him with its picture of delightful little beings lit by glowworms and towered over by an intrepid barefoot girl. She'd clearly never been in a house that had been picked up and shaken by spiky giants. Never been stared full in the face by something alien and inimical and felt in her marrow an echo, like recognition, that scared her shitless, as it did him.

After phoning work and telling them he was indisposed for the day, he'd just begun at the A's of *The A to Z of World Fairies* when a flood of light fell across his table. The street door flung itself back, smacked into the wall outside. Plaster crunched, and the panes of glass set into the door gave out a thin protesting creak. "Oh, sorry! Sorry all. Don't know my own strength!" The woman who burst through in the wake of that thunder stood blinking in the pub's comparative darkness, smiling vaguely at every nook where something moved.

Her hat wasn't the only thing that reminded Ben of Crocodile Dundee, but it was the first. The big floppy leather hat, with its band of twisted leather, seemed to have been made for corks. The fashion statement carried on beneath it: baggy khaki shorts over stick-thin legs; grey knitted socks drawn up to her prominent knees and secured there with garters, the ends of which dangled out of the turned-over inch of sock top. A pedometer was strapped on one skinny wrist and a something-else meter on the other.

She hitched her bags more firmly onto her shoulder. The massive camera case bulged, other cases dangling from rings and straps all over it, like a big black spider carrying its young on its carapace. Binoculars around her neck, map in a see-through plastic map case with a compartment for a compass.

Ben pulled his book closer to himself, raising it up like a shield. All around the room a fluttering of newspapers indicated other people doing the same. A universal shifting on the barstools turned drinkers' shoulders towards the door.

Crazy woman alert, Ben thought, just as she pulled up a chair at his table and dumped her many bags on it. He closed his eyes, pretending not to be there, as she gave an appreciative groan and stretch. She had the lined arms—all sinew and sag— of an elderly woman, and the voice of a duchess. "I think you must be Mr. Chaudhry. How d'you do? I'm Phyllis. Phyllis Mountjoy, don't you know. With—"

"Don't tell me." He got up to take the offered handshake. It was like holding on to steel pistons inside a thin chamois leather bag. "You're with Matlock Paranormal. I'm beginning to recognise the signs."

The hat landed on the table, obscuring his book and overlapping his plate. He blinked—he had somehow not imagined the impeccably cut silver bob of hair, or that she had paused to put on baby-pink lipstick before going out for a hard day's ramble. "Is that rudeness, young man? I believe it is." Periwinkle-blue eyes ringed with faded white. Her twinkle had something hard edged about it.

"I *was* being rude," he said, thinking it out loud, "but it's true nevertheless. You all have an air about you. An air of—"

"Not having time to waste on fools?"

Ben might have said "pathetic defiance". An air of knowing what the world thought about them and not caring. Not even alternative chic. More like the mere antithesis of style. But the way she put it was as though she had taken that verdict and turned it inside out, made the world wrong and herself the only sane person in the room.

"Well, no more we do." She put her hat back on, took up her numerous bags and scooped up the gin and tonic that had appeared for her at the end of the bar. "The beer garden is safe too. Let's go outside."

"Do we have to? I get heat stroke—I think I've got it already just walking here. And the level of particulates in the air is well above average today. And I'm not just talking pollen. Ey-up, you must be Ben."

The newcomer was a plump, ginger-haired youth, wearing a Metallica T-shirt. His mascara only threw into higher relief how ghost-pale were his eyelashes. The pockets of his skinny jeans distended two or three inches out from the rest of him, crammed with rectangular objects. A silver skull dangled from one ear and failed to make him look even passingly hard.

"Wotcher. I'm Stan. Chris said we should come over and look at you, so I'm looking. I hear you need a bed for the night, but you can't stay round mine. My dad wouldn't like it, and I'm attached to my peace and quiet, so no hard feelings, but tough."

"I've fallen into the valley of the nerd." Ben straightened his tie and tugged his cuffs to lie more smoothly over his wrists. He rubbed the black onyx of his cufflinks as if for luck, although he didn't believe in luck.

"Yeah." Stan beamed, blue-white skin under a polished copper top. "And in the valley of the nerds, Stan Grimshore is king. All right then. Outside if we must."

Outside meant a slatted table under a stand of three oak trees. Theirs was the only table unoccupied, chill in the shade and spattered with white droppings from the colony of starlings who chattered and hopped about the branches above. Stan's skin—apparently—was too delicate to risk out of the shadow, in the penetrating UV light of a mild British summer day.

"You're probably thinking I'm a vampire, aren't you? My friends do, when I tell them I don't go outside in the sunlight."

"It...wasn't the first thing on my mind." Ben riffled the pages of his book, looked at over-pretty illustrations and instructions on how to contact the realm of Faerie, and wondered what he had done to deserve this. Across the table from him, Phyllis had leaned down to pick the wide leaves of a weed that grew amongst the roots, using it as a napkin to clean her seat. Once that was done, she unzipped her bag, brought out the body of a camera, and then a great compound lens, almost a foot long, assembling them together and adjusting the settings of the camera with the ease of long practice.

"So what do you do, exactly? Both of you?"

The heavy black eye lifted from the table, swung up towards the sky. Click, click, click and "damn". She lowered it reluctantly, still looking up into the cloudless, featureless blue. "Twitcher," she said, with a sip of her G & T. "Bird watching initially—did you see that? That was a common egret. Not so common around here, I can tell you."

"You bird watch for Matlock Paranormal?"

"No, I UFO watch for them. Also developing techniques for photographing spectres, spirits, etheric vibrations, whatever you wish to call them." She raised her eyebrows and smirked. "Ghosties. Elusive beasts, but that's the fun of it."

A bi-wing aircraft pottered across the sky above them amid sparse wisps of cloud. Down here, a waitress passed with two plates of Cumberland sausage and chips, and the couple over by the back gate struggled to make their toddler unlock her legs long enough to get them through the bars of a high chair. Stan had brought out a Nintendo, and the tinny sound of Sonic the Hedgehog mingled with the squabbling of birds from the tree above.

"You see a lot of them?" Ben asked, feeling cast adrift with no outboard and no idea of a destination. "Ghosts, I mean."

"Oh yes, hundreds." She might have been talking about the difficulty of getting good staff, the tone was so nonchalant.

"After I rigged up the filters. Didn't see none before that." Stan didn't trouble to look up, frowning over the little screen.

An abandoned chip at the end of the bench drew a starling, the whirr of its wings almost touching Ben's face—wind and the softness of feathers down his cheek—and then it buried its thornlike beak in cold potato, its claws scrabbling on the wood.

"Stan's our technical expert," Phyllis explained. "Quite a wizard with microchips. I believe the ghost filters were a school science project?"

"I.T. Simple really, though. Stands to reason—it always gets cold when ghosts are around. Yeah? Everyone agrees on that. So makes no sense to be photographing in the visible-light range. They're going to be low energy. Infrared and that. You're looking for something that's taking in heat rather than giving it out. Find your moving cold spots and Bob's your uncle."

The hair on the back of Ben's neck stirred as a second starling brushed past him, almost close enough to touch. It landed by the first, cocked its head to look at him. Its eye looked swollen, liquid black like a bobble on a blackberry. Ben's internal seesaw of disbelief and fear began to tip slowly back towards terror.

A third bird landed soundlessly next to the others. Phyllis uncoupled the lens from her camera with businesslike quickness, slapping on a mushroom-shaped monstrosity capped with crosswires. She aimed it up at the tree, and so of course Ben had to look too.

They were all silent now—the starlings—standing side by side, ranged along the branches of the oaks like sentries. Still, unmoving, with those black pebbles of eyes unblinking, their beaks slightly open and the wormlike tongues within curved like scythes. He thought the rest of the world went silent in sympathy, that all over the beer garden motion stopped, beaded condensation did not drip, poured gravy stopped midair.

Click, click, click, click. Phyllis moved like the progress of a glacier. When she spoke, her voice boomed and Dopplered like a whale's voice underwater. "Go inside, Ben."

He thought he'd leapt to his feet but found the unfolding seemed to go on forever, could feel every little fire of synapse and muscle. All the web of connections that made up his body and mind shuttled madly back and forth while something else pressed on it. Something from the tree. From the massed birds' open mouths, unified, came a cry like spreading ink. He could feel it rushing towards him, black, see the turbulence of the edges, the way it fanned out from the tree. Black and sharp and colder than zero degrees Kelvin. Water vapour fell out of the air as snow as the shockwave of it approached.

And he was still standing up, still forcing one neuron to fire after the next. It was going to roll over him, freeze him solid, steal every one of those sparks of soul. And maybe, he thought, with dreamlike icy certainty and terror, it would piece them together again somewhere else, graft them onto a sculpture of wire and bone and call it by his name.

"I said move!" The hand around his wrist was like a hit of cocaine—pure speed rushed up his arm, snapped him, slapped him out of it. It had taken eternity for him to get to his feet, it took a millisecond to dash headlong for the pub's back door. The black flood of sound came curling after him, white fume at its edges steaming. Stan, panting next to him, pewter-ringed hand clamped around his, chanted, "Get the door open. Get it open, fucker!"

And Ben grabbed the wrought-iron fancywork of the door handle, thinking only to twist it, get inside, but as soon as his fingers touched the iron the spray of darkness broke like a wave, spattered over their faces in a hundred chattering cawing noises. The starlings burst up from the tree in a skirling flock that made the toddler laugh and clap her hands. They were dark against the sky for a moment and then they wheeled, broke apart and flew away. The world was dull and safe once more, and welcome.

Ben held the door open for Phyllis, then closed it very firmly behind them all and staggered into the snug. There the jukebox was playing "Poker Face" by Lady Gaga, and Chris stood nonchalantly against the bar, looking calm and warm and solid as gold. "All right?" he said. "I took the liberty of buying you all a drink."

Chapter Five

Flynn reached the city under the hill just as the sun was going down. It teetered for a moment on the horizon, like a shield of brass, gilding the long grass and poppies that swelled over the artificial mound. It made the armour of the guards who stood to either side of the massive gape of door shine orange amber as flames, and the limewashed lintel behind them look like a single ingot of hammered gold.

They held drawn swords in their hands. He felt their watchful gazes flick over him, observing, weighing him, judging if he was a threat. One of them smiled as he passed between them into the mouth of the tunnel. The other inclined his head, very slightly, and he wondered what it meant.

Trying to guess why you're back again, I expect. You could have run that time.

I could have run any time. It's a funny sort of prison, Skip, a world. No matter where you run to, you're still inside.

There was no interpreting the guards' expressions. The smile could have meant anything from "better luck next time" to "behold our mighty power, puny human. You will never escape." Best not to think about it, really.

Is that why they let you rattle about like a marble in a tin, then? Because they like to see what you'll get up to next?

It's as good an explanation as any, isn't it?

There was something depressing about reverting to talking to himself after that brief afternoon where he'd had a real-life, flesh-and-blood conspirator to chat to. A hostage, she'd said.

That meant, surely, that Oonagh wouldn't have hurt her too much, wouldn't have risked the wrath of her powerful friends. At least, that's how it would have worked at home, amongst people he could understand. Here, who knew?

At any rate, he would not worry about her. He'd had to walk back from the clearing where they'd met, and it had taken two days. If worry had been appropriate, it was probably too damn late by now. Another one of those things that couldn't be helped, like powdered eggs and friends gone down in smoke. Funny how war put an end to all that connected civilian thought, all those expectations that life would be reasonable or predictable. Funny how it had turned out to be a good preparation for living in this place.

He passed between the elves' bright blades, the skin between his shoulders trying to ruff up, like a wolf's mane, as if making himself look bigger would help. Inside, one long street curved gently away to the right, paved and roofed with creamy sandstone.

The light was twilight blue and shone like a mist about him. He could see it eddy at his passing, wash into the great warehouses that opened on his left, where grooms were at work cleaning saddles the size of Spitfires. There was always a hammering there, metal against anvil, and in the farthest darkness against the outer wall hung rows of skinned cows. The light moved through their jaws like breath and settled like dew on their staring eyes.

He'd been this way a number of times now, in and out of the city, and seen the guards and the grooms, but he'd never yet seen their mounts. Sometimes, though, if one stood with their back to the wall on the right of the entrance, one could feel the stones tremble with the bass metallic scream of what could have been an animal's voice. Or that of a prisoner.

No, not a prisoner. He'd already told himself not to think of that. Humming "Keep the Home Fires Burning" under his breath to distract himself, he walked briskly down the centre of the street. The faint curve of the single path was barely discernible now. All outside landmarks were stripped away as he passed from the district of storerooms and shopkeeper's houses into a ribbon of parkland lit by lanterns. It didn't do to look too closely at the flowers—glistening things that nodded like bells, and like bells gave out a faint music. They were the photographic negatives of the bluebells that had carpeted Sumala's glade, delicate, white, half-illusory and everywhere. He was glad to walk out into the playful white marble of the public baths, wash the oversweet stink off his face and thread his way through naked nymphs and sharp-faced lads clad only in their ankle-length hair.

Do you have a plan at all?

His mental picture of the skipper had turned ghostly, as though that glimpse of him grown mysteriously old—positively middle aged—had rubbed out the edges of his memories. It was suddenly very apparent that he was talking to a figment of his own imagination. Funny that, too. He hadn't thought that finally seeing the man he loved again would make him feel so very much more alone.

As the road wound on its southernmost curve, he passed through the district of feasting. He grazed as he walked, picking up fruit, bread, cheese. He'd given the meat a pass ever since it occurred to him that he didn't know what kind of beast it had come from. Walking past a group of lounging, beautiful women, blue and gold as lapis lazuli and with eyes like aquamarine, he plucked the goblet from one of their hands just as the rim touched her lips.

The taste was of bitter honey and there was a little kick to it. Not enough—not as much as the whiskey he would have preferred—but enough to let him set it back on the table smartly and bow, smiling, ready to fight or apologise or run, depending on what the occasion required. "Thank you, ladies. Now, anyone want to tell me about the queen's hostage? Girl called Sumala? Hints always gratefully received."

Indigo hair slid forward over their faces as they bowed their heads. The one farthest away from him opened her golden lips, but it was only to sigh as they all, in unison, pointedly looked away.

It wasn't only the skipper who felt like a ghost at times. Flynn pushed on, stealing food and drink practically from the mouths of the diners—it was, he reckoned, the only way he knew it wasn't poisoned—and the strongest reaction he ever got was a shrug of weary exasperation. He might have been a wraith.

At a table beneath an awning in the malachite courtyard to his right, a young man with hair like moonlight and midnight skin struck up a tune on the lyre and sang a deep, sweet song about being drowned at sea.

Flynn stopped while the unearthly music woke a yearning in him, shades of desire and regret, like the shades of grey on a dove's back. The world slowed and speeded past him in ribbons of light, and then he thought, *Snap out of it, old son,* in Skip's voice, shook himself and found the light had dimmed and the crowds around him put on their nighttime plumage, more subtle, more silvery than the day. "Bugger."

God knew how many hours he'd lost, bewitched and bewildered by the song, but at least it had given him an idea. So he was ghostly to them, was he? Then he knew who to haunt.

He made another quarter turn of the city—this one slightly shorter as the road spiralled inwards to the great hollow at the centre that was the throne room. The Gate of Brass, the first of the seven great defensive gates that closed the only road, was shutting for the night. He stepped through ahead of the last guard and watched the bolts fall and the locks turn. When the guards ducked into the guardhouse to his left, going on all fours through the knee-high door, Flynn followed them. As they pulled off chainmail, he walked into the off-duty crowd. Sat down in someone's seat, meeting no more resistance than scowls.

"What is it with you people? Am I a guest or a prisoner?"

The tables were long, flanked by long benches. Flynn found himself in solitary splendour as the guards ceded him both table and seat, chose to remain standing. There'd been something in the room he recognised—a kind of wartime camaraderie—and his presence had burst it into smithereens. All of a sudden he'd had enough, enough silence and sneaking, enough half glances and averted eyes.

"Well?" The outer door darkened again, and when he turned to look, a yellow-green boy was straightening up there, pulling off his helmet and watching the room with wary eyes. His mail coif jingled in his hands. His gaze seemed, just for a moment, to seek Flynn out, but then it balked and slid away. He licked his lips, and at that small sign of weakness, Flynn launched himself back to his feet, crossed the room at speed as if hurtling down into a diving run, got the creature by the elbows and drove him into the wall. "Well?"

Yellow eyes should not look innocent or afraid, not with that golden sparkle to them. They should look like the eyes of a toad, a snake. Not like a child's. The arms beneath Flynn's grasping hands were thin as twigs and trembled. *New recruit*, he thought, *bloody little sprog.*

There was no stirring behind Flynn. No one was coming to their companion's rescue, even though he could see in the willowy boy's eyes the reflection of a dozen interested spectators, sitting back, watching the show.

"You're a..." The boy gulped, turned his head to the wall and as he did so the light flowed a little more clearly across his face, picking out the bones, the smooth cheeks and fullness of the mouth. "I'm not supposed to say. You're a potentiality, nothing more. You need to be left alone to become."

He was a girl, Flynn saw with a jolt of shock and concern. Not just a raw new recruit, but also a thin, scared-looking girl. And no one appeared to give a damn about her. They looked on, as avid and interested as gamblers around a cockfight. He wondered how far he could go before anyone intervened on her behalf. Who would stop him from doing anything at all he wanted to do to her if they had been given orders to leave him alone?

She closed those yellow-green eyes of hers and breathed out a long sigh of resignation. He let go and stepped back. Sometimes he hated these people, hated them so much. All of them were as cold as their icy queen. "Bread and circuses all around, eh? All right then. Sit down."

He indicated the nearest bench. Like any table in any mess, it was cluttered with plates, tankards, discarded gloves, the boards of games he did not understand, and wedged between a cup and a gauntlet, a pair of dice. "How about, instead of beating some answers out of you, we have a quiet game of pontoon. Every time I win, you have to answer a question." Yes, this was more their sort of thing, Flynn thought, noticing the stir of interest about the room. More apt to engage their attention. Cold bastards.

"You answer it honestly, mind you."

"And when you lose?" This one must have been their squadron leader. He was disturbingly humanlike, his skin brown as autumn oak leaves, his eyes as green. Flynn had long given up noticing when the creatures were beautiful—they all were. It became unimportant after a while.

"You choose," he said, and swallowed down dread. Something about the man brought out his competitive side. He didn't want to look afraid. But bloody hell, he also didn't want to allow any of them the initiative. They had minds like sharks and expressions equally full of teeth.

"Very well. Tell me how you play this game."

Flynn weighed the dice one by one in his palm. They felt all right, though he didn't pretend to have the kind of expertise to detect a weighted die simply by touching it. What the heck—he was committed now. "It's simple enough. We each take a turn. We add up the value of the dice. After 16 we switch to one die. You can stop playing whenever you like—if you get a 19, for example, you can elect to stick there. The person who gets closest to 21 without going over wins. If you get higher than that, you lose."

"It's just luck? No skill involved at all?" The elvish officer sneered.

"The skill is in your choices."

"Isn't it always?" He sat down opposite Flynn and reached out a long hand for the dice. There were snakes tattooed along his palm and flowers around his fingernails.

"What should I call you?"

He had a long face, with a pointed chin. Not wide enough for the mocking smile that seemed to be his permanent expression. Flynn hadn't forgotten that he hadn't stirred a finger for his cadet, wasn't tempted to give him the benefit of the doubt so far as character went. And when he said, "That should be your choice," Flynn was tempted to gift him with a name like Arsehole or Bastard, but he weighed his chances of getting out of there alive against the satisfaction and said "Serpent" instead.

Serpent smiled once more and tossed the dice. They played silently, in the centre of a ring of enthralled gazes, while the willow girl picked up an abandoned pitcher and went round filling tankards, with a look of intent interest on her face. "Twenty," Flynn said at last. "I'll stick with that. Let's see you do better. No magic, mind."

The name was apt. Serpent hissed through his clenched teeth, as if Flynn had made a remark about his mother. His throw bounced angrily off the side of the table and rolled into the ashes of the hearth. "Twenty-three."

"Tell me where you are keeping Sumala."

Serpent's laugh was like the boiling of a kettle, a wet, bubbling sort of sound. "In the dungeons," he said, his smile brighter than a welding torch. "Your turn to start."

"That's not…" Flynn kicked his own ankle under the table as the onlookers burst into musical laughter. He'd forgotten the other rules of this game, the unspoken ones. They would be as unhelpful as they could. His questions had better be more specific than that, more watertight.

His mouth was dry for the next round. Luck had always been with him in this game. But in this world, how far could he trust it to hold? He got an eighteen and cursed, not daring to throw again. Serpent got a twenty-five.

"Can you take me to the dungeon where she is being held?"

"Yes."

Oh, bugger! Word games, damn it. He should just have gone on squeezing until Willow had told him what he wanted to know. Then he wouldn't have had to sit here and listen to them all having fun at his expense. He handed the dice back. Third time was the charm.

Fifteen. He rolled again. *A six, come on, give me a six.* And it was a three. Again. Serpent flicked the foam off his beer into Flynn's face, and the look in the green eyes was hard as flint. Harder, hard as tinted diamond. There was death in his gaze.

The die spun on its point, tilted over and landed on a six. Twenty-one. Serpent's turn to set the conditions, to name the prize.

"Well." He lounged back against the wall, put his feet up on the table. "What should it be, do you think? He wagered whatever I asked. What shall I ask? His soul? His eyes? We could make a new set of dice out of the lenses of his eyes. That would be pleasantly ironic."

"My lord." Willow stopped by Serpent's chair, standing to attention like a WAAF recruit. "We can't tell him to do anything. That's the decree. He is to be free to do whatever he wishes. We can't interfere."

Serpent gave her an oddly searching look, as though he didn't know her, didn't know what to expect, was weighing his options in a place of some delicacy. It was a look a politician might have worn, interrupted in his speech by a hard question from the audience. "We haven't interfered," he said finally. "He has entered this contest of his own will and now receives the reward for which he bargained. This is his own doing."

"But if we blind him, we interfere with him."

Flynn tried to see through the words to the underlying attitude—to figure out what they wanted from him. But it was hard to work on the larger theory with the imminent threat of blinding hanging over him, unresolved.

"You're just philosophising," Serpent said, his mouth drawn down into a curve like a staple at the sides.

"I am trying to save you from making a grave mistake." Willow gave Flynn a sideways look, which might have been admiration, might have been gratitude. He realised with some surprise that she had understood he had done her a good turn by suggesting a game rather than merely beating the information he wanted out of her. Now she was trying to repay him with one in return. Her nervousness seemed to have entirely disappeared when she turned back to Serpent. She even laid a hand on his arm, in a way that felt far too familiar, even condescending, for a sprog to her CO.

"I think the human has tricked us. He knows that the queen has said we are not to do anything to him. She has said we are to let him do what he wishes without opposing it. We are not to take his choices from him, nor to act on him. He acts, we do not hinder."

"What do *you* care what the queen has said? The queen is..." Serpent stopped himself, with a glitter of annoyance like the green flare of a bomb marker through fog. "Entitled to obedience, of course."

He was lipless as a serpent as he turned to Flynn and said, "Clever. You bargained on us not being able to get in your way. You knew that if you asked us to choose, we would have to give the choice back to you. Quite admirable thinking, for a human."

It would have been, Flynn had no doubt, if only he knew what the hell the pair of them were talking about. Still, the blinding seemed to have taken a backseat. "So?" he said, trying to encourage them to explain it a little more.

"So tell me what you wish us to choose."

He'd lost, and in losing the game, he seemed to have won the battle. Bloody creatures, one couldn't make head nor tail of them. "You will take me to where Sumala is being imprisoned," he began, "and—"

"No 'ands'. One answer per question. Those are the rules. Very well, get up, we will go now." Serpent kicked the legs from the chair on which Willow had curled, sending her flying. "And you can get out of my sight and stay out. Do not think that your allegiances will protect you should you ever come into my territory again. You spoiled my sport, and the gods themselves, were they still alive, could not stop me from making you pay the full price."

The dungeons lay beneath the throne room but were accessed by a door in the side of the final gate of the city—the Gate of Will. It was made of crystal, and the door opened only by the power of command. When it sealed itself shut behind Flynn, leaving him in sudden impenetrable silence, embedded like a fly in amber, he had some misgivings.

Below, a spiral staircase wound widdershins into darkness. Serpent trotted down it on light feet, even the small of his back giving Flynn the impression that he was smiling. He had not brought a torch or given Flynn to understand that he would need one. Flynn followed him into a hole like that of Alice's rabbit.

He set his hand to the wall and went down. The light flowing through the door fell off almost immediately, and blackness pressed on his eyes. Ahead, he could no longer hear the light footfalls of the elf. He lost track of time as he descended. His knees, thighs and ankles protested, and at the faint pain he thought, *He's taking me to the centre of the earth!*

The air had the musty scent of recently disturbed dust. Particles clogged his nose and tasted in his mouth like talc. Cold seeped through his flying jacket, an underwater, damp cold, like the moist press of earth at the bottom of a grave. He thought of calling for Serpent, thought again—he was not yet that desperate.

Just as he'd convinced himself that he'd been lured into a trap, been given the sort of Sisyphean task that must be setting the guardroom in fits of laughter—set to walk down a stair that went nowhere, forever—there came a glimmer of grey light. It showed a ring of large flagstones and a doorway at the end of the stair. When he ducked through, he set a hand on the wall and felt the vibration and faint sound of running water. It was the only sound.

Ahead of him stretched a single huge room, carved up into a chequer-board by stone tables. On each table lay a figure, like a funerary statue, on their backs, hands folded on their breasts. Hundreds of them. The colours looked stony too in that grey light. Darkness above them, veins of crystal winding down from each table into a grid on the floor, and all the prisoners on their tombs, their eyes open, but their chests not moving. They looked newly struck down, peaceful, without a wound on any of them.

The skin across Flynn's shoulders itched as the hair tried to stand on end. He couldn't tell if the cold moisture on his face was dew or sweat. The weary light fell from steel stars embedded in the distant roof. They shone in groupings which may have meant to represent constellations, but which he, with three years of night flights behind him, could not recognise. Grey light spilled out of them in a fog that slowly sifted downwards to pool in a still lake just above the corpses' faces.

Not corpses, he reminded himself, wishing for the imaginary voice of his skipper, the familiar comfort of it. Not corpses, prisoners.

Ahead of him, Serpent paused at last. They had walked together perhaps a mile, through sleepers spaced a bare four feet apart. The narrow path from the stair glimmered a little where the tributaries of crystal had formed up into broader runnels that threaded back to the gate. But the room itself stretched away beyond sight on every side.

"How many of them are there?" Flynn whispered, turning to the elf for the comfort of another living thing. His voice sounded obscenely loud, as if he were swearing while other people prayed.

Serpent just gave him that narrow, pointed smile and gestured with the tattooed hand. Here, two ranks in from the path, Sumala lay, motionless as all the others, her open eyes staring at the strange stars, all the little bells of her headdress silent and her body not stirring even to breathe.

"They're dead." Flynn turned a circle, aghast. "You've killed them all. Killed her too. Why?"

"You won an answer and I've given it. I'm not obliged to give you anything more."

Serpent swept Flynn with a contemptuous look, withering him with scorn from head to foot. "But I will tell you for free that you are the most ignorant being I have ever met. I'll be glad when they let me kill you, as should have been done at first."

His scathing glance drifted off the end of Flynn's foot to the floor, and there it stopped. Everything in him tightened and went on alert. Flynn could see him vibrate with urgency like a pointer dog spotting a fallen bird. He thought, *What?* But had the sense not to say anything. The guardsman had forgotten him, let it stay that way. He had at least raised a doubt that the girl wasn't dead, no matter what it looked like.

Following Serpent's gaze, Flynn saw white dust on the floor like scattered flour. White dust, glittering slightly with flecks of steel, settled out of the air even as he watched, blurring the edges of his footprints behind him. Beyond Sumala rows of empty plinths went on for another mile or more, and between these the dust lay soft and thick as snow, so what...?

There were paw prints in it.

The small padded footprints of some sort of animal—a cat, perhaps, or a kitten. The next sound was a musical, metallic tearing as Serpent drew his sword. The blade picked up the grey light and glittered with it as Serpent hunkered down and put his free hand on the crystal edging of the path. "Guards to the dungeon! We have an intruder."

Some kind of intercom, then? Flynn took a second look at the layout of the room, seeing the inlaid crystal afresh, not as decoration but as wiring. The chamber was a machine of some sort, and one did not need a machine to dispose of the dead.

"Scared of a kitten?" He laughed, covering his pause for thought, watching the blush of anger turn the tall elf's face the colour of mahogany.

"Out." Serpent gestured with his free hand towards the stairs. "Get out now. This is none of your concern. Nothing of what we do is your concern, Ghost, more fit to be a human slave than to blunder around in the business of your betters. Flit off somewhere else now. I've work to do."

He stalked the trail of footprints, his own feet leaving no mark in the dust. Somewhere, in the darkness to the northern side of the chamber, there came a scrabbling sound, and Serpent cocked his head, triangulated, and was off, running between the plinths, drawn sword in his hand, at a speed that bemused Flynn's eye, made him see a constant band of motion, heading north.

But there was another, coming towards him. The blur stopped, resolved itself into a tiny animal, a kind of weasel, he thought, with black-and-gold fur and socks of white on its clawed feet. It bunched itself up to flee again, and then looked up and saw him. Gazing down, he met the metallic yellow eyes and hesitated. Didn't he recognise them? Hadn't he seen them before somewhere?

As they stood looking at each other, the air in the chamber shivered, and Serpent was there, smiling. He did nothing but smile, Flynn thought with sudden anger, and yet there was nothing friendly, nothing amusing about him. His smile made his whole existence an act of sarcasm.

The little animal bolted forwards, set its claws in Flynn's trousers and climbed him, worming its way inside his Mae West. He could feel the pricks of its claws through his jacket, and the panting warmth of its breath.

"Well, if you choose to put yourself between me and my prey..." Serpent laughed, drew back his sword, and Flynn ducked down into a rugby crouch and rammed him. It was like colliding with an enormous bird—the feeling of not enough weight, of something delicate and breakable and fragile, knocked over because he was not taking care. The sword passed over his head, and as Serpent recoiled, slamming backwards, not letting go, it whispered back past Flynn's cheek and opened a shallow stinging cut there. Blood mixed with the sweat on his face.

"You can't interfere with me!" Flynn yelled, grabbing Serpent's sword arm, squeezing tight. He could feel the bones bend inwards from the pressure of his fingers. "Drop it. Drop it, damn you! You can't hurt me. You can't stop me. So drop the damn sword right now!"

Under his weight, the elf writhed, fluttering, his face contorting from the pain. Flynn held his sword arm down with one hand, the weapon clanging forlorn against the floor. He shifted to replace his hand with a knee, brought the other knee into the centre of Serpent's chest. A man would have bucked him off easily, but the elf had no such strength, didn't even have the strength to breathe beneath his weight. Flynn got both hands around Serpent's throat and was struck anew by the feeling of spun-glass fragility, weightlessness.

Serpent pulled desperately on his hands with fingers as frail as icicles. His very helplessness made Flynn ease off, kick the sword out of reach and let him breathe again.

"I can't stop you," he said, "can't interfere." The blood in his mouth was a thin, bright orange, like the blood of a housefly. "How sporting does it make you, then, when you do this?"

Flynn took a deep breath and watched as Serpent choked down another breath. From inside Flynn's jacket, the creature wormed its way down his sleeve, emerged across the back of his hand, and sank its teeth into the flesh just below Serpent's undefended eye. Disgusted at it, he swept it away, gave the struggling elf what seemed to him a punch on the jaw that even a girl would have been hard-pressed to feel and watched him slump into unconsciousness with a feeling of revelation.

All this time he thought he'd been a helpless prisoner of war, left to kick his heels in a prison camp, and now it seemed he had more going for him than he'd suspected. He wasn't a hostage after all, but some kind of player in this game—one who was expected to do something important and must be left free to do it. And he had more weapons in his arsenal than he had supposed.

A stir in the corner between the path and the base of one of the plinths caught his eye. He looked and was just in time to catch the ribbon of shadow and light that was the weasel changing into the lanky yellow-green form of Willow. She scrambled to her feet and gave him a feral look, wild and wary, "You heard him call for the guards. They'll be coming."

"I'm here to rescue Sumala." Flynn didn't have time for astonishment or even curiosity. "That one there. Is she dead?"

"She's not dead." Willow plucked at his arm. There was bright orange blood in the corner of her mouth. He could see why she did not want to meet the rest of her companions again.

"But there isn't time. We can come back. Please!"

"They can't do anything to me," Flynn said, testing out this new and welcome thought. "Even if they find me here, they'll have to leave me alone."

"Yes, but not me, and I helped you. I was sent to help you." She had begun walking backwards, still with her hand tangled in his sleeve. He let her guide him away from Serpent's fallen form, back onto the path.

There was a footfall on the stair, the sound of it echoing loud and vulgar through the hollow chamber. Someone said, "Ssssh!" and Flynn allowed Willow to pick up their pace as he followed her directly east, threading between the stone tables. Losing himself amongst the dead.

"They're not dead," she repeated, as if she had read his thought, or—more likely—his shudder. "Come on."

Grinding slow but fine like the mills of God, Flynn's thoughts finally caught up with what she had said to him earlier. "Sent to help me?"

He'd thought their meeting accidental, but when he looked back, remembered that she had come in after the final guard, that she had attracted his attention by trembling when later she had not been nervous at all, and that she had spoken back to Serpent not like an underling but like an equal, it fitted. In intervening to help him, she hadn't been paying him back for his kindness at all. She had been sent for the purpose. "Who by?"

Shadows now blocked the exit by the spiral stair. The tearing silk sound of swords being drawn, and then four tall figures bowed themselves through the low archway and straightened up, looking around. It seemed all of a sudden an inappropriate place to ask questions. Willow thought so too, she broke away and dashed through the deepening shadows, he had to race full pelt to keep up with her, and behind him he could hear the rushing noise that was four heavily armed guards running faster than he could see in pursuit.

At the edge of the chamber, the floor sloped in a concave curve up to become the wall. The room was a huge bubble, he saw—a single massive semicircular bubble of stone underneath the throne room. Ribbons of crystal snaked up the walls and spread like rivers amongst the grey stars. Willow had knelt where two tributaries of those rivers met on the floor, forming a triangle with the base of the final stone table. The man who lay atop this one was scarcely recognisable as a sentient creature. Carved out of jet, and with a coating of ash. Flynn took a double take at the horns, the bat wings and the long claws on each finger and shivered. Crikey.

Across the chamber moved the blurs of the guards. He set his back to the wall and clenched his fists, feeling quite the Superman. But then there was a click, and he looked down to find Willow already only visible by the hair, descending another flight of stairs while holding open one of the flags of the floor. It was pitch dark down there, but the oncoming guards glittered with a suspiciously chain-mailed gleam. Thinking of punching a million rings of metal, Flynn crouched down, leapt over the edge of the trapdoor and let Willow close it behind them with a snick.

The darkness was total, but the sound of the river much, much clearer. "Can you see?" she asked, and when he whispered, "Nothing at all," she took his cuff again and ducked under his arm, placing his hand on her shoulder.

"It's only a little way down."

There was a smooth stone jetty and what he guessed was a boat. When he stepped into it, it bobbed like a cork, and the sound of water rushed on either side. They cast off, and he felt wind, cold and wet against his face. He counted heartbeats, then lost count as they sped through the underground dark. Eventually, when there was no sign of pursuit, he said again, "Sent by whom?"

The darkness thinned. A speck of light in the distance rushed towards them, burst over them—a cave in the side of the palace mound, overhung by trees. They rushed headlong from the copse, went wheeling and tumbling down reefs of white water among meadows of long grass and reeds, away from the palace and out, until they came once more under the shade of the distant forest.

"I'll show you," she said. "It isn't far."

A half hour later, they moored on the banks of a small clearing. The shingle beach was covered in small stones of all colours. An alder hung over the stream, with its roots in the water and its leaves rustling in the faint breeze. In the clearing, blond meadow grasses rippled, and poppies and cornflowers gave the whole thing a sense of tapestry. The forest that surrounded them was dark green, and the scent of it blew sporadically lush and cool through the predominant smell of sunshine and heather.

"Here." Willow leapt out then hauled the boat farther up onto the shelving beach. Flynn scrambled out to help, and as he was doing so, the light altered. The daze of sun through leaves gave way to a more steady glare. There was a sucking sound, and the sand and pebbles shifted beneath his feet.

"Well done."

Flynn let go of the boat's prow and turned at the sound of a woman's voice. There had no one there, he would have sworn it. Now, barefoot in the edge of the stream, stood a tall woman with skin like snow and long, long black hair. Her eyes were black too, without iris or white. She wore a sweep of white gown and a girdle of leaves, long and narrow. The pouring black hair was held back by ropes of flowers. Daisies and forget-me-nots and the little sun faces of dandelions.

"What the...?"

She smiled. Quite a different smile from Serpent's. This was gentle, regretful and carried a sense of age. Perhaps it was the look of patience or wisdom that she wore on a face handsome, not beautiful. He liked the look of her but knew better than to read anything into that.

"Welcome, Navigator," she said. "Perhaps we shouldn't stand with our feet in the water, I know that humans find that uncomfortable. Shall we?" She gestured up the bank to the meadow where he saw a blanket had been set on the grass, and shadowy servants were even now putting down bowls of fruit, goblets of wine. "You are very welcome here. I have long intended to speak with you."

He trudged up the bank behind their graceful steps and noticed that her robe didn't even bend the blades of grass over which it passed. It was some kind of fog, he thought, some kind of white water, held suspended in an unaccustomed shape. "Oh yes? I thought I was not to be interfered with? They call me Ghost. Treat me like one too."

"It's an interesting name." She swooped down to sit on the white wool of the blanket. "Do you think it's apt?"

"I'm sorry?"

"Would you say you were alive, Mr. Flynn?"

He laughed and then remembered how, in that first waking, he had thought he was in heaven. He'd been wrong though, surely. "I'd say I was, yes."

"Or dead, perhaps?"

The amusement was a little bleaker this time. "Is this Hell? Is it some kind of purgatory for people who couldn't make up their minds between good and evil?"

Sympathy in her smile. She inclined her head slightly and offered him a plate of strawberries. "No. This is a world set sideways to your own, but it is not an afterlife."

"Then yes, I'm very much alive."

"That's what I thought." She leaned back on her elbow and sipped at wine the colour of rubies. The scent of it poured slowly out of the cup and pooled on the ground between them, a heavy, honey scent. "I have not spoken to you before because you were aimless, drifting about our world like a cloud, blown hither and yon by the winds.

"But now you have begun to act. It has seemed wise to me, therefore, to tell you something of the world in which you find yourself. Our problems and our...oppression. Unlike Oonagh, who keeps you in ignorance, I wish you to be better informed. For we should be allies, you and I. We have common cause. I am Liadain, leader of the resistance, and if you will help me, I will find you a way home."

Chapter Six

"Well, this is it. Home sweet home." Chris launched Ben's bag into the hall with scant regard for his netbook or aftershave, followed it with a couple of the ghostbuster devices from the back of his van. Two up, two down, the little grey stone cottage squatted in the centre of a yard full of abandoned machinery and brambles. A dry stone wall enclosed the garden and butted onto the road where a wrought-iron gate closed a serried rank of spears against the world.

All around the house, summer trees whispered like the sea. Moving water slid behind the back garden, and a runnel broke off to encircle the house. A paving slab formed a crude bridge over it, between the front path and the porch.

If Ben opened the gate and stepped outside, onto the road, the stars glared at him, the smudgy light of the lamp rolled and dripped like water vapour, and in the corners of his eyes, he caught dim silver tendrils of light writhing over the distant hills. If he stepped inside, he saw rust and weeds under a mundane sky. Cheery blue paint peeled from the front door and fell into the warped wooden porch, where Ben barked his foot on a rucksack full of bricks as he went inside.

The lampshade in the centre of the front room shared Chris's fashion sense—a dusty cone of mustard-yellow velvet with tassels.

Ben picked his way between piles of books. A coffee table, made from a sheet of plywood set down on four packing crates, was piled high with magazines and dirty plates, pamphlets, stones and strange devices.

The sofa sat sagging, its red-velvet upholstery balding beneath pens and a pile of ironing. The ironing board stood in the corner by the television where the window gaped uncurtained on a view of black Pennines against plum-purple sky.

"I wasn't expecting visitors." Chris folded down the board and leaned it against the wall.

"I can see that." Ben peered through into the kitchen. Much the same, the clutter flowed over work surfaces. More books, interspersed with cups. Upstairs, a closed door must be the bedroom because the other open door was the bathroom, where the peeling paint was joined by a scattering of black mould around the frosted windows and above the bath.

Downstairs Chris had pinned up a large bath towel over the curtainless window and turned the television to a report on last year's Chicago World Music Festival.

Ben remembered, all of a sudden, that he still hadn't said thank you to Chris for riding to the rescue, for turning the terror of last night into the mild embarrassment and curiosity of this one. He wouldn't say thank you, of course, but he took the can of beer Chris held out and drank.

Moving the pile of laundry to an empty spot of floor in front of the hearth, Ben slumped onto the sofa, watched the TV intently as a man under a green spotlight played an Ethiopian krar.

Chris lowered himself gingerly to perch on the edge of the cushion next to Ben, and he was glad to be distracted by the straight man's discomfort. Without the beer he might have said, *Don't flatter yourself. You're not my type.* With it—and the seven other pints he'd sipped relentlessly over the course of a day imprisoned in the pub—the lie seemed too complicated. "You'll make someone a terrible husband," he said instead.

It was a tactical blunder. Chris chuckled and leaned back. With him sprawled across the cushions, there seemed suddenly far too little room on the sofa. An inch or so between Ben and the older man, and their auras must be running together like spilled paint because he could almost feel the electrical storm of Chris's thoughts, the fire and pulse of muscles and beat of his blood like a counterpoint to the melody on the TV.

He shifted, uncomfortably, thought about dirty plates and whatever it was that was sticking into his back, managed not to think about being hounded by legends. A tight lid on his thoughts kept him just about calm, but the balancing act was getting trickier every minute.

"I know it looks like a mess." Chris reached behind Ben and worked a metal staple out of the fabric. "But really it's a sort of distributed filing system. Everything's got its place. Sorry about the settee by the way. God knows why they thought it was a good idea to stuff it with wire. I should have wondered why it was free."

Something jabbed hard under Ben's right thigh now, like a bony elbow. Feeling under his leg disclosed the end of a spring, and then a second one, back and to the left.

"That's why that end gets used as a laundry basket." Chris shrugged. "But it's fine. I'll stick my feet down there. This side's not so bad. Guests get the bed, of course. Shall I show you?"

A clean bedroom with a worn green carpet and a bed with sheets, blankets and coverlet in place of a duvet. Wooden bedstead and another packing crate beside it as a side table. The bedside light with a Tiffany lampshade and a photo beneath it in an antique silver frame.

"I go out for a run first thing in the morning," said Chris, looking out of the bedroom door as if he could thus make the idea of another man in his bed disappear. "You'll be fine as long as you stay inside until Grace arrives. She's coming here first thing. She'll get you sorted out with the same sort of protection the rest of us use, which will mean you'll be okay to start living as normal again tomorrow. This house is safe too, but don't let anyone in who doesn't look like a Nigerian woman in a dog collar. Clear?"

"Yes, sir!"

Chris risked a look. Something about the light and the late night softened his face, smoothed the edges of his cheekbones and dimmed the hazel of his eyes to umber. It occurred to Ben that he looked tired, like a man who needed rescuing himself, and he had almost swayed forward and smoothed his thumbs comfortingly over the prominent cheekbones when the man stepped back abruptly and said, "Well. Good night."

The thud of an airing cupboard opening and the soft, muffled sound of a pillow falling to the floor. Silence—he would be gathering up bedding—and then the creak of feet down the unvarnished wooden stairs.

Ben sat on the edge of the bed and picked up the photo. Seven men in flight suits, helmets under their arms, stood in two self-conscious rows in front of the massive wheel and wing of an old-fashioned propeller plane. The photo had been tinted sepia to look more antique than it was, but showed a much younger Chris, his face lacking that touch of trademark cynicism, standing in the centre of the pack. All the men were grinning as if they'd snorted jet fuel and were higher than kites on the joy of being alive.

Looking at it any longer felt again too much like trespass. He set it facedown on the table and went to bed.

With the light off, the glow of the orange streetlamp filtered through the thin curtains, the bedroom too was a sepia-tinted photograph, like something washed up from the Edwardian era when time went slower. The bed had not been changed, and as he nestled into the heaviness of the blankets, Ben found himself surrounded by the smell of Chris. It was unpleasant in a way quite different from what he would have expected. He liked things clean, he would have preferred to sleep in clean sheets with the lavender and camomile scent of his own bedding. Yet at that pervading smell of Old Spice, shaving foam and sweat, it was his heart that protested, not his delicacy. He wrapped his arms around himself, put his cheek in his own hand and pretended they belonged to someone else.

Twice now he'd been attacked, twice badly frightened. It would have been nice not to be alone in the middle of the night.

Restlessly, he plumped the pillow and turned over. In the distance on the road into Matlock, a car passed, and the light of its headlamps travelled across the walls in a slow silver sweep. The photo frame glistened. Downstairs, he could hear the creak of the sofa. Then a *gloing* sound and a subdued curse. The weight of the blankets lay on his chest like a hug, and if he pulled the sheet up over his head, he could imagine arms around him. His imaginary lover was all darkness and smoke, the touch of his hands tender.

As warmth and drowsiness began to overcome him, his thoughts drifted. The loneliness that nestled like a pocket-sized black hole in his chest opened up and blossomed. His mind conjured the picture of that elvish knight, the pure intent on his face as he leaned forward, gaze cutting through Ben's skin, seeming to peel back his skull and expose the thing that lay in darkness there. What would it be to make love to such a creature? Surely like being a caterpillar, paralysed by some wasp's venom, feeling its larva hatch out within and begin to feed.

The thought returned him to full alertness with a fast-beating heart and a sense of being smothered in the heat. Turning onto his back, he pushed at the militarily tucked sheets at the bottom of the bed, getting his feet out into the air.

Somewhere in the house a clock ticked with a deliberate, old-fashioned tock. Chris's frustrated sigh echoed up the central stairwell, followed by a rustle and what must be the papery slide of one of those piles of pamphlets and magazines being kicked over. It felt as if it had always been the night, and always would, but when Ben rubbed his sanded eyes and looked at his watch, the little green light only said 2:43 a.m.

The texture of the brown half-light in the room altered. When he sat up, he saw that light was sifting through beneath the closed door. The television came on with a loud hiss of static, turned down with an apologetic swiftness. *What the hell,* Ben thought, lonely, heartsore, scared and tired, *he can only say no.* He swung his feet out of bed and padded gently downstairs.

In the light of the standard lamp, Chris sat on the floor, propped against the recalcitrant sofa and swathed in a blanket like a biblical character in a toga. His sandy hair stood up from one side of his head in spikes and lay squashed down on the other like a corn circle. A bare foot poked out of the end of the blanket, a glimpse of striped pajama trousers. The white vest he wore on top hugged his shoulders and chest. Ben would have put good money on it feeling soft as the shirt he had worn earlier, over corded muscle and hard bone.

Not that he was looking, of course. Not that he could tell from Chris's prickly stillness that Chris had heard him come in and knew that he was looking.

"Listen." He leaned against the doorway, trying hard to be unthreatening. "Why don't we just share the bed? That sofa's a death trap. I won't do anything, I promise."

Chris looked up from the remote control in his hand and smiled. Weariness and the enchantment of poor light made his expression look fond. Something affectionate and wry that belied the sting when he said, "Famous last words?"

This time Ben did say, "You're not *that* hot, you know." Which got him a laugh and Chris unfolding to his feet with the startling smoothness of a sword being pulled from its scabbard. He'd looked boyish on the floor, rumpled and domestic as something out of an Enid Blyton adventure story. Standing, with the blanket trailing from his crossed wrists, he might have been a senator caught in the act of stabbing Caesar—vivid and alive, virile and unmistakably guilty.

Well, and so he should be guilty, homophobic git, Ben thought, closing his unaccountably fallen-open mouth, and then his eyes, in case Chris could read his thoughts. He turned around abruptly. *See, I'm insulted. I'm not in any way hiding anything that must look painfully obvious in these shorts.*

Welcome to one of the world's worst ideas.

"If you're sure. I admit I'd underestimated the vicious nature of the sofa. And I'm getting a little old for the floor."

The bedroom was a different place with two of them in it. Chris's every movement seemed to make the air swirl. Ben could have sworn the man was the centre of a kind of golden maelstrom. He had stridden fast up the stairs, hopped into bed and was facing the wall, covered up to his ears in blankets before Chris closed the door behind himself. And yet as Chris snapped off the light, settled onto the edge of the bed, then clambered in, gingerly, careful not to touch Ben anywhere at all, Ben felt as though a strong light shone on his back. Questing fingers of force seemed to curl over him, all honey and tingle, and he burrowed closer to the mattress, partly to get away, partly to feel, just for a second, touched and embraced, even if it was only by nubbed cotton sheets and a tired mattress.

"Good night."

"You too."

Darker now and warmer, and the burning chill and weight of the singularity in Ben's heart was held away from him by the sound of Chris's breathing, the tiny movement of the bed as his chest rose and fell. The burning awareness of everything Chris did went out slowly like a tide receding. In its place came comfort. Just as he'd hoped, it was much better not to be alone tonight.

Sleep came unexpectedly easily, soft and heavy as a snowfall of feathers.

Chris dreamed of Geoff. The last hotel they'd stayed at, the morning of the last day of leave. Sunlight like searching fingers through the white curtains, and he stirred, drowsy and aroused, the taste of beer still in the back of his throat. Geoff lay with his arse tucked into Chris's lap, and that was a fine thing to wake to, rounded and smooth beneath a single layer of thin, soft fabric. Breathing out, a yawn and a sigh of contentment combined, he snuggled closer, reached out and pushed up Geoff's pajama top so that he could slide a hand beneath it and explore the soft skin, card through the wiry brown hair of his chest, half in need and half in simple affection.

Geoff arched his back, pushed himself closer, giving a lazy growl of encouragement, his voice deep and hoarse with sleep and bliss. Chris had turned his attention to the buttons now. A line of them down the pajama top, and he celebrated the undoing of each one by pulling the collar farther down at the back and kissing each inch of exposed back. God in heaven, the man had a back like Michelangelo's David, curves and hollows of muscle that might have been carved from marble.

Marble? Still and cold and reluctant? Where had that imagery coming from, when the two of them were so pliable and human and eager? The thought was like the first intimations of cramp, faintly troubling, easy to ignore in favour of the sweet lance of pleasure as they moved together. Squeezing his eyes tight shut against the broadening light, he bit along one shoulder, closed his mouth on the nape of Geoff's neck and sucked, worrying the skin gently with his teeth.

It had always made the man wake up fully, lose control, flip them both over and pounce. Chris expected, hoped, to find himself overpowered in short order, pinned, his wrists held above his head, and Geoff looking down on him, pleased with himself, smug and challenging and possessive.

Instead, this morning, Geoff shuddered at the touch and all the demanding tension left his muscles as he seemed to flow into liquid, yielding surrender. The rush of joy and delirious power fought with that intimation of wrongness when Geoff gasped, and his voice no longer sounded like his own.

There was no fly button, and when had Geoff ever worn shorts like these, stretchy knitted material like the fabric of a T-shirt?

But what the fuck did it matter when he was this close, and the man under him was making breathless, whimpering, needy noises and trying to hump the mattress? He pushed the shorts down and his own trousers in the same motion, and there was the touch of skin, slick and slippery with sweat. He bit down again and his not-quite-phantom lover cried out, in a noise half-pain, half-bliss.

Someone was enjoying themselves, obviously, so that was all good, yes? He closed his hand around the man's prick—hard, it was so hard it must hurt—stroked in time with his thrusts. The man rocked back into him, and it was sweet and fast. Prickle and copper taste in his mouth, fire in his spine and black, devouring need in his belly, balls tight as fists, and he hadn't had a dream like this for three years. So very…

He came with a bursting heart, pleasure like a rush of terror, as though a trapdoor had fallen open beneath him, plunging him into the short fall and the snap of the rope around his neck.

Real. It felt so very real. Because it *was* real. Because this was not a tissue of his old reminiscences and his dirty imagination, it was the shudder and then the shocked stillness of Ben Chaudhry in his arms. It was the clear light of a summer morning in the Peaks falling over Ben's rucked-up shirt. The bruises beginning to spread on his brown skin, the slow and careful way he turned his tousled head and blinked open eyes that were soft and black and puzzled.

God above, Ben had been asleep too; all that need, all that responsiveness had come out of his own dream world. Somewhere where he was being touched by someone who wasn't Chris—someone he wanted.

Ben's brows pinched together, his forehead furrowing, the muzzy vagueness of sleep disappearing, and he was beautiful. So young and fresh and naïve and…and so very taken advantage of.

Chris scrambled to the edge of the bed, hurled himself out into the still-chilly room. He grabbed a dressing gown, covered himself up.

"What…?" Ben's voice was nothing like Geoff's, lighter, a

young man's tenor, it sounded lost and confused and a little
betrayed. As well it might, considering that the boy had put
himself trustingly into Chris's hands for protection. A client. A
man half his age and one who had made it quite clear he
resented and disliked Chris. All that distrust he should have
been working to combat...all proved correct with one moment of
half-conscious selfishness.

"I..." He backed towards the door, not sure if he was
chivalrously protecting the boy or merely running away. "I, I'm
sorry. I'll go. I'll go out. Get out of your way. Grace, Grace can
help you. Oh God, I'm sorry. I'm really sorry."

He closed the door behind himself, bounded down the
stairs and bundled himself into yesterday's clothes. Yes, he was
a coward. Yes, he should stay and talk. He should do something
to help, be there in case Ben called the police.

He jammed his feet into trainers, opened the front door,
slung the rucksack full of bricks on his back and set off on his
morning run, head down, feet flying, trying to outrun guilt and
shame and memory, and even the nagging feeling that running
away like this was the worst thing he could possibly do.

But he was doing this for Ben, wasn't he? For his client, for
the man who had trusted him too far. So that Ben could pour
out the whole story to Grace and be gone by the time he got
back. So the boy need never look him in the face again if he
didn't wish to. And, God above, why would he?

Chapter Seven

The door slammed and Chris's hurrying footsteps bounded down the stairs. Ben felt an impulse to launch himself out of the bed, catch the man and demand some kind of explanation. But the impulse burst as soon as he saw the time on the clock. Five thirty a.m.? No. Nothing in this world was getting him out of bed before six fifteen at the earliest.

He lay back down, pulled the covers over his head to keep out the lemon-yellow sunlight that was making the striped walls look so cheery, closed his eyes.

The dark behind his eyelids was still soft and inviting, and his body hummed to itself with satisfaction, feeling boneless and inclined to purr like a cat in a warm lap. After a little while of drifting, waiting for vanished sleep, he put up a hand and felt the bruise on the back of his neck. Even the pressure of his own fingertips there, sliding over the sensitised flesh, made a tingling swirl of pleasure curl through his veins and seep out from the pores of his skin.

Good way to wake up. Unexpected, certainly, and goodness knows who Chris was dreaming of, because that abrupt departure had not been the sign of a man at ease with his actions. But he was warm, and he felt good, and he was certainly not in any mood to complain. Now if he only got breakfast in bed as well out of the deal...

When he opened an eye again, it was quarter to eight. He was going to be late for work and his charitable mood had given way to irritation. A power shower later, shaved and dressed in clean clothes, he'd worked up enough of a head of steam to go downstairs and face the inevitable conversation. *Listen, we were both half-asleep. These things happen. It doesn't mean you're gay, all right? And I won't tell anyone. Let's just rewind to the part where you spent the night on the sofa.*

He came downstairs into grey light and closed doors. Ben pulled down the towel from the window and folded it, finding an alcove behind the TV where it could be put away.

Beer cans on the floor. Without thinking, he took off his suit jacket, gathered up the cans, the dirty plates and cups, that pizza box from the corner, half-buried in CDs, containing a crust and a crumpled sheet of tinfoil which had clearly, at one time, been wrapped around garlic bread.

The kitchen door pushed open at the pressure of his foot. Here too the blinds were down and the light dim. He emptied the overflowing bin bag from the bin, deposited the pizza box inside, tied the corners and replaced it with a new one that he found—as he had expected to—beneath the sink.

There was bacon in the fridge, milk and a loaf of bread, instant coffee in a blue pottery jar by the side of the kettle. He opened all the cupboards, found frying pan and oil and salt.

Strips of bacon sizzling, he ran the water and washed the first batch of crockery. Sunlight poured through bubbles as the kitchen warmed and began to smell of toast and bacon, hot coffee and artificial soapy pine.

Eight o'clock and no Chris. Ben revisited his thoughts about how serious this morning's frolic must have seemed to the other man. It'd been fun, hadn't it? They'd both enjoyed it—he certainly hadn't been mistaken about that. And everyone knew that waking up was tricky, when you had a warm, willing body in the bed with you and your inhibitions not yet up to speed.

I'd do it again. No question.

But he wasn't Chris, was he?

He found tomato sauce to go with the bacon sandwich, ate, and then washed another batch of plates. Putting the vinegar, the pickled onions, the spare pot of coffee and the soy sauce away in a cupboard left the surfaces bare enough to clean. There, that was better, apart from the inevitable piles of books and the engine in the middle of the floor.

With a fresh coffee in hand, he ventured back out into the front room, folded the bedding and took it upstairs to the airing cupboard, paused on the way back to look at the front door. Had that been the sound of a car door? Maybe Chris had driven off to do something manly and was now returning with sump oil under his fingernails and his heterosexuality intact.

A different generation. Not one which took these things quite as lightly as Ben did. As he waited for footsteps on the path he took another look at the living room and thought, *All it really needs is bigger bookshelves. Maybe a couple of filing cabinets. I could fix real curtains over that window in five minutes.*

Taking this lightly, are you?

The thought was like a goose walking over his grave—that same unsettling wave of cold, the realisation that nothing after this thought was ever going to be the same as it was before.

And then the doorbell rang. He jumped so high the coffee sloshed out of the cup and spattered a purple pamphlet titled *The Cryptozoological Times, part VI: Mothman and the Goat-sucker, entity or apparition?*

Not Chris, then. Chris would hardly have rung the doorbell of his own house. Which meant it was this Grace person... Or something more sinister. He dived into the kitchen and, rooting through the drawers, came up with a paring knife with a blade four inches long and a wicked needle point.

The bell rang a second time, and a woman's voice called, "Hello! Are you in there?"

Blade held behind his wrist, he turned the knob of the lock, opened the door a crack and peered through.

She had pink hair. Only Chris, he thought, would not think that was worth mentioning. Hundreds of tiny pink braids, tight to her scalp, tied at the back in a bun like a Catherine wheel. She wore a purple hippy skirt and a velvet waistcoat atop a pink clerical shirt.

Somewhere between himself and Chris in age, strong faced and very dark skinned, she had bright intelligent eyes and held a white robe and a green stole, embroidered with a gold cross at each end, over her arm.

"You'd be Ben." Her broad, Cockney consonants took him aback, he'd got so used to thinking of the Peaks as a million miles away from London, too far away to communicate or visit. "I'm Grace. There should be a secret handshake, but I never could get the hang of them. Is Chris not in?"

"He... Um." Ben stuffed the hand with the knife in it into his pocket. The knuckles grazed something rough and cold, unexpected. He brought out the nail he'd forgotten from yesterday, still embedded safely in its cork. "He had to go out. Maybe you should hold this."

She took it from his hand and smiled, keeping her lips pressed together, only the skin around her eyes wrinkling in amusement and, he thought, approval. Nothing uncanny happened when she touched the iron, so he guessed she must be who she said she was.

"Good idea. So can I come in?"

"Of course."

He backed into the hall and watched as she swept inside. The fringes of that long, improbable skirt dusted the skirting board as she passed into the living room and perched, with the air of one long familiar with the sofa, on the edge of the table, putting her vestments and the nail down next to her. "Someone's been tidying."

"That would be me." He wondered if he should offer coffee or if she, as a much longer-term friend of Chris's, should be the one to do so. "Tidying tends to happen around me, when I'm thinking of something else."

"Well, you've certainly got enough to think about." She moved past him into the kitchen and brought a teapot out of the one cupboard he had not looked in—because he had been so sure it would contain only the vacuum cleaner. When she put the kettle on and added tea bags, he thought that was his question answered.

She set a cup of tea in front of him with an almost sacramental gesture, as though it were a chalice. "Or at least, I assume so. I didn't get the full story of what's happened to you from Chris, but he wouldn't have alluded to life-threatening circumstances or dragged me away from my family at a time like this unless it was urgent. Besides, whatever happened, it must have been big. It must have frightened you"—she waved a hand around the room, this stranger's room—"to make you agree to this."

"It did," he agreed, and took a chocolate biscuit from the barrel. "Though it runs out of my fingers when I try to believe it. I know it happened. I know I am here because of it, but it's hard to bring myself to describe it to you, in case you think I am mad."

"And it's hard to believe that if I, or Chris, can take you seriously, we can possibly be sane either?"

"Right."

"Are you a believer, Mr. Chaudhry? I haven't seen you in church, but perhaps you are a Hindu? Or Muslim?"

"I'm not much of anything." This morning's irritation returned, a slow itch of annoyance under his skin. "My family converted to Christianity before they left India, but that was before my time. Their reasons were...political. Not a matter of any great conviction. They left me to make my own mind up. So far I haven't seen any need to bother."

"You never thought of Christianity yourself?"

"Why would I, when I'm gay?"

He hadn't meant for it to come out like that—like a clenched fist. But she was right, he was scared, and angry because of it, and ready to knock down anything that looked like a threat.

If only Chris would come back. Something about the man's rudeness was reassuring. He had a capable air. Ben had felt safe when he was around. It would have been nice to have him here to taunt, when the vicar got started on the hellfire and sin of his "lifestyle".

"There seems a lot of that about, these days," she said, which wasn't much in the way of condemnation. But the lines at the sides of her eyes smoothed out, leaving her without a smile for the first time in the conversation. She put her cup down gently in its saucer and put on the white robe.

Folding the stole in the centre, where there was a third cross, she kissed it there, right on the embroidery and passed it over her head. The little cross rested exactly in the place on her neck where Ben's bruise nestled on his.

"It's a shame you don't have faith," she said. "That would make this stronger. As it is, I will have to give you something else, like a talisman, whose power will be enough to protect you.

Something strong enough to counteract your lack of personal belief. Do you feel able to kneel?"

"Do I have to?" He was not happy with her assumption of authority, the easy, confident way she did it, as though backed by something larger than herself.

"No, of course not. It's traditional to bow your head, to show humility—you are asking for something, after all. The Lord doesn't *have to* give you anything. This is not magic we're doing here. It's a request for help. But if you don't feel capable of being humble, simply standing there will do."

She hoisted up the white robe to draw a small book out of her skirt, and from the other side produced a hip flask and a tiny silver instrument that looked like an egg whisk. "Oh, Lord, who parted the Red Sea to draw your people out of slavery in Egypt..."

I'm not one of His people, Ben thought, trying to beat down the squirm of resentment. *My ancestors were never in Egypt.*

"Who commanded the raging waters to be still..."

Neither were hers.

"Bless this water to your use..."

Neither were Chris's, come to that. And how bizarre is it that we're all supplicating a tribal god, and it isn't even the god of any of our tribes?

Water spattered into his eye, landed cold on the corner of his mouth—little droplets of water hitting him like pins as she circled him, dipping the whisk in the flask and flicking it at him. He was showered by holiness, put out his tongue and licked just in case it tasted like gin.

After the third pass she paused in front of him, folded her hands and began a long prayer to which he didn't listen. Behind him, the door from the kitchen to the garden ground open, scraping over the lino. A thud and a ceramic clinking noise, and when he looked back, there was Chris, sweaty, red faced and ill at ease, putting down his brick-filled rucksack just inside the door. Never mind the water and the hocus-pocus, Ben suddenly felt a whole load more protected.

Chapter Eight

They didn't like each other. Chris mopped his streaming brow on the tea towel and, catching Ben's disapproving look, flung it onto the floor in front of the washing machine. Damn. He'd hoped they would—hoped it would all be out in the open now and Grace in a position to negotiate between the two of them, like a referee or a chaperone. Or a priest. Hoped that, at the very worst, she'd be Ben's champion, ready to take over responsibility for keeping him safe, even if the first evil thing she had to drive away was Chris himself.

"All right then?" he said. Not the most eloquent inquiry, but he badly wanted to be assured that it was. How could he have done such a thing? And after he'd deliberately let slide so many chances to tell Ben, *You want to stop assuming things, son. I'm not now and never have been straight.*

Grace took off her alb and folded it with reverential care. Setting it down near the toaster, she put her prayer book and stole on top, pulled out a glass vial from her waistcoat pocket. "Have you got that little funnel you use for the meths stoves?"

He brought it out of the drawer and passed it to her, trying to decide how upset Ben looked. The young man was composed. But in the short time they'd known each other, he'd rarely been anything other than composed. He reminded Chris of a Victorian photograph he'd once seen, a visiting Indian prince seated beside the queen, she looking dumpy and housewifely, he devastatingly elegant, with the beauty and arrogance of a falcon.

Grace bent her head over the tiny funnel, fitting it into the neck of the vial, pouring in water from her flask. Ben turned, and his soot-dark eyes looked warm, amused. *Mysterious.* Chris clamped down on *alluring*, dropped his gaze and ground the heel of one foot into the toes of the other, because he'd just spent a large part of the morning trying to outrun feelings of that sort. He shouldn't be encouraging them now.

Ben studied the gesture of self-control. His mouth turned up at the ends. "Thinking bad thoughts, Wing Commander?"

Arrogant little sod. What did he expect Chris to say with Grace in the room? Oh, Ben might have poured out the whole story—the boy was young, and youngsters these days had no shame when it came to sex...

Wait, though, that was an interesting thought. Youngsters had no shame these days, and there Ben was, smiling like he'd got one over on Chris. It came up like the lava in a lamp, shouldering everything aside with a great glossy welling up of relief; Ben was smirking.

And smirking was not, perhaps, the expression of a victim, of a man betrayed. Not even of a man embarrassed and ill at ease. If anything, Ben was exuding the smugness of a man who'd found buried gold and intended to keep it all to himself.

"Bad thoughts, Mr. Chaudhry? I never have anything but the best of thoughts, and my instincts are splendid."

"For an old man."

Oh, Chris swallowed. That was...uncalled for. And rather delightful. "If you have complaints, I will of course try harder next time."

"Harder? How much harder?"

Grace set her flask down on the work surface with a click, leaned back, crossing her arms. They both started guiltily. Just for a moment it had been as though she hadn't been there at all. "I don't think I want to know what this is about." She pursed her lips, raised her eyebrows, then snorted, blowing out exasperation through her nose. "I can see I'm in the way. Here."

She handed the vial of water to Ben, who sniffed at it cautiously, the little plastic stopper held in his other hand. "It smells of snuff. I thought you said there wasn't any witchcraft in this."

Grace chuckled. "I think it's funny—holy water in an imp. The smell does cling, though, even when you've used all the perfume up and washed the bottle twice. Think of it as the odour of sanctity. I know I do."

"And this"—Ben looked askance at the tiny test tube full of water, with its plastic lid and remnant of torn-off label—"will protect me from...them...so well I can go back to work?"

"Yes." Grace poured out a cup of very stewed tea and gulped it down. "It needs to be on you at all times, though. I suggest you sew it into one of those tennis sweatbands that goes around your wrist—something you can sleep in. Don't take it off. If you've had the sort of fright that makes coming for help to Matlock Paranormal seem sensible, then you don't want to risk ever putting this down. Not until the larger problem is sorted. All right? And bear in mind that you haven't even addressed the larger problem yet. That has to be done if you're to be secure in the long run. This isn't a solution. This is just buying you time."

Ben looked at the door with an expression of uncertainty. Chris had not shut it properly and the wind, gusting over the peaks, kept opening and closing it—a stripe of bright morning and the skirl of cold, granite-scented air, and a creak and thud as it shut again. "What do I have to do to get rid of them permanently?"

"You could convert." Grace refolded her arms and the brief

moment of cordiality was over.

"Even that might not help," Chris said. "Remember Tam Lin? The old star on his brow? But they still grabbed him and held him."

Responsibility hit Chris like flying into turbulence. There was nothing beneath his wings holding him up. He fell, heart in mouth, hands slippery on the joystick, brought the nose up, increased speed and won through, plunging back into confidence on the other side. They would not get Ben. He didn't know what to do to prevent it, but he *would*. Dying in the attempt was acceptable, but failing was not.

Wiping his hands on his shirt, he wished for a shower. Wished, in a moment of weakness, that he had left all of this alone, as the RAF had advised—or that all of it would have been content to leave *him* alone. But that way lay madness. You couldn't un-see what you'd seen, or un-know what you'd known. Besides, he'd never have met Ben if it wasn't for *them*.

Grace took him by the elbow and hauled him physically into the garden, leaning back on the door to force it closed. "Chris, what are you doing?"

"Hm?"

"I saw you looking at him." She'd lowered her voice to an urgent whisper, and the effect was to make it hiss like the wind in his ears. "What were you doing in there? *Flirting?*"

"If I was?"

"Well, I'm shocked. You know the church's position on these things. A man can't be blamed for how he's made, but you have the look of a man who is contemplating acting on it."

"Grace, this is none of your business."

"On the contrary, it is very much my business. It is my business as your priest to ask you to refrain from sin. And it is my business as spiritual adviser to Matlock Paranormal to tell you not to mess around with your clients, especially when they've come to you in fear and trust, in a life-threatening position, looking for your protection."

The sun flashed in angry disks from the mirrors of her skirt, but her voice softened. "I know you know that, Chris. I wouldn't have got involved with your work if I didn't know you were a good man."

A gentleness that was one step away from pity, harder to take than outright rebuke. "Besides, there's every chance he's not thinking clearly. Do you remember how you felt when you found out these things were real? I do. I ran headfirst to anything that could take my mind off what I had just learned."

From the other side of the garden wall came a cawing of crows. Light danced green and gold on moving leaves. Through the channel he had laboriously dug around the outside of the wall, a tributary of the river Wye poured, gurgling. Chris looked up at the bright, empty sky and tried to remember that what he had made for himself was a refuge, not a trap. She had a point. She always had a point.

"I'm saying this as much for you as for him," Grace went on. "Perhaps he's the kind who won't care too much if he uses you for a week or so to take his mind off things. But I know you are not. And when his problem is solved and he wants to forget all this, I see you being badly hurt."

On the other side of the river, the roar and grumble of a tractor engine heralded the appearance of a harvester in the field of yellow hay. Chris squinted across the distance, watching it. Let her get it all out at once. Easier for him to respond once he'd got the full picture.

"Perhaps too," she concluded, putting a hand gently on his wrist, "he is putting a brave face on things, and he is in fact the kind who will look back and say 'I was vulnerable and alone, and he took advantage of me.' I worry about that too. For him, and for you."

"You're done?" he asked when she'd finished, looking down from his contemplation of the far field. "Message received and understood, Padre. You have to say these things. I know that. I have to say we're both old enough and ugly enough to look after ourselves, but I'll bear your words in mind. Let's leave it at that, yes?"

"Meaning you'll do exactly as you please?" She took her hand back, folded her arms.

"Meaning I'll do what I think is the right thing."

She laughed. "Well, that's as much as I can ask. Shall I show myself out?"

"No, I'm…" He opened the back door, conscious again of the need for a shower, breakfast, time to think. "Coming back in anyway. Thank you for the morning visit, and the chat."

This time she grinned, showing her badly chipped teeth while she gathered up her vestments and what remained of the holy water. "You don't get one without the other."

"You keep me honest," he said, leaning in to kiss her on the cheek. "I appreciate it."

Screwing up her face, she pushed him away. "Ew! Shower!" and laughed. Waving to Ben, who rose from his spot on the bottom of the stairs to see her off, she said, "Don't do anything I wouldn't, now," and was gone, revving off down Aston Lane, down towards Matlock.

"Now there's a scary lady," said Ben, not entirely approvingly. "So what does that mean? I can go now?"

Ben's overnight bag sat in the hall beside him. Some time ago, Chris had been on a stained-glass window-making course, and the fruits of his labour were now set into the fan window of the door. Lustrous ruby red and tangerine light striped Ben's downcast mouth. The playfulness of earlier had gone without a trace, and what remained was the sombre, polished young bank clerk who had opened the door to him yesterday.

"You can, yes. If that's what you want." He was an old fool to drag this up, to insist on words, but Grace had rattled him, to tell the truth, and he wanted this out, honest, unmistakeable. "Listen. I'm sorry about this morning."

"Are you?" Ben rolled the little vial of holy water between his fingers, gave a false, belligerent half smile. "Because it gets in your way when you try and look down on me for being gay?"

"You and that attitude," Chris marvelled. "Always on the attack."

"Oh yeah, and you can talk, Mr. Straight as a board and, guess what, twice as thick."

But Grace was right, he'd felt this himself—the uprooting of everything he knew, and the urge to pick fight after fight afterwards until he'd fought himself back to normality, tested everything and everyone for their strength, their reliability.

"I never told you I was straight, Ben."

"You damn well did!"

"I did not. I just didn't tell you I was gay. There's a difference. And frankly it's not something I'm in the habit of telling people."

Ben's hands shook. Chris noticed with approval that he tucked the vial into his top pocket carefully before he clenched them. "You didn't think it was important for me to know that before we *went to bed together*?"

Oh God, but that brought it home. Chris's turn to slump down on the bottom step and put his head in his hands. "I wouldn't have done anything. I didn't mean to do anything." He laughed at how pathetic that sounded, phrased it again in a way that made it worse. "My intentions were strictly honourable."

Ben kicked the door, stood looking at it for the space of two quick breaths, then knelt down and attempted to remove the scuff his black polished shoe had left on the wood with spit and his handkerchief. His first laugh was hard edged, like the sound of a bursting balloon, but the second far more natural. "It's just that you found me so irresistible?"

The soft curl of his hair was glossy as ravens' wings, and his fingers long and elegant. The side of his mouth had a chiselled, sculpted look that made Chris want to reach out and trace it with his lips and tongue. "There's something in that idea. I didn't see you doing a lot of resisting, yourself."

Tucking the hanky away, Ben looked up, smiling now, onyx eyes warm. "Well, it's nice not to have to pretend any more that I haven't noticed you're hot."

"I am?" Chris studied the floor, feeling embarrassment and pleasure scorch skin that had chilled under his damp shirt. Things *had* changed since his day. He and Geoff would never have said such things, even in private.

"You're supposed to say, 'and you're the most ravishing thing I've ever seen, Ben. Care to join me in the shower?'"

"I am?" Chris repeated, flummoxed. He pulled himself to his feet and felt again how clammy he had become. His muscles twinged, and he thought of Grace's words. This morning had been largely involuntary, but for anything that happened after, he would have no excuse. "I think I…I think I ought to give you a few days to think that offer over. No sense in rushing into things."

Chapter Nine

Light squeezed around the edges of the front door. The tiny hallway, just big enough for a phone table and a coat hook on the wall was like being folded in the pages of a book, cream paper on every side. Ben caught a glimpse of his own face in the mottled, dusty mirror that hung above the table and was shocked to see himself look so lost, so unprofessional.

Smoothing his face as he might have ironed his trousers, he leaned down and picked up his bag. "So that's it, then? You take the advice of your priest. Nail yourself back in your closet, and I go to work. Then what? Like she says, this isn't a solution."

The flask of water felt strangely cold against his skin, as though he were carrying an ice cube in his top pocket. It had a tingle, like the taste of sugar-free peppermints.

"Well, yes. You should be safe enough today to go about your usual business. I can come around this evening, bring a couple of sledgehammers. Get started on dismantling that extension."

Chris smiled cheerily enough, though his gaze was focussed on the line of putty around the window, rather than on Ben's face. He seemed unconcerned at the thought of Ben venturing out alone now that he had his holy relic to protect him. But Ben couldn't place much faith in the protective abilities of a teaspoon of water in an old perfume jar. Besides, how could Chris stand there, still looking flushed in his wet shirt, and expect him not to haggle a little on the matter of the shower?

"What if I want to stay? What if I was to insist we go upstairs and get naked, and I screw you hard in the shower while the water falls warm around us both, my fist in your mouth so you can't say anything stupid."

Chris got up, stepped back, while something flickered tawny-gold at the back of his eyes, and those sandy brows rose to cling to his hairline.

"What would you say to that?" Ben let the bag fall, closed the distance between them. Chris retreated farther, his heels knocking against the skirting board, shoulders against the wall. The handrail of the stairs, poking into his lower back, made him arch outwards, exposing belly and groin to Ben's fascinated gaze. Ben's spread hands settled on his chest, the texture of the shirt as though it dissolved between them, leaving hot, damp skin exposed.

Chris's eyes were hard and sceptical, but his mouth had gone soft. He didn't raise his hands either to pull Ben closer or to push him away. Ben blanketed Chris's body with his own, felt the sharp gasp through his own torso, telling, defenceless. His to do with whatever he wanted. And it felt good, so good...

"I would say I don't appreciate you using me as a distraction. I'm not here to help you prove that you're still in charge, Mr. Chaudhry." The contemptuous voice shoved him backwards better than any amount of force. He could feel the sting of it like a split lip. He reeled away, confused and hurt and yes, also uncomfortably ashamed, stood looking down, breathing hard, trying to will back the flood of imperious arousal.

When he dared look up again, it was into a smile. "Besides..." yellow morning sunlight on a hard expression, unyielding but wry, "...Grace'd have my balls if I touched you, and I'm more afraid of her than I am of you, Ben."

Oh so here came the seeds of that little chat they'd had, the two of them out the back. Spindly saplings of hellfire and guilt and duty. "What does she know?" he said. "Why shouldn't we?"

"Too many reasons to count." Chris straightened his shirt, backed up the stairs, his twist of grin unravelling into something softer. "She's right. You don't know how much of this is fear talking. Maybe when the problem's solved we can go out for a drink. Take it from there. But pushing it now... It's a bad idea."

Outside, a thin whistling whine went by overhead, and the shape of the light changed, the bars that filtered around the door strobing and flickering, green gold, choked with dust. Ben watched it, in case it was the precursor of something uncanny coming through the door, and while he was distracted, Chris took the chance to disappear upstairs.

He guessed that counted as a "Goodbye. Go to work." And left alone to face the outside world again, Ben could admit that maybe fear was a part of it. Maybe this awkward, rude, wrong-footed *thing* that was going on between him and Chris seemed more attractive to him because it took his mind off the threat and fatal lure of the unknown. But did that make it wrong? Did that mean he should let it fall apart, the wing commander retreating into the prickly defensive dark of his closet, and Ben left to his own devices again? And it wasn't that he was desperate and lonely...

Well, maybe it was that he was lonely. Had been lonely ever since he moved back up here, all his school friends gone away and not enough resilience in him since the bomb to make more. His life had been on hold ever since, suffocating in its respectable regularity, and now things were moving again. In a weird way, Chris was the most fascinating man to cross his path in years. It seemed a shame to let that go. But he knew a definite no when he heard it, and he wasn't going to try to negotiate that.

The water came on above his head, making the whole house hum with the sound of thundering gas boiler and speeding pipes. He found the phone book and rang for a taxi, straightened his hair and tie in the mirror. Since it wasn't going to get any easier, leaving, he opened the door at once, stepped through and let it snick shut on the Yale latch. There. Locked out. Even if he was tempted to go back, argue again, to ask Chris to come with him like some sort of miner's canary, he couldn't do it.

The back door's open, though.

He shook his head at the wheedling voice of his own cowardice and stepped over the narrow runnel of glinting water outside the front door, going down to the gate. Iron railings—it felt better to hold on to their slightly rusty points while he watched the road for his taxi. The day was already beginning to warm, and around the house the moving canopy of leaves smelled of cut cucumber. A syrup scent came up from the riot of purple Himalayan Balm that choked the river banks. Swans, on the water, were black and serpentine like miniature Loch Ness monsters.

Ben clutched his bag, set his jaw, and determined that he would not be needy and frightened. They thought he was safe, did they? Then he would act as if he was safe. When the taxi drew up, he left the shelter of the gate, plunged into the undefended day, and looked back through his window as they drew away to see whether Chris had watched him being brave. Maybe there was a shadow, looking out of an upstairs window. Maybe that was his imagination too.

"All right then, Ben?" Mrs. Stilman put down the stack of direct-debit forms in their pigeonhole and headed for the kettle at the sight of him. She dropped tea bags into two cups, added two spoonfuls of sugar for herself and topped them up with water. "Had a bad day yesterday?" She swept him with an all-body peer—he would have bet anything she could estimate his weight to the nearest pound by the tightness of his sleeves and the way his shirt creased where it tucked into his belt. "I must say you're looking a bit peaky. One of these twenty-four-hour colds, was it?"

"Skiving off, so I hear." Paul breezed out of his office in time to prop a hip against the tea table and ostentatiously admire his heavy gold cufflinks. His smile was full-fat with satisfaction and malice. "Spent all day in the pub. You needn't deny it. Our Dave works in the kitchen there and saw you, talking to that nutter and his chums."

"I wasn't about to deny it." Ben wondered why he had been so keen to return to work. "I had...a bad day with the flashbacks. I couldn't have worked, but I wanted to be where people were in case I injured myself."

Paul uncoupled himself from the table in a rush. His lips were plump and pink—much like the rest of him—and twisted with disapproval. "Oh yes. I'd forgotten about your loony episodes. So much for the 'extraordinary promise' you were supposed to display in your interview. Here." He pushed the pile of files he was carrying towards Ben. "I'll want these done by lunchtime. And I mean twelve o' clock. I'm lunching with the chairman, so if they're not done, I'll know who to blame."

He oiled back into his office with a good approximation of his usual self-satisfaction, but nothing could escape Mrs. Stillman's powers of observation. "Ha! That ruffled his feathers all right. You'd think flashbacks were catching, the way he reacts. Sorry to hear they're still not gone, though." She pushed over a flimsy box of white cardboard, opened the lid to display a cinnamon whirl, a pecan slice, a *pain au chocolat* and an iced bun. "Here, have a Danish. I didn't know whether you were coming, so I got the usual."

"Thanks, Mrs. Stillman." He pulled the cinnamon whirl onto a paper plate, carried it to his cashier's cubbyhole, right next door to hers. With a click and a hum, the distant rotating doors began their daily turning and the leaflets that lined the walls shivered in their wire holders.

Mrs. Stillman clipped a long restraining chain of faux pearls and jet onto the ends of her glasses and poised them on her nose. The thick lenses magnified the creases around her bright blue eyes. "That's Enid, Ben. How many times do I have to tell you?"

It occurred to him with a lurch of shock that she must be in her forties—not very much older than Chris—and he was glad his ritual denial had the force of habit behind it. "It doesn't seem right, Mrs. Stillman. What would your husband say?"

Chuckling, she bit into the *pain au chocolat*, stripping the pastry away from the lines of bitter chocolate, saving those for last. "He'd say the days I was mad enough to mean anything by it were long gone. Shame on you for thinking otherwise."

Ben smiled and bent his head over the pile of status reports Paul had foisted on him, writing a succinct summary of the portfolios of some of the bank's largest clients in bullet form on a separate piece of paper.

"I don't know why you put up with him." Enid leaned over to deposit a paying-in envelope in the sack between them, stayed there poised like a pointer dog over the papers. "That Paul. Slimy bastard had me doing all his work when he first joined, now he's moved on to you. You shouldn't have to handle this stuff—that's high-level stuff, that is—not without a raise, anyway. You should tell him where to stick it."

Ben connected his next customer with a loans advisor and thought that perhaps a man with fairies at the bottom of his garden ought not to be too inflexibly formal. He swapped his black pen for a red one, looked up at the clock and was surprised to see two hours had gone by since opening time. "Well...Enid..."

She giggled like a woman half her age at the sound of it, and Laura and Don at the next two desks leaned back to raise their eyebrows at one another, asking to be let in on the joke. He distracted them with the remaining two pastries. "Well, Mr. Bothy was always going to do well. He's the manager's nephew, after all. I don't see myself winning if I fight him."

"That's so..." The unfairness of it reduced her to making inarticulate hissing noises through the new teeth she'd recently had implanted at the cost of enormous money and pain.

Ben marked numbered x's in red pen down the side of the relevant photocopies and listed their vital statistics beneath his bullet-point presentation. Then he tucked the originals into five different folders, labelled with a system that only he understood.

"And to tell the truth, I don't care. I never meant to be a banker anyway. It—this job—I only meant it to be a stopgap thing while I got myself sorted out. What I really want is to find something musical to do, an orchestra to play in or a recording studio that needs an engineer. I don't want to get so bedded in that I can't leave at a moment's notice if something like that comes along."

Enid gave a *hm* of wry laughter. "Not to be a killjoy, but when I joined I thought, 'It's only 'til the modelling career takes off.' And here I am, twenty years later, too tired to care that sometimes dreams don't come true. If you really think you've got a chance, you want to go for it now while you still can."

It had the same flavour as what he'd thought about this morning in Chris's hallway—change, and the fact that although it was scary, it was exciting too. That perhaps he didn't have the option of hiding from it any longer. "You might be right." He made another indecipherable mark on the papers and grinned at her, suddenly hugely amused. "But I'll tell you what, when I leave, Paul will realise he doesn't understand his own filing system and he can't do his job without me. He's going to be in deep trouble, and I can't think of a nicer person for it to happen to. Teach him to do his own work in future, I hope."

"You're a wily one." Enid laughed.

"Actually I think that's why he doesn't like me mentioning the flashbacks. I think he maybe knows already that he relies on me too much and, if I go mad, his career goes down the pan."

Enid finished dealing with a customer who wished to take five pounds out of four different bank accounts and pushed back her chair, biting her lip. "I just told him to pull his finger out and do his own bloody reports. But I wish you luck with the long-term plan. Speaking of mad, though. I don't want you to think I am. But...well. Have you ever...?"

She pulled her faded brown ponytail over her shoulder and picked at the split ends. White, frayed hairs landed and were lost amid the shaggy raglan of her cardigan. "Well, I know you *have* been down in the basement. Course you have. You didn't...ever think there was something odd down there?"

"What d'you mean, odd?"

"Yesterday—" She broke off to polish the inside of her window with a yellow cloth. The single customer left in the atrium drifted down the walls of leaflets. He picked up *Mortgages Made Easy* and *Income Tax for the Self-employed*, looked up, saw Ben watching him and scurried swiftly away.

"Yesterday," Enid tried again. "While you were gone..." Her explanation failed at the same point. She glanced nervously over her shoulder at the door into the bank proper—the old building that the customers never saw. "Look, can you put your notice up for a moment? Don and Laura can hold the fort. I want to show you something."

Inside the bank proper, a corridor of white doors faced onto a passageway paved with faux-medieval tile. At the end of the passage a barred window was all but choked beneath a climbing rose. Dead heads scattered brown petals onto the floor. The dark mouth of the downward stairs smelled fermented sweet.

A wind moved the tangle of twigs and the thorns scratched against the bars like claws. Enid stopped at the head of the stairs and shivered, wrapping her arms around herself, hands tucked inside her cardigan. It was cooler here. Much cooler than the stifling cubbyholes out front. *The whole breadth of the building is between us and the sun,* Ben thought, leaning down to pick up the flaccid petals, roll them into a ball, and throw them outside. They felt unclean against his fingertips, damp and cold like the eyelids of dead men. As he was turning away, rubbing his fingers on his handkerchief to take the taint away, they blew back in, still furled around each other, crinkled from the squeeze of his hand.

He was bending down to try again when Enid plucked at his arm. "Don't!" Her spectacles gave her fish eyes, liquid and huge as a guppy's. "Just...don't. Come on. I think it's going to happen again. I wish it wouldn't, but I think it is."

The rose petals unfurled behind him. As Ben followed her

into the basement, they blew in ever-expanding spirals along the corridor and tumbled sweetly down the stairs.

"Can you feel it?" Enid asked. The stairwell was painted white, but generations of passing feet had ground a deep greyness into the treads. Generations of supporting hands, trailed along the wall, had smeared the paper with a matching grunge. Enid's breath came in hissing bursts, and she put her kitten-heeled shoes down with aching care so as not to make a sound.

"Feel what?"

"I don't know! Anything. Can you?"

At the bottom of the steps, the basement stretched, arched like a medieval undercroft. Strip lighting hummed above them and poured harsh blue light on sweating walls. The photocopier bulked black to their right—about the size of an altar—and for a moment Ben saw boulders, a ring of grey boulders set upright in tussocky turf, a long processional way leading out of the cellar, up into a great, white bowl of a hill, midsummer sunlight dazzling from white lime and close-cropped grass, while the year teetered on its axis and a thin, sweet, six-note tune played over and over again on a flute made out of a man's leg bone.

Ben closed his eyes, opened them, and the double vision disappeared. The sunlight and the hill and the music were gone, replaced by burning iodine light bursting from the photocopier as it took copy after copy of nothing. The florescent lights flickered, pulsed. A whine like a surgeon's needle went through the back of Ben's eye, and then the bulbs popped one by one, the most distant first. Lightning and showers of glass and a wall of darkness behind them rushed towards him. He saw Enid showered with splintered glass while she stood and screamed, saw her, one fist jammed in her mouth to stop the noise, edge forward, her hand stretched out towards the plug.

Sparks swarmed about the contacts of the shattered light bulbs above her head. Sparks arced out of the socket in the wall. Ben closed his eyes again, put one hand over the vial of water in his shirt pocket and lunged past Enid, laying his other hand flat on the plastic top of the photocopier's cover.

It ended with the abruptness of being struck unconscious. Darkness. Then daylight filtering down from upstairs, grey by the time it got there, laced with spider webs. The sharp, throat-catching reek of fear from Enid, and Ben realised, from himself too. He took his hand away, briefly, panic hammering under his breastbone, wound tight with the need to slam it back, keep it there, keep the thing down. But nothing happened. Glass crunched under Enid's feet as she lurched towards him and grabbed, held on tight, holding herself up.

"I...oh," Ben panted, glad himself of someone to cling to. "I gather that wasn't what happened yesterday?"

"No, it was...um. Cold. I heard...um. Whispering. It came on twice—the copier, I mean—and then it stopped. It was cold and there was music."

The grey underground light darkened and strobed as bodies moved on the stairs. Don first, with one of his precious golf clubs clutched as a weapon, Laura a step behind him with a determined expression and a can of hairspray. They reached the bottom step, took in the broken glass glinting on every surface like frost, Ben and Enid with their arms around each other. He could see them thinking, *Compromising position? Assault?*

Laura held out her hairspray two handed, elbows locked, like a pistol-wielding cop on an American TV show. "What the fuck's been going on down here? I want the truth now. Don't mess me around."

Ben caught Enid's eye, saw his own manic glint reflected.

She pressed her hand over her mouth, but the laugh emerged as a thin mouselike squeak. He thought it was the most hilarious thing he'd ever heard. They were led out of the basement shaking and weepy with laughter, and given a biscuit and a nice cup of tea.

"It's a scandal, that's what it is." Laura had platinum-blonde hair with iron-grey roots and favoured snug purple tops. Weekly visits to one of Bakewell's tanning salons had left her orange as a flowerpot, but she had a monumental aptitude with the computers and an empathy with everything electrical. Perhaps she'd felt on an instinctive level the rioting of tortured electronics beneath her, because she'd accepted the "power surge" explanation instantly and was running with it. "The wiring down there is so old you wouldn't believe. I shall take this up with the union. It's all very well putting new circuits in for the vaults, but if they're not going to check how compatible they are with the old system... You could have been killed!"

The laughter had worn off now. Ben clutched at his teacup in desperation, trying to pull some of its warmth into himself. There was a tingling in the palm of the hand he had pressed over the vial, and a shudder, undetectable to anyone but himself, through his every muscle. The worst thing was, he thought, remembering how it had all stopped at his touch, the worst thing was that he probably couldn't have been killed. But Enid could.

Would they have come through her to get to him? Would they even care that she had nothing to do with this—whatever this was? And what about everyone else on the staff? Did it care about any of them either?

"Why don't you both take the afternoon off? I reckon they owe you that for the shock."

"I think I will." Enid's hair had frizzed out about her head as though she'd been rubbing it with a balloon. She tried to smooth it flat but it wasn't having any of it. "I'm on the well-dressing committee this year. It'd do me good to go and choose flowers. How about you, Ben?"

"Yes." He swallowed. His mouth hurt, the gums achy, his tongue prickly and sore. "I think I'll go home. I've got stuff to do there that I can't put off any more. I've left it too long as it is."

Chapter Ten

Flynn took a strawberry from Liadain's hand. It tasted of summer, and a little of regret. Just an edge of 1939, sitting outside St. Johns on the Backs, with cricket being played within earshot. He put the berry back on the plate, half-eaten, pushed it away. Dreams in the food, and no chance to simply enjoy a decent, untampered-with strawberry for its own sake. God, he hated this place.

"The resistance? Resistance to what?"

"You aren't hungry?" She gathered her skirts under her. The hem rode up over what should have been an ankle and disclosed the tapered, earth-stained end of a root. Then she stood and looked entirely human again. "Then walk with me for a short way, and I will tell you everything."

That would make a change. Slightly disturbed at the understanding that he was talking to the alder tree beneath which they had moored, Flynn got up, wiped his sticky fingers on a handkerchief and smiled. Those Greek chaps had not mentioned roots in their depictions of nymphs. Either the Greek type were considerably more perfect, or the poets' imaginations had carried them away. He suspected the latter.

"We are in enemy-occupied territory here, Mr. Flynn," Liadain said, and her dignity rebuked him. Nymphs should not make one feel one was being looked over by a girl's mother for signs of suitability. Her scrutiny was gentle and her face was kind, but he felt he didn't want to get on the wrong side of her. "Queen Oonagh and her forces at the palace, they are invaders.

Usurpers of the throne of the Sidhe. They are from Germany originally."

His look of scepticism seemed to amuse her. She gave a gurgling laugh, like water over stones. "Oh yes. We have a great deal more common cause than you might imagine. Come."

Here in the meadow the sun was warm and bees drowsed amongst the many flowers. All around, the grass sloped up to trees. They walked along the borders of the river, beneath a red-leafed maple tree, about whose boughs honeysuckle twined white and amber. The scent was like a body blow.

"Where are we going?"

"Just over there." She pointed to where a small dry stone wall meandered through the trees. Moss grew on it. The river passed through a gap in the stones, and a smoke of vapour and sound of churning on the other side seemed to indicate a waterfall. The haze drifted above the stones and made it hard to pick out what lay beyond. Liadain walked up to the wall, sat down on its sun-warmed stones and patted it. Obediently, Flynn sat too, and as he did so the haze parted. He took in a deep breath that seared his lungs like gas. "What the…?"

Beyond the wall lay ash mottled with the dust of what might once have been trees. Darker patches showed where there had been fires, long ago. Charcoal dust filled the wind with tendrils of darkness. There was indeed a waterfall. The water plunged down into a basin far below, and a petrochemical haze floated above the stones and burned his mouth when he breathed it in.

Beyond the basin of white water lay a huge dam. The churning noise came from water wheels, whose great fins seemed made of obsidian, black and glittering. A road stretched out from the dam downhill into a valley built high with skyscrapers of smooth, grey rock. A scurry of people looked like termites from up here, but Flynn could see what looked like the emptying of labour camps in the morning when everyone shuffled out under machine-gun guard to man the factories of war. On a clear night, under a bomber's moon, this would look just like the industrial heartland of Nazi Germany writ large across the face of a fairy tale.

"What?" he said, too flabbergasted to formulate a proper sentence.

Liadain's smile came again—that compound of wisdom and pain, endurance and something he now suspected to be outrage. "You have been living in the palace, Navigator. You have run freely through the palace grounds, where the elite of our world spend their ill-gotten time without a thought to those who mine for them. You have been able to ignore it."

She twitched the edge of her skirt just enough to show, again, the tapering tip of a root. "I, however, am anchored in this land. I feel it. I taste it. I hear it screaming as Oonagh's people despoil it not only of every mineral, but of every moment, every second. There are patches here a million billion years older than the ground on which we stand now. Those places will never be healed, though we wait until the sun burns and the dark comes.

"While I work in secret against her, I must bow and scrape and pretend to be a loyal member of the court. One who has put the past behind her and forgiven invasion, robbery and rapine. There are spineless worms enough among Oonagh's nobles who have accepted her rule and are happy to grovel in exchange for power. This is the mask I must force myself to wear. But how can I ever truly forget or forgive when they keep on tearing our land to pieces? It was never theirs to despoil. They have no right. They must be stopped."

Flynn had begun to pick out details now, grey buildings

against black ground, strips of light, as grey as the light of the stars in the dungeon. About two o'clock from where they sat, a factory blew out smoke the colour of moonstone. A degree or two clockwise from that, a wide-open plain was covered in metal blobs, like drops of mercury pressed down from above by an inquisitive finger. Some looked about the size of a small house, some—as well as he could guess from here—were more aircraft hangar-like in dimension.

"They must have been here a hell of a time to build all this," he said. "Years. And you're sitting here having a picnic? This resistance of yours, you must have had plenty of time to dig in, do something. Why aren't people talking about you? People don't stop talking when I'm there—Ghost, you know— and yet I haven't heard a thing about you. What have you been doing all these years?"

She rose and pointed out the very place he'd been examining. "You see that? It took a century to build, and it wasn't here yesterday."

"I beg your pardon?"

"You have it." Rising, she led the way back through the forest to her clearing. It seemed a kind of paradise now, and he tipped back his wine gladly, letting it soothe the tightness in his scoured throat.

"I mean," he said, "I don't think I follow you. Don't understand what you just said."

It was a very gracious smile, but he found himself getting tired of it. "We mine time there," she explained, clearly stopping the conversation down to his lower intellectual level. "Think of it like this. If it takes a hundred years to build an airfield like that, and you happened to have a hundred years in a bottle, available for immediate use, you could take a hundred years, and yet build it in an instant. Time is one of our most precious resources. With it, one can achieve everything else."

Flynn thought about the cave again. A hundred years of his life, gone in a few minutes of torment. Yes. She had a point. But what he said was "Airfield?" Because he had certain fixed ideas about elves, and elves in planes was not one of them.

"Indeed. And the worst of it is there is no longer the strength in the land to fuel them, yet still she builds on. A waste of time and power that we cannot afford to spend. Only a foreigner could do it. If she were our real queen, connected to the land by blood and spirit, she would feel the desecration in her own form. And she would heed the cries of her people. Instead, you have seen what they are to her—cogs in a machine to be worked to breaking and then discarded."

Flynn thought about the factory workers in the Ruhr, on whose heads he rained down fire on a nightly basis. He always hoped that when they came to the Pearly Gates, saw all history stretched out before them, saw their own actions clear, they wouldn't mind so much having died in the cause of freedom. But finding some way of allowing them to live in that cause instead would have been better. "Are you telling me this because there is something I can do about it? I can if I will—this kind of thing is why I joined up. But what can I do? You haven't told me that."

"It's...complicated." She broke a loaf of white bread and offered half of it to him. Wary of losing himself in dreams, he shook his head, echoing back her slight smile.

Putting it down, she folded her hands in her lap and took a deep breath, like a storyteller about to open with *Once upon a time*. "Let me tell you what I know. When Oonagh—that isn't her real name, by the way. She changed it to try and curry favour with the old ones among us. She used to be Askatla when she was young enough to be honest." Liadain gave a quiet laugh. "But there I wander into ancient history and off my path. I was telling you of the prophecy. When a new queen comes to the throne, the seers of the realm are instructed to foresee any threats in her future and to council her on how to circumvent them. This was done for Oonagh when the old queen retired to the hills.

"It is the way of these things that seers will come out with something obscure and ambivalent, which they can later twist to make it seem applicable to whatever comes. This time, however, they were unusually specific."

"Oh yes?" It had become very hot in the field, particularly as Flynn was wearing every stitch of his flying kit from parachute to thermal underwear. He considered discarding some of it, but he'd put down a single glove on his first day here, and it had been stolen, and for what seemed weeks afterwards his dreams had been invaded and his energy drained. The final insult came when he was controlled like a puppet and made to dance on one of the market stalls. So public a performance that Oonagh had intervened, broken the spell and told him to take better care of his belongings in future.

Better to swelter than risk that again, but he took off his flying helmet and held it tight in both hands while a grateful breeze cooled his damp hair. "So what did the prophecy say?"

"As well translated into your language as I can." She gestured, and Willow rose from amid the bracken and began to clear away the remnants of the meal. "This is what it said: *Out of time, he who guides the thunderbird will save you. Alive or dead, he who guides him will thwart you. Neither dead nor alive, he will be your shield.*

"As I say, it was more detailed than is common. Not more immediately comprehensible."

Flynn laughed—it seemed he wasn't alone in being frustrated by the lack of straightforwardness in this place. Only after he laughed did the meaning begin to suggest itself to him. "You think the thunderbird was a Lancaster?"

"We were sure on that point. The queen had her diviners hard at work for some years on the puzzle. I shall not trouble you with the craft of it, weaving down the lines of the web. As a human, you do not have the subtlety to understand even if I tried. But yes, by the end of the process we knew the thunderbird was a Lancaster. We knew, indeed, that it was *your* Lancaster."

She leaned forwards and fixed him with a look he thought was meant to be sympathetic, but there was too much eager interest in it for that. "That was the final time one of the ships in her airfield was used. She armed it with fire and sent it through into your world to collect you and to dispose of the unnecessary remainder."

He scrambled to his feet, sweet green grass under him and rustling leaves and sunshine all about, and his head full of fire and screams. "You? It was you who shot us down? Saved me, let the other chaps burn?"

She leapt up to put a hand on his arm, black eyes wide with sympathetic pain. "No, not me. She. Askatla—Oonagh. She believed that by taking you out of your own world, bringing you here, she could solve the puzzle—she could make you neither living nor dead, and thereby turn you into her protector."

Flynn threw his helmet on the ground. "You—I mean, bloody fairies? What had any of us to do with that? I can understand the Germans killing us. You—"

"She."

"Had no right. We weren't at war. We'd never done you any harm. We didn't even believe in you. You had no right. No right!"

"That has never stopped her," Liadain said gently. "Do you find it so surprising that one who will do what I have shown you to her own people should also treat yours as disposable trinkets?"

Her long fingers curled about his elbow and felt unyielding as twigs—which was, he presumed, exactly what they were. "Let me show you. Let me show you it closer."

She was tugging him to his feet. He crammed his helmet back on and followed, remembered screams repeating like a gramophone record in his mind. He was only peripherally conscious that he was being led back to the wall, but when he stepped over and found himself on a narrow thread of bridge above an abyss, the survival instinct of today snapped him out of it.

This hadn't been visible from the other side of the wall, a crack, barely six feet across, where the barren black land had fractured all the way through. He could see out into space simply by looking down. The waterfall arched over the gap, picked up particles of smog and fume and fell into a collecting pen whose metal walls faced outwards into the oblivion of that drop. A number of dull twinkles in the distance indicated where other narrow bridges stitched the two continents together, and evidently they shared their air, but...

"Is this all that holds them together?" he asked, startled out of rage and into curiosity and awe.

"Yes. These are the fracture lines where the world has been so exhausted by her mining that even the forces of gravity have been depleted. You see a place crumbling into nonexistence while in the cities and the palaces the Ylfe and their sycophants use this power to fuel their dreams. Hold on to the rails now until we are farther across."

On the other side, a line of posts indicated a walkway where his feet only sank ankle deep into a powder that lifted and scattered at every footfall like talc, but burned in the back of his throat like nerve gas.

"You need to see this—to understand that you are not the only one she has wronged," Liadain said, still seeming to drift weightlessly above the ground. Where she walked, the dust settled a little, brushed by the water of her gown. "To put your ordeal into context."

Flynn didn't want to put his ordeal into context, didn't want to be told he was a small cog in a big machine. He wanted—a childish desire, but his—a bit of sympathy, a chance to put down the nightmare and heal. He didn't want elvish politics and responsibilities. But another thought forced its way into his mind and made his eyes water—fortunately the dust could be blamed for that. "He who guides the plane and he who guides him? That means the pilot and the navigator, yes? That means you have plans for the skipper too?"

"Oh yes." She led him down many stairs to the side of the waterfall basin where a lake the colour of thrice-used washing-up water churned mountains of grey foam amid the oil slicks.

From there, another walkway descended into the industrial valley. Liadain held out a hand before he stepped on it, and there whispered by him two shadows who went down first. He looked back and saw two more. Shadows of men without anything substantial to cast them.

"Don't be alarmed." She must, again, have caught either his apprehension or his flinch. "They are dreamwalkers. They have bodies, but the bodies are asleep in a safe place. We're going into a desperate place, there will be desperate people, and the dreamwalkers will keep us safe. Best to be prepared."

"Oonagh has plans that involve my skipper?" Flynn

repeated, thinking about the industrial draining of time—that glimpse of Skip gone suddenly old. The thought was as corrosive as the spray that kept stinging his cheek and making his clothes smoke and stink. Had they drained him of twenty years in a few seconds? Was that what had happened? Bastards!

"Oh certainly." Liadain stepped off the last riser, onto sleek black paving. Silent when she trod on it, it rang like struck crystal beneath Flynn's foot, soft-soled boots notwithstanding.

"You and your friend are both involved in this—how would you put it—up to your necks. These days not even she would spare the energy to bring a man here on a whim. You are both important, and more, you are both already falling under her control."

"That's tosh," he said, trying to stand up straight on the sleek, melted-glass surface. Some kind of park or public square, he guessed, from which radiated a score of streets so narrow he could have trailed his fingers down the fronts of the buildings on either side.

From above it had looked like a Nazi work camp. Down here it looked much stranger. There was an organic quality to the walls—like the walls of wasp nests—as though they had been masticated and spat out. Liadain, with her roots, and the dreamwalking bodyguards seemed reassuringly normal down here.

"Where shall I take you first?" she asked, with the air of a tour guide. He wasn't sure if she was talking to him or to herself. "I want you to see everything, so that you know what I am fighting for. More—so that you know what I am fighting against."

The sunlight barely penetrated down the threadlike streets. Above him, covered walkways had been spun from one side to the other, cutting out even the thin band of sky. There were doors enough, even the occasional window, behind which shapes moved in formless grey light. But not a weed underfoot, not a garden, not a flowerbox, not a single line of washing hung out to dry. Five steps in, and his world became grey. The scent of fuel clung to everything, a zinging, metallic, kerosene stink that he could feel crawling into his clothes, his hair, worming its way under his skin.

Liadain's colour too had changed. Her robe dirtied and the daisies in her hair turned to wilted weeds. Her ribs rose like opened bellows as she drew in air. He thought about the dust underfoot, the powderlike barren dust that blew endlessly about his ankles, and how it might be—as a tree—to get your roots deep in that.

Like having your nose and mouth stopped up with sand. Whatever she was showing him must certainly be important. She wouldn't put herself through this if it wasn't. "I'd like to see those flyers," he said. "Elves in planes? It takes some getting used to, that idea."

"I thought we would agree." Even her voice had lost its rounded music, sounded whispery as the wind through autumn leaves. "What need do we have for any of this? Elves in planes, indeed. It's not our tradition, and it is bought at too high a cost. I would mend this...if I was queen. I would make all our land...flower again like the meadows about the palace."

She bowed her head into her hands and just breathed, and he said, almost involuntarily, "Look, if it's making you ill, let's go back."

She straightened up, pushed her long sheet of hair behind her ears, dislodging withered brown grasses, and smiled bravely. "No. You must see whatever you need to see. I will recover later. Only think—I am not the only tree which rooted in this land of old and can do so no longer. Look there."

There was a stump at a crossroads. He looked once, saw a torso, the arms and legs sawn off, the head lolling, still grotesquely alive, open mouth full of a hornet's nest. His heart choked him. He stumbled, looked again, and it was only a tree stump, covered in ashes, with a hole in the trunk from which the flies buzzed. "God!"

"Much of this destruction was caused in the war the former queen fought against our gods. You can imagine, perhaps, the profligate use of power that required. We cannot look to the gods for aid now. We must help ourselves, and even stoop to asking others to help us. I do not enjoy humbling myself or my people in front of you, human."

That too he understood. Suppose Hitler invaded, built factories, turned Britain into an enormous workhouse, starved her people into submission and put them to work for his obscene purposes? Flynn wouldn't have wanted to be the one who had to show the Yanks around and beg them to get involved. A welling up of sympathy for her surprised him. "I'm not judging," he said, "I'm just looking."

"Here then." They turned another of the endless corners, into a slightly wider lane that ran uphill towards the mount on which the metal bubbles rested. What he had thought was the wind was closer here, and he realised it was the sound of a million voices inside the termite-mound towers. Down from the airfield echoed shrieks and screeching of metal, the din of massive hammers, a whine like that of a starter motor, and above all of it loudspeakers blaring out a music of harps and harpsichords and the skirling of high-pitched uillean pipes.

Flynn stuck his fingers in his ears and walked on.

At the airfield they were challenged for the first time by an elf as silver grey as the machines he guarded. Long pewter hair streamed over eyes the colour of rain. Tattoos down his neck and under the collar of his jumpsuit—tattoos of vines and wire. After a quick talk with Liadain, he put down the spear he carried and regarded Flynn with what might have been interest.

"You're a flyer yourself?"

"Navigator."

"What do you fly?"

"A Lancaster." Just for a moment, he'd forgotten where he was. The grey elf in front of him had the air of a squadron leader. It felt like coming home to talk to him. Flynn had to throttle back a great desire to report. "It's a..." he held his hands wide apart, "...a big bomber. One of the biggest."

"This is our biggest." The nameless elf threaded his way through loops of paths, above which the featureless squashed metal balls and discs floated like balloons. Their surfaces, seen close, were opalescent. Flynn could see a blurred reflection of himself as he passed them. He fancied they turned and looked at him, as curious about him as he was about them.

The elf walked to the edge of the hill that bordered the plain of ships. He took hold of a thin crack which ran from head height to the ground, flipped it back with the easy motion of a man opening a tent door. And a tent door it was—or rather a dust cover, a sheet of gauzy material, to which the ever-present dust had clung, making it look like a mountain. Flynn walked in and found in front of him a spherical ship that might have been a small moon. When he touched it, he had again that disconcerting feeling that it was watching him. He pushed, and it moved, a little. It was like bouncing the Albert Hall on a racquet.

Good Lord! Suppose he did help them? Liadain had open disdain for these things. Surely she wouldn't mind giving one or two away? He could take them home, give them to the war effort. "What weapons does it carry?"

"This one, none. This is a palace."

"This is hers."

Both Flynn and Grey stood with their hands up, lightly touching the metal sphere. It felt like laying your palm on a sleeping dog, comforting, warm. There was even a pulse. Liadain kept her hands bunched at her sides. "This is her escape. She knows that the land cannot endure much longer. She builds this so that she can fly somewhere else, begin the process again."

"If you want fighters, these may be more to your taste."

Sleeker, the fighter planes were also a lighter silver, more heavily shaped. Indeed they put Flynn in mind of nothing more than giant arrowheads. The shape worked for him. He could almost see how it would soar and dive, spiral and speed, blinding the eyes of the searchlight crews and the flak gunners beneath. Would flak even penetrate that liquid metal skin? "And what can they do?"

Grey saw his wonder and smiled. It wasn't done to make snap judgements in this place, but Grey's was the most likeable smile he'd seen in this world... Except perhaps for Sumala's. And thinking of Sumala gave him a pang. Not much of a knight errant, was he? Leaving her lying still as a statue in a room full of corpses and running off to play with the aircraft. Not exactly chivalrous.

"I don't know your system of measurements." Grey set a hand on the nose of the nearest fighter, and the skin of it became transparent. Flynn had a glimpse of what looked like jewellery—gold wire, gems, a crown, before the mercury dazzle flashed back into place. "But it will fly faster than sound through air or the void, level mountains, vaporize seas."

He walked to the perimeter of the airfield and looked out.

Flynn noticed the sweep of pearls piercing his ear from lobe to tip, and the earplug he wore like a larger stone, helping him block out the cacophony of the workers. "No one will be able to withstand us," he said, zeal in his clear grey eyes. "There have been questions in my mind, at times, about all this. But now it's clear the queen knows what she's about. We have sacrificed much, but we will gain more. And by the sword—the way it used to be done. The way it is done still, in your world."

Flynn felt as if he had kicked out the escape hatch and plummeted. His feeling of fondness, of fellowship with Grey abruptly sickened him. It was all too easy now to see the creature in a Luftwaffe uniform, silver glints at his collar. And yes, perhaps he'd be one of the gentlemen of the air, jousting in his silver planes. But that made it no better.

Level mountains? Vaporise seas? No. Where was the honour in that? More likely he'd be one of those bastards who sneaked in in the dark, unseen, unheard beneath the roar of the Lancaster's engines, and emptied his cannon into the unprotected belly of the kite. Slid away again, never in a moment's danger as he consigned a whole crew to burning alive.

Flynn took another look over the airfield, and the workers' quarters that surrounded it. The aristocratic poise of Grey with his clean clothes and his earplugs to blot out the screams sickened him suddenly. All those hives, where the injured rotted in the streets, where no one dared show his face... Perhaps the parallel really was as exact as he'd thought. That was Britain under Nazi occupation.

Well...Faerieland under Nazi occupation, to be more exact. And the palace with its exquisite grounds, they were paid for like this—by enslaving first their own people, and then aiming to do the same to others.

"I..." Nausea choked him. No, if there was some strange mirroring here, some way in which the human world guided or influenced these creatures to imitate its own savagery—even if there wasn't and it was their own savagery—he was as downright against it here as at home. This would have to be stopped.

He looked at Liadain and could see, beneath the deepening grooves of her fatigue, that she had observed and approved his decision. But they couldn't talk about it here in front of Grey.

"I...am feeling a little ill. Could we go back?"

"Of course." She moved off, and when she was at a distance, Grey took him by the elbow, leaned in. His breath was chill as sleet against Flynn's cheek, and smelled of sorrel.

"Navigator," he whispered, "have a care of that one. She... I don't trust her."

It was, in its own way, a vote of confidence.

Back in the meadow, Liadain excused herself for half an hour to stand by the waterside in her tree form, her roots deep in the water. Flynn passed the time in wondering if he could sneak back to the airfield and steal one of the fighter planes. They had such an awareness about them—it felt as though they would have to want to help. And even if that could be achieved, he was no pilot. He didn't have the first idea.

But if he could get the skipper here...? Skip could fly a brick if you only glued wings on it. There was an idea to hold on to, just in case.

But the thought sparked an association, brought back something Liadain had said before they went down to the industrial plain. When she came rustling back, revived and beautiful, green water weeds like embroidery about the hems of her skirt and buttercups in her hair, he said, "And what about the skipper? You were going to tell me something about him. Watched, you said. The both of us."

"Indeed." She motioned to him to follow her across a pebbled ford in the river, over to where reeds hissed in flat lands full of shallow pools. "What would be the point of a prophecy like that, if one followed up only one of the threads? Oonagh brought you here to make you her champion. And she, even now, is working on your friend to bend him to her cause."

"She won't have any success there," he said, feeling sucking mud under his feet. The water poured over his boots and soaked into his socks. He felt something wriggle between his toes. "If ever there was a man who went his own way, that would be our skipper."

Liadain smiled. "But you are both such knights errant. Of course she won't go to him and say, 'Give me your help to attack my neighbours and establish my sovereignty over them.' She will find a way of making him feel he is going to the rescue of the innocent. Only when it's all over will she reveal to him what he has really achieved, and laugh. You must know her well enough to admit I speak the truth."

And he did. He had no ill treatment at the queen's hands to hold against her. But she had laughed so hard at his early attempts to escape. Every time he tired of his life of ghostlike drifting through the halls and byways of her kingdom and returned to the throne room to see if she would tell him something—anything—she had watched him as if he had been created with the sole intent of amusing her. Humour in her eyes, a smirk never far from her lips. If she enjoyed his loneliness, frustration, anger, how much more would she enjoy his despair?

"Do you know what her plans are for him?"

"I do."

"Tell me."

"I'll show you." Liadain led the way to a perfectly circular pool. The sky reflected so clearly in it, it was as though the ground beneath had disappeared, a hole had been cut out of the world and replaced with silver clouds. When Liadain set her foot in it, no ripples showed on its surface. When he looked down himself, he could see no reflection. His feet, beneath the water, might have been severed at the calf.

"Oonagh has an ally," Liadain said, her whispery voice scarcely breaking the great silence of the moor. No bird cried, and but for the slimy things in the mud, nothing stirred. Flynn drew his flying jacket close, even though he wasn't cold.

"His name is Chitrasen, Lord of the Gandharvas and the Apsaras. He rules a large country in the middle of whose bounds stand our equivalent of the Himalayas. For reasons I can't explain to you, unless you understand our technology and our physics, this makes his land the perfect place for the launching of Oonagh's ships. He is reluctant to despoil his own land as she has destroyed ours, but he is willing enough to provide launching places in return for a share of the spoils."

"Chitrasen?" Flynn sat down on a fallen aspen tree, which just touched the circumference of the pool. It seemed polished, as if it had been used for the purpose many times before. "I think I've heard of him. Where have I heard of him?"

"From his daughter." Liadain looked happy, up to her knees in mud, though strangely no shorter. She adapted herself to the terrain, or it adapted itself to her, it was hard to say. "Sumala."

"No," Flynn said it automatically, but his logical mind almost approved of the idea. Hadn't she lured him with chatter and nudity and bravery, and then done that thing to him—that thing where he'd looked in her eyes and he still couldn't remember what had happened next. "Why? Why would..."

"Oonagh doesn't know what you are going to do. Nobody knows until you do it. You are a potentiality waiting to happen. She expects you to do something which will save her, but what if she has miscalculated? Better, then, to give you an ally who will keep track of your movements, aid you and be in place to thwart you should that prove necessary."

"But that's nonsense," he said. "If that was the case, why would she round up the girl and put her in prison, or whatever it is she's done to her?"

"You are supposed to free her." Liadain shook her head with a sound like the sea. "Then you would have been comrades in arms, bound by a shared adventure. It is powerful, here, to have gone through a story together, and the sleeping princess brought back to life by her swain? That is a powerful story. Your fates would have been linked ever after. I knew you would try to rescue her—knights errant, remember—so I sent Willow to prevent you and to bring you here instead."

Of the two of them, he liked and trusted Sumala more. Why, he couldn't have said. Perhaps because she seemed less plausible, less unruffled—because she'd been angry and trivial and noble in the face of danger. And possibly because she'd been wearing no clothes, though he'd have preferred if that hadn't been a factor.

"Your word against hers there," he said. "She told me she was as much a prisoner as I am. And given that she's currently under wraps in the dungeon, there's got to be a modicum of truth in it, yes?"

"I don't ask you to accept my word." Liadain made a sharp beckoning gesture, full of authority, and the shadow under the oak elongated, darkened, stood upright. It reached out an insubstantial hand in which something brilliant glittered. When Liadain took it, it proved to be a tiny box carved out of a solid ruby. As the shadow guard tucked itself back under the tree (Flynn drawing up his feet so they wouldn't be embedded in it), she opened the box and took out a tiny pinch of brown, brittle dust. She offered it to him as though it was worth more than a handful of diamonds.

As it bloody is. Flynn rubbed his wrist where the nails had gone in. *I wonder who had to suffer for this batch? Can't be many volunteers for the job.*

"I offer you the chance to see. The Apsaras rarely involve themselves in the doings of mortal men, but when they do, it is because they have been sent by the gods to confuse them. To blind them by lust and lead them by the tail in whatever direction they wish the man to go. They are subtle and apt to become whatever their victim finds most distracting. You feel the tug to rescue your damsel in distress even now, don't you? And your friend... Well, his nature is different, but his temptation is fitted to him."

Flynn went cold all over. Did she mean what he thought he meant? How could she know? Would she use it for blackmail against him?

It was an instinctive, foolish flinch in this place where the inhabitants could be whatever they chose and didn't understand the distinctions of flesh. Bigger things were afoot, but still he wished she wouldn't talk about the skipper so. Careless talk cost lives, and all that. He reached out and let her tip the brown dust into the palm of his hand.

"Look."

This time when he scattered the ashes, the whole surface of the pond changed. Below him, when he looked down, were red-

and-white tablecloths, candles in silver holders, the tops of waiters' heads. Smoke from candle flames rose to roll over the mirror of the water's surface.

The skipper sat at a table close to both door and window. His feet were stretched out in front of him, crossed at the ankle in relaxation. He wore civilian clothes and smiled a lot. Sometimes he even laughed.

Across the table from him, the light tangled in the raven-black hair of a young man Flynn recognised. He too laughed, at ease, beautiful and relaxed though he seemed to be wearing only an undershirt and shorts. Flynn looked at the profile— clear-cut lines and long black lashes, a mouth like a bow, generous and sensuous and perhaps a little sullen. *Cruel,* he thought, feeling something boil in his chest like tar.

"Do you see that aura?"

Once Liadain had pointed it out it was hard to miss. The young man was swathed in it like a tight-fitting suit of silk— indigo and gold, purple as midnight, gilt as the sun.

"He may look human, but he is one of Chitrasen's people in human disguise, sent by Oonagh to guide your friend in the paths she wishes him to tread. I wish," Liadain sighed with a sound like the sea. "I wish I could offer you proof."

Flynn tucked his hands into his armpits and shivered as his understanding of the world reshaped itself nauseatingly beneath him. Like seasickness, he'd only come to terms with one wave before the next one hit. "I don't need proof."

He remembered Sumala on top of the tree, chanting *show me the nearest kin of mine.* Remembered too the face he'd glimpsed there. Liadain couldn't have known, couldn't possibly have known. She must be telling the truth. God help him. The face he had seen in Sumala's vision was the same man he saw there now, so happily chatting with the skipper. Light in both

146

their eyes, and Skip's fair skin pink across the cheekbones so the freckles stood out.

The man with Skip was Sumala's closest kinsman, and that meant the skipper was in serious trouble with no idea how deep.

"Tell me what I can do to help."

Chapter Eleven

Chris rubbed his gritty eyes and swallowed the last mouthful of his third cup of coffee. This early in the day the Red Lion was pretty much his to call his own, but for the barmaid. She kept the coffee topped up between stints in the kitchen and long periods of sitting with her stilettoed heels up, headphones in her ears, reading *The Da Vinci Code* at a rate of a page an hour.

Listening to the tinny beat of the music from her earphones, he could sympathise with the rate of progress. He looked down again at the accounting notebook, all lines and columns and subheadings, and realised he had forgotten to carry over the subtotal of hall rental until June and add to it the fifty pounds he had slipped to Stan to compensate the lad's parents for the amount they spent on electricity and strange electronic components. His crew might all be volunteers, but it didn't mean he wanted them out of pocket because of it.

He fished in his pockets for receipts, spread them out on the table in front of him and tried to remember what they were for. That one at least, folded into four and still otherwise uncrumpled, was the receipt for the box of chocs that sat in its plastic bag by his feet. Better not put that on the business accounts or Grace would have his guts for garters.

Yawning, he put his head in his hands and rubbed small circles over his eyebrows. He felt muzzy and confused and worried and itchingly alive for the first time in years. Aware of himself, physically, as he hadn't been since...

Since the hospital, in fact. Since he'd woken up in a hospital bed to find that was the beginning of the nightmare rather than the end.

Chris pushed his chair back and got up, stretching against the pull of muscles protesting his long run this morning. The memory of this morning with Ben blushed in his stomach like an ember. If he breathed on it, it flared into life, filling him with tingling heat and hunger.

So he shouldn't be taking time out from his accounts to think about it, should he?

The hissing *tink* that was all he could hear of the barmaid's music was the only sound in the sleepy room for a moment, and then on an impulse, he went over to the jukebox and looked through their "nostalgia" collection. Maybe losing himself in the past a moment would help him to forget how Ben had looked this morning, impeccably shaved, impeccably dressed, cufflinks at his wrists, wearing his well-cut suit the way men used to wear their clothes, in Chris's day, with elegance and understated style.

Chris fed the machine with coins, waited while it ticked through its thoughts, and almost winced under the onslaught of homesickness and trumpets. She had a voice like a bugle, Vera Lynn, and what had happened to that accent, the speech that said you cared about every word enough to pronounce it correctly?

He sat down at his table again—not even his table, just a table he used, in a pub where he was tolerated with scepticism. Best he could reckon, he was somewhere around forty years of age, and he didn't know what future they'd been expecting, Geoff and he, but this wasn't it.

Oh, and he shouldn't be indulging himself with regrets and nostalgia like this. Maudlin and no damn good to anyone. But they'd never expected to live through it, that was the thing. *We were supposed to go together, you and I. I wasn't supposed to have lived on, alone.*

And perhaps he hadn't fully accepted that he had, until now. *"My fist in your mouth so you can't say anything stupid."* He took a great gulp of air to slow the bound and thunder of his heart, just at the thought of it, and whatever he had *supposed* in the past, he *was* alive, the blood rushing in hectic delight through his veins. And he didn't know if what he felt was more anticipation or guilt.

Chris fished his phone from the pocket of his jacket that hung over the back of the chair, passed it from hand to hand as he wondered if he should call Grace for a bit of spiritual strengthening, or Ben for... To check if the protection was holding. Yes, that was a good excuse. Call him, offer to come around and help with the demolition job. And if they found themselves, afterwards, a little filthy and sweaty and badly in need of a shower, then...

Then he would try to remember that Ben was a client, and all those other things Grace had said that seemed so sensible at the time.

He thumbed the cover of the phone open, and simultaneously—it felt as though the small movement had caused it—reality seemed to turn itself inside out. His ears popped and a wave of cold travelled up from his belly button to the roots of his hair. The music stopped. Something grey, like water, pressed on his eardrums and his eyes, and a light shone from above him and danced over his hands.

He looked up, and above him and to the right, where the steam from his coffee had condensed on the glass of one of the pub's elderly pictures he thought he saw—just for a snatch of a second—blue sunlight behind the outline of Geoff's head. Then it shifted as the leaves danced, and very dimly he made out Geoff's face, looking out of the picture as if from a mirror. Geoff's expression was strained, horrified, hopeful. He was trying to speak, but no sound came through.

Chris dropped the phone—didn't feel it fall from his numb fingers. He scrabbled to his feet, climbed onto his chair and then the table, trying to get level with the picture, the window, the whatever it was.

But when he did, there was nothing there. Spiders, cigarette smoke yellow on stippled plaster, a long trailing end of grey cobweb, and only his own face reflected in the grimy glass above a group photo of the 1898 pub skittles champions. "Flynn?" The nickname came to his mouth natural as breathing. More natural, in fact, for he'd forgotten how to do the second, remembered it only when it choked him when he tried to speak again. "Flynn, is that you?"

A long silence. A cautious footstep and cleared throat behind him made him realise he was standing on the table, talking to the wall, with his face pressed up against the glass and his fingers white-tight against the frame.

He eased them off, heard the last few bars of music "...some sunny day" and focussed on getting down, his wobbly legs making that quite a task if he wanted to do it without falling on top of the barmaid. Karen, her name was Karen. He knew that, because she was Stan's older sister, and he really didn't want her spooked to the point of carrying tales home.

"Should you have medicine for that?" she said.

Geoff! Chris made it to the floor safely, staggered to his chair, sank down there, shaking. That had seemed so real. So real!

Could he be alive? Could he be? The man at the hospital— patient, official, inflexible—had said no. Lost, all of them. Every

151

one of them dead: Flynn and Tolly, Red, Archie, Occe and the Yank. All of them, burned up into greasy black ash. Only him left.

But what if the man at the hospital had been wrong?

The shake worked its way into an all-body shiver. He tried to pick up the phone, dropped it again, and she put it on the tabletop in front of him. "I'll...um..." he said. "I'll, um, call a friend. Don't worry. I'm actually not mad at all."

Yes. Well, that was convincing, wasn't it?

"Could I, um. Could I have a..." Whisky was what he wanted, but not what he needed. Something to sharpen him up, not dull him. Something to just let him get a hold of himself and then he'd be rolling. "Another coffee? Dozing off at my books there, sorry. Probably asleep on my feet."

He hit the speed-dial for Phyllis. "Phil?"

"Oh, you always phone just in the middle of *Doctors*."

Daytime soaps. A wave of furious cold went over him, left his lips tingling and his heart athunder. He stood up, squeezed the side of the table in a death grip. He didn't throw either the phone or his empty cup, but he was very tempted. "Phyllis. This is urgent. And personal. That communications device Stan has been working on? I know you've been testing it for him. Is it still with you?"

She sighed. Some rustling and a click later, she said, "There. That's the VCR on. Now what was that? You want Stan's etheric radio? Yes, I've got it. Where do you need it?"

"Red Lion ASAP."

"Got that. You need the ghost camera too?"

"Oh..." This time the wave of cold felt like nausea, sucked all the strength out of him, leaving him collapsing back to his seat. Did he want the ghost camera? The flying, impatient hope, the barely held-back razor wire of hope and joy and fear, exquisite and agonising, faltered in its grip on his soul. He wrapped his hands around the cup of coffee Karen offered and tried to absorb the impact of the thought.

Because it could be a ghost. Even if it really was Geoff and not his own conflicted imagination, it didn't mean that the man had to still be alive. A ghost would make so much more sense. "Ah. Yes. Please."

"Be there in ten minutes. Try not to disturb anything in the meantime."

Obedient to his instructions, he sat and sipped his coffee while he waited, concentrating on beating back the trembling of his hands. *Breathe in, two, three, four. And out, two, three, four.* Carefully feeling his heartbeat slow and stabilize, he wrapped up all that yearning and loss, regret and hope, to be dealt with once he knew exactly what had happened.

She made it in eight, and it felt like eternity. "Well, then. Help me in with this, if you would." The camera on its tripod to set up, the laptop and the bulky server, microphones and screen that Stan claimed would enable messages to be sent from one dimension to another.

A few lunchtime customers had begun to trickle into the bar now and form a ring of interested onlookers. "Don't know why we let you lot in here," said Karen, bringing Phyllis her usual gin and tonic.

"Nonsense. You couldn't pay for this kind of street theatre." Phyllis faced the curious onlookers and drew herself up, looking very pony-club in her pink twinset and pearls. "'Spect you people want to know what's going on, eh?"

The idea that the entertainment might talk back, might even, God forbid, call for *volunteers from the audience* made the onlookers flee to the bar or the beer garden. Chris took a deep breath, tried not to sound too pathetic when he said, "I did mention this was personal, Phil. I'd appreciate it if you didn't treat it as a learning experience for the crowd."

"Never known you to do personal." She set the camera in its tripod, attached it to the server with a long cable, and attached that to the laptop with another. Brought up a green-tinted, dim image and a scrolling screen of code. "So what am I looking at?"

"It came from the corner there. The picture." He pointed. She panned the camera slowly along and up. Grubby smoke-stained wall showed on the screen as featureless grey green, and there was no change at all as she swept the lens over the picture and off the other side. "Maybe a little farther up?"

"Just the picture, Phil. The condensation on the picture."

But she ignored him and quartered the ceiling regardless. The cobwebs showed as hair-thin lines of light. Bright white against the dull background. "That's because they're lived in." Phil put her wellington-boot-clad foot on a blue velvet seat and hoisted herself up to peer more closely at the photo, check the spiders at rest in the corners of the frame. "Not getting anything paranormal, though."

"No movement there at all?" he asked, though he could see for himself on the computer screen that the picture was as unmagical as its surroundings. "Not even a glimmer?"

She changed the filter on the camera lens, twice. Held up a number of boxes that appeared to do nothing more than click briefly. Chris brought the stone out of his pocket and looked at the wall through that. Nothing.

Wiping her hands on her linen slacks, Phyllis flicked through a suite of other programmes, looked at the results of the EM pulse, infrared and ultraviolet flashes, displayed the results in a variety of easy-to-read graphs. Then she sat down and propped her wellington boots on the footboard of the table. "Well, I have to say, it's all very much what I'd expect in here. Since Grace put the wards on this place, it doesn't even have the residual background readings you'd expect on any piece of merry old England. What did you see?"

"I..." He rubbed his fingers through his eyebrows, making the hairs stand up, then smoothed them down and reached out to turn the computer off. Static hissed and crackled through the speakers like the sound of wind on trees. Then a crack and a pop as the screen went black and the drive inside whined down to silence. "I saw a light. A man's face—as if it was reflected in the glass of that picture. He was trying to tell me something."

Now the crisis was past, it seemed he didn't want to talk about it after all. But Phil took a large swallow of her G&T, reached out and closed her bony fingers over the back of his hand. "Personal, you said."

The touch broke something in him. If Ben had been there, he'd have said something awkward, accusing, something Chris would have had to rally strength to deal with. Phil's sympathy did the opposite. Appallingly, he felt tears come to his eyes. The table blurred beneath his gaze, and he covered his face with a hand, quickly, so that she didn't see it. "You know..." He coughed the tremble out of his voice. "You know the incident that got me demobbed?"

"Shot down, you said."

"Yes. And my navigator was killed. I thought. I *thought* he was killed." He glanced up, and she turned away quickly, as if to avoid seeing him so nakedly grieving, so exposed. He was glad of the tact at the same time that he wanted to grab her and force her to see what he had seen. "I just saw his face, reflected in the glass. Tell me, Phil, that he might not be dead after all. Tell me that I didn't imagine it."

Her fingers tightened on his. This time when he looked up, she held the gaze. There were white rims around her irises where the colour had faded out over time, and her skin looked like tissue paper drawn precrumpled from its box. He wondered if she would tell him some comforting lie, rejected the thought—she was too much of a lady for that—as she gave a small, sad smile.

"I don't know, Chris. I'd expect there to be some evidence if anything had really happened." She sighed, "And you told me yourself you've been having flashbacks. I can't help but think that this was an unusually upsetting instance of that. Has something happened recently that would make you think of this man especially now? Stirred up some old memories? The mind can be a funny thing."

Chris set his elbows on the table and held up his heavy head in his hands. On the triangle of dark wood beneath him, someone had scratched *Lara 4 Robbie*, and he wondered if that mark too had outlasted the love it commemorated. He grabbed a damp beer mat from the end of the table and covered it up while below his lungs the hope that had been painfully beating died and began to rot. It felt as though—if he reached in to the cavity of his chest—what he found there would ooze out over his fingers, sticky as tar.

Because the mind *could be* a funny thing, and if he was hallucinating Geoff's face, it wouldn't be so surprising, just at the moment when that old wound felt like it had a chance to close. When everything in him was shifting and reorientating itself on a new target. Could be his feeling that he hadn't done enough. Could be guilt talking, using his old lover's voice. He'd ballsed up other hopeful starts since, unable to finally let go. Why should this time be any different?

"You might be right." He braced up a back that was beginning to feel old, cramped and compressed by too many
156

years and too much time on the floor last night. He missed his sleep these days too, when he used to be able to fly all night and spend the days at the pictures or the dance. "Intimations of mortality and all that. Besides, Ben Chaudhry's problem has me on edge. The Good People—I can't stand the bastards. It's always bigger than it looks with them."

"That business with the starlings now." Phyllis accepted the turn of the conversation gracefully. "I'd say that was an abduction attempt."

It was like being on a beach when the tide went out. Every time he found a new place to stand, the sea sucked it out from under his feet. For a moment he felt hopelessly pulled under. Might as well breathe the water in, accept there was nothing he could do and wait for them to take away another person in his life he cared about.

But no. They should not get Ben. He was not ready to roll over quite yet. "Abduction? That's a lot of trouble to go to over one blocked path. You sure?"

She turned the laptop back on, angled it into a deeper patch of shadow and brought up a slide show of pictures—a clear shot of a tree leafed with solemn birds, and then an expanding bubble of interference, like a sphere of static and dust motes and plasma, everything within it distorted as if underwater. "Fairly sure. Creepy business with the birds. I don't see what that was about, if they could waltz past the wards as they pleased."

"Then I saw in his hand a little thing, like a nut. It was so small I wondered that it did not fall apart. I asked him what it was and he replied, It is everything that has been created. It is the whole created universe."

"Beg pardon?" Phyllis gave him one of her famous looks. Had she not been retired, he thought she might have rapped the desk smartly with a ruler to wake him up.

"Lady Julian of Norwich," he explained. "She was a medieval visionary. She was given a tour of Heaven and Hell by God, and at one point stood outside the universe, looking down on it. That was when she saw that it was as small and fragile as a nut. It's all a matter of perspective, yes? Perhaps the elves found a way to smuggle their own dimension through our wards by having the birds swallow it. It would be tiny as a seed, inside the mundane little bodies of the birds. The wards would only see the creatures from our own world and miss the invading universe inside them.

"I always liked her, you know. When she visited Hell, she made sure to come back and tell the world that it was empty. Very reassuring, I always think."

"No." Phyllis knocked back the dregs of her drink and craned her neck to look at the menu of lunch options chalked up on the blackboard behind the bar. "That's all too mystical for me. But what I want to know is, why? If you're right, that was some trick. Can't have been easy even for them. What are they getting out of it? Why him?"

She flicked through to the final picture—Ben, startled and frightened, bursting through the door into the pub's muted indoor light. "And here's the point I have to show you this. I think there's something strange about him. See that aura? Lots of purple and gold. Would you say that was normal in that situation?"

Chris pinched the brow of his nose. It didn't seem to do much to cut off the incipient headache. And this was why he should take Grace's advice and make sure not to get involved with a client—because he already didn't want to discuss Ben in this kind of context. Like a problem to solve, like a clue, a lead, a potentially guilty party. "He has the Sight. It's got to make a difference."

"Perhaps. And perhaps you should ask him if he's encountered the fae before. Get some family history. Maybe they gave him a gift that they now want to take back? Maybe he stole it. Lots of checking up to do there, I'd say."

Even being pulled out to sea had its advantages, it seemed. "You may be right. Ha. Well, you *are* right." Was that an excuse, even a duty, to see more of Ben? He rather thought it was. "Leave that to me."

Phyllis laughed. "You know, I thought you'd say that."

And he wondered, as he gathered up his tax returns and notes, if she'd been talking to Grace. All of this to cope with and he had to handle coming out as well? *Fantastic timing there, Padre. Thank you so much.*

Chapter Twelve

"And then it exploded! All the light bulbs blew, *pft, pft, pft,* like that." Ben put down his sledgehammer to mime bursting spheres of glass. It was the first time Chris had ever seen him so animated, using his body to express what words alone clearly couldn't convey. He had also put on shorts and a reflective jacket, steel-capped boots and a hard hat, and the effect, along with the dirt of falling rubble, was to make him seem like a different man. One who couldn't possibly coexist with the mild-mannered banker of yesterday.

"I'm telling you, there was glass everywhere. It's a wonder we weren't cut to pieces. Is this sort of thing going to carry on happening wherever I go? I'm a danger to my colleagues and my employer."

Another man would have said friends, Chris thought, taking a swing at the last remaining section of the wall. The jolt of impact up his arms and through his shoulders felt satisfying, and there was a great deal to be said for watching the cracks spread through the mortar, hitting again and hearing it start to slide, jumping out of the way of falling bricks, red dust settling over all and turning the sun to blood. He loosened the final few surviving pieces with a series of sharp blows, then set the sledgehammer down and picked up the bottle of water.

His mouth was full of dust. He rinsed—water fresh as dawn in his parched mouth—and spat, trying hard to think of anything reassuring to say. "Let's get this done, all cleared away and the peace offerings put out before we jump to any conclusions. If it carries on after that, yes, we have a problem. But it may not."

Brick dust made the white roses outside the exposed sitting room blush pink. All the grass had a layer of it, looking like a scene baked in terracotta. Inside the house, Chris impressed but not at all surprised to see that the room was completely empty, and a street door with a serviceable lock had replaced the glass-panelled internal door which had separated the extension from the rest of the house when last he visited. That was very like Ben, Chris thought. He was thorough. He planned things through and acted on them in order. And maybe he needed to know all the worst possibilities for that capable, organisational brain of his to figure out what to do even against something as nebulous as a threat from the fae. Panicking did not appear to be his style.

Ben too set down his sledgehammer, came close enough to take the water from Chris's hand and swig it. They stood together quietly, watching the cars ease slowly past along the road, watching the drivers watch them. Ben took off his hard hat and scrubbed at his flattened hair. "You don't believe that," he said.

"The truth? No, I don't. I think we're in deep trouble."

"You say 'we' so easily." Ben's brows twisted into a downward pointing arrow. "When what you mean is that *I'm* in trouble, and the person I've asked to help me with it has no clue what to do."

"Heh." Chris too rubbed some of the brick dust out of his hair. "How about we start with pizza?"

"Is this one of those 'come to the pub' things, which really means 'you're in imminent danger of a fate worse than death, but I'm trying not to alarm you'?"

Unsettling hallucinations and premonitions of doom aside,

Chris couldn't stop himself from grinning at that. Ben had such an attitude. It reminded him of himself in pilot training, seeing how far he had to push to get a reaction, testing where limits were, so he'd know—if ever it came to it—who were the weak points in the squadron. Who would help him, and who would be likely to suggest ditching the crate in the sea rather than face a dishonourable discharge at home.

He shook himself. Memory lane. Yes, that should have a new door and a padlock applied to it too. It did no good to venture down there these days.

"No. This is one of those 'I'm starving, let's eat' things. Thought we could get some food, have a chat."

Ben's eyes rounded in a look of mock surprise. His hand gestures had fallen off again, his hands lay uncommunicative by his side. Chris had the feeling that a wall of glass had come down between them. "A date kind of chat? Or an interrogation kind of chat?"

He tried to make his smile in return look unthreatening, suspected it only looked false. "A little bit of both."

Ben's gaze said nothing at all. He went into the house, returned uncoiling the flex of a masonry drill. "Pass me that baton."

They propped the separated ends of the wall with scaffolding, then fixed heavy blue plastic sheeting over the gap to keep the weather out. Chris cleared all the fallen bricks into a wheelbarrow and thence to a pile against the garden wall while Ben cleaned and packed away all his tools.

It was late when they'd finished. The sky glowed above them in a curve of deep, rich purple. Stars shone between long wisps of cloud that reflected the final beams of the sinking sun in blowing tatters of peach and gold. The peaks loomed over all, their silent black crowns like holes in the luminous sky. But cars flicked steadily past the house, blurring into lines of white light, and of red, and at the base of the hills the streetlamps and windows of Bakewell were pale gold and saffron in the gloom.

"All right?" Chris asked as Ben stowed the last item and locked the door behind him. They fell into step, walking through the mild summer night side by side, with the trees that lined Ben's road rustling overhead, and a student party filling the quiet with the music of Miley Cyrus and laughter.

Ben's step slowly lengthened, and his shoulders came down from around his ears. He gave his all-but-inaudible laugh—the one that was nothing more than a quick whistle of breath through the nose. "Apart from being sore and covered in brick dust and scared out of my wits? I'm fine."

"Pizza okay? You don't want a…" Chris's involuntary pause for thought brought the smile further out from hiding on Ben's face. It was faintly mocking but Chris welcomed it anyway. "You don't want a curry?"

"Pizza was invented in India, you know."

It almost fooled him, the deadpan delivery. His face had slipped into the expression he would have used to say *No, really? I never knew that!* But something in the apple roundness of Ben's cheek and the challenging brightness of his eye stopped him, left his eager expression to collapse into a grin. "You're having me on."

"Nearly believed it though, didn't you?" Ben stopped to pry a pebble loose from the bridge, drop it through darkness into the sliding silver shine of the river. In the streetlamp's light he looked as though he were carved from amber, a precious thing. But the breeze tousled his black curls around his face and made shadows flicker across his smile.

As they began walking again, Ben's right hand made a tiny

little twitch and Chris could have cheered. Despite the bank of trees with their roots sunk deep in the stream on their right, the long grey velvet of meadow on their left, where two massive oaks filled the night with whispers, Ben was beginning to relax.

As they passed the fork of Station Road, the trees were left behind, only honest grey northern houses now on either side, and as the lit front of Bella's Italian restaurant came into view, Chris too let out a breath he'd scarcely been aware he was holding. "I have to admit I'm horribly out of touch. These days, if it's not spooky or otherwise paranormal, I regard it as very much not my business."

Ben's laugh was audible now. He led the way into the restaurant, settled himself behind a table dressed in a severe white tablecloth and slid a sidelong glance at Chris while he pretended to read the menu. "You're such an old fogey. Do you study that, or does it come naturally?"

Chris was unaccountably insulted. He thought he'd passed so well, adapted to the point where he fitted right in. He stiffened and looked down to smooth his napkin on his knee. "What gives it away?"

But Ben's gaze was warm. The tasteful orange-scented candle between them honeyed the dark brown of his eyes, added little tints of gold. His hard defensive smile had softened. "Everything."

A waiter brought red wine, poured it into elegant glasses for them, and the gurgle of liquid, the ruby glow and sudden scent of tannin and blackberries got tangled up in Chris's mind with the very edge of Ben's mouth. There, where the lips turned in with a little tuck that deserved to be immortalized in sculpture, chiselled into marble, or licked open, forced to gasp and part and yield...

The smile curled farther up, and Ben's tongue crept out

and moistened his lower lip. Chris almost jumped at the flash of fierce erotic delight, wrestled down the urge to grab the young man by his shirt, pull him outside and take full advantage of that mouth in the nearest patch of shade.

As Ben laughed, Chris wrenched his gaze away, coughed, raised the menu between them like a shield. "So, Phil—Phyllis, that is—asked me to get some background details from you. You...um..."

Yes, work helped to put the distance back between them, to close up Ben's expression and restore the wariness on his face.

"You have an unusual aura, apparently. She wondered if you'd had other experiences with the People which might explain their interest in you. It's unusual for them to be this blatant in this day and age."

By the time the waiter had taken his order for steak in a cream pepper sauce, put out cutlery and bread rolls, he was feeling almost collected again. If only the table had not been so narrow that his knee brushed against Ben's whenever he moved, everything would have been under control.

"So tell me about yourself. Is this really your first brush with the paranormal? What about your parents? Might they have handed something down to you, something that the Good Folk now want?"

Ben's pizza arrived as he thought about this. He sawed it into tiny pieces with his mouth shut tight. *Ashamed? Embarrassed? Or hiding something?*

"No, you're right." When the great disk had been fully dismembered, Ben put down his knife and sighed. "I can see that you need to ask. Just don't snark, all right? I put up with your bad jokes and remarks about me, but don't say anything about my mother and father, because I won't have that."

"What kind of a person do you think I..." Chris began. Then

he remembered Grace on the phone—her assumption that he made a habit of insulting his clients. "Hm, well, scratch that question. But yes, I swear it. Scout's honour."

As he'd hoped, this brought a small unwinding. Ben bent his head to hide the smile, and his knee drooped against Chris's under the table. "Well then. My grandparents came to England just after the war. They were...trafficked? Rescued. By a Christian charity working with persecuted people in Uttar Pradesh."

He snapped out a sigh, looked up. "I shouldn't be so bitter. They were very grateful to leave. They were always very grateful. But everything was so strange to them here that they huddled together with their fellow emigrants for comfort.

"My parents saw that as not going far enough. They didn't come all this way just to remain in the same position—clearly associated with the same caste—here in England. They thought the way to leave it all behind was to become English. So I was brought up in a white district, in a white school, with white friends. Instead of being persecuted for my caste, I was persecuted for my colour, with no community beside me to whom I could turn for solidarity."

His mouth was hard now as that of a warhorse accustomed to a spiked bit. He pushed his plate away, bent his head over his empty hands and gave out a grim, enduring silence. Feeling helpless and guilty—trying not to be angry about it—Chris reached out and covered Ben's open hand with his own. Maybe he could return the favour Ben had done him in the pub, hold the young man back from the onslaught of too many memories.

It seemed to work. Ben lifted his head and looked at where they touched, breathed out that little snort of cynical amusement. "I should be grateful too. I live in a country where you can do that and not even understand what you've done.

Even your priest—she thinks I have the right to talk to God. That I won't pollute him. That he can bear to look at me. I should be thankful."

This was not what Chris had come to learn. He floundered in deeper waters than he had been prepared for, struck out for something that seemed to make sense. "I don't like being told what I should and shouldn't feel either. So you're a contrary bastard—tell me something I didn't know."

The waiter returned, spotted the joined hands and favoured them both with a two-inch recoil and a nervous look, as though he'd suddenly noticed there were a pair of zombies sitting in his restaurant, discussing where to find the best brains. Chris jerked as the impulse to snatch his hand away fought with bloody-mindedness and the knowledge that that would look even more incriminating.

"I don't think we'll bother with dessert, thank you. But you can get me a coffee." Ben disengaged himself and offered the man his plate. They smiled together with relief as he gathered up crockery and left, double quick.

"You know, it's a good thing you're not a doctor. With your bedside manner, the patients would be offing themselves in a rush like lemmings."

"You didn't have any complaints about my bedside manner this morning."

The waiter had not made it out of earshot and this caused him to jump so sharply that all the knives rattled on his armful of plates. He grabbed them tight and legged it in a way that was absurd and funny and really quite annoying all at the same time. Not malicious enough to be dealt with as an insult, but blatant enough to unsettle.

Ben must have been watching him closely to unravel Chris's thoughts from his expression. "After a while you don't even notice," he said. "Or you do but it fades down to something easy to ignore." He smoothed and refolded his napkin, putting it neatly between the cruet set and the vase of flowers. "So is that it? Business over, we can go back to the level of personal insults and sex? It's really quite fun watching you flounder."

"Is it?" All right, there was awkward and charming, and then there was plain insensitive. "Not quite so amusing for me, however. No, we're not finished. You didn't answer my question. Please do so now."

In the act of taking his cup from the waiter, Ben put it down with a smack. Coffee sloshed out and filled the saucer, but everything else about him tightened, neatened and drew together, wire thin. "Yes, go ahead and take it out on me. All right then, no. I've had no experiences with elves before. I don't know about my parents. They never told me they had seen anything, but I don't believe they would have spoken about it if they had. I don't know why my aura upsets you, but I'm not to blame for it. Perhaps it's just one more way in which I was born wrong."

He pulled out his wallet as another man might have pulled out a gun, took out a twenty and slapped it down next to the chrysanthemum in its bud vase in the centre of the table. Scraped his chair back...

"Wait!" Chris lunged out of his seat and grabbed the back of Ben's gritty black Nirvana T-shirt. Ben paused, gently set down his upraised foot and gave Chris a bland look over his shoulder. "Let's...ahm...start that again, shall we? Let me just..."

He rooted in his pocket for change, calculated how much he owed and counted it out in coppers and two-pound coins. By the time he'd finished, there was no tug on the T-shirt in his hand and little lines had sprung up about Ben's mouth as he tried to smother a laugh. "You should get a purse."

"Yes, I should."

"One of those little leather ones that you could rootle in for hours at the head of the checkout queue in Tesco's. You're the least cool man I've ever met."

Unlike the last, this jab hit no nerve, leaving him free to grin and reply, "Indeed. I believe you said I was hot."

"Yes, well, I am bonkers."

It felt better, outside. It shouldn't have—it made no sense that the peril of the midnight hour, water and the uncanny stars should feel less threatening than the fact that the restaurant staff were undoubtedly passing comment on their every move, right now. But it did. Some forms of conditioning clearly still ran deep. Chris pursed his lips and blew out a long whistle of relief. "Mad? Tell me about it."

"Well, it all began when I saw the terrible thing in the woodshed."

Laughter tasted like the wine, fruity and bouncy. He tried to choke it down, but Ben's sidelong look was so delighted, so proud of himself for the terrible, terrible joke, that the humour kept wriggling out of Chris's grasp, getting the better of him. He stopped and laughed until his face ached, letting Ben guide him by the elbow off the road and into the shadow of the trees. But there he sobered, in the dark, feeling the blind awareness of the oak settle watchfully about him, hearing the shiver of the leaves. He was off balance between hilarity and suspicion when Ben pushed him back against the trunk of the tree and kissed him hard.

It hurt. It hurt that he could want something so much, that it could be simultaneously fanfares and fireworks all over his body while under his heart a black singularity of pain compacted his backbone and made his lungs ache. He couldn't... He just couldn't.

Mysteriously, his hands had bunched into the back of Ben's T-shirt, drawing it so tight it rode up and exposed his waist, his belly button and the handspan of flesh above the waistband of the shorts that clung to his hips. Chris was as psychic as a brick, but he knew if he shifted his grip to Ben's waist, felt the bare skin warm against his palms in the cool of the night, this kiss would turn into the fastest hand job of his life. And he couldn't do that. Not on the first day for fifteen years on which he'd seen Geoff's face.

"Don't..." He reasserted control over his arms, wound them inside Ben's grip and broke it, shoved Ben away. "Don't. It's too—"

"Is this because I told you what I was?" Dark skin and black T-shirt blended into the oak shadow and moonlight, so that Ben's suspicious fury was little more than a glitter of eyes and a line of blue starlight along one high cheekbone, and Chris almost said, *It's not you, it's me*, but caught himself in time.

"No," he said instead, resorting to honesty—his brain too scrambled to do otherwise. "It's certainly not that. You're brave and clever and beautiful and too good for me. But I... It's complicated."

"*Why* is it complicated? Why isn't it the only thing about this situation that's simple?"

Dear God, where to start? Ben had not moved away, still close enough to touch or punch whichever way the mood swung. Chris snugged an arm around his back, drew him close and rested his forehead in the hollow of Ben's shoulder.

Ben twitched. "Sex is complicated but hugging isn't?"

And the absurdity of the whole thing made Chris laugh. "I suppose that is going at the problem arse over tit. It's complicated because..." *Fifteen years ago a guy I shagged for a*

170

couple of weeks died, and I haven't got over it yet. No, he liked Ben but he wasn't giving that bit of information up to be ridiculed by anyone.

Because my people don't trust you? No. It wasn't true anyway, they were just being thorough and he couldn't blame them for that.

"Because you're scared and lonely, and who's to say you're not throwing yourself at an old man because you think it'll give me more motivation to protect you. Or just to take your mind off things."

Ben pulled away. The night air was suddenly cold on Chris's cheek. The tree whispered above him, its swaying branches creaking like arthritic joints. It smelled of moss and damp, but there were stars caught in its canopy amid the moving shine of moonlight reflected from the river. Here under the foliage it was almost completely dark, and silent. Ben's heat and presence oozed out of him like honey from baklava, and Chris thought, *Damn. You ruined a perfectly good romantic moment there. Focus, idiot, how many more of them are you likely to get in your life?*

"I think..." he scrambled to recover what he could, "...it's to do with you being a client. And also that I really don't do casual. In fact this has already gone beyond casual for me."

"It has?"

Ah. So he'd said that last bit aloud, had he? A brief feeling of panic was cut off by the tentative touch of Ben's hand at his waist. A sigh and then a brush of warmth on his ear as Ben misjudged his position in the dark, tried for another kiss. It didn't seem to matter that out on the path a dog walker was looking nervously in their direction. They could just mind their own business for a moment while he negotiated the fact that something seemed to have softened in the enveloping night, even the chuckling river turned down its volume. "Yes, it very much has, Ben. I...like you. I'm very afraid for both of us. This is going to hurt."

"What if I wasn't a client?"

In the tricksy blue twilight, Ben had now found the angle of his jaw. He half-expected more kisses, was thrown for a loop to feel the young man's long, narrow fingers brush gently, almost tenderly, up his throat, scritching through his evening stubble. Oh, that ached. That ached like the first step on a newly healed leg, like the disbelief and desolation lying in wait beneath love, that makes it so sublime. He fought the desire to close his eyes, tip back his head and surrender. "Huh...er...how d'you mean?"

"You're volunteers, your team?"

The nod caught the fingers under his chin, kept them there, warm and hard against his Adam's apple. Nice. He could get used to that. "Yes."

"Then let me join up. There's training, I presume. Some kind of physical? They'd be able to run all their tests, poke and prod me all they like. And then you could do the same later in the privacy of your own home."

The little, tentative blossoming within him curled up tight again and withdrew, like the flower of a sea anemone brushed by an intrusive finger. Ben's suggestion was practical. Suspiciously practical. He'd receive training, all the knowledge and technology at their disposal—even if that was all made in woodwork class by Stan. He'd be at the heart of things, with someone always there to turn to and Chris wrapped around his little finger—or some lower organ. Great idea. Highly pragmatic from his point of view. Possibly even a benefit from Chris's, make Ben easier to keep an eye on.

He was a stupid old fool to have thought for a moment that there could be some genuine affection under it.

"What, it's too super-secret to let me in?" Ben misinterpreted his pause. "You've got to be in MI5 or the Masons?"

"I think it's a good idea."

"Got to swear a pact? Then you'll take me round the secret base under the Red Lion? What?"

"I said, 'I think it's a good idea.'"

Since a professional relationship seemed to have been re-established, Chris levered himself away from the tree and plunged out into the citrusy light of the single yellow lamp that lit the path back.

Ben followed, looking bemused. Maybe even touched. "You said yes?"

And at the look in his eyes the tide changed, the sea warmed again and that tender thing inside Chris's hard shell unfurled, just a little, to test the water. Ben was practical—he already knew that—it didn't have to mean it couldn't coexist with something else. "Of course I said yes. We get to know where you are, and I get to see you more often. Why wouldn't that be a splendid idea?"

They walked in silence over the ancient bridge, Chris imagining what it must have been like to see the elves in their riding. That must have been something. Say what you liked about the bastards, they were like sharks, like wolves. No matter how deadly, the world would be a poorer place without them.

"What is it?"

"Hm?"

"The tune. You're humming something. You must be feeling mellow."

A quick jog over the desert of tarmac that was the wide

road junction on the corner of Bath Street, and Chris chased down the music that had been going through his head. The music for a dance called Bideford Bridge, but there was another secret he couldn't see this relationship surviving. "The tune's called 'The Fairy King'. It must have reminded me, as we came over the bridge. Though I believe it's a fairy queen we have in Bakewell."

Ben giggled, a ridiculous *tee hee hee* that made Chris stop in the street to figure out what he'd said. Fairies? Queens? …oh.

"Hahaha. Your face!" Well, it was a night of firsts. Chris couldn't recall having seen such an open smile on Ben's face before. Worth a certain amount of tasteless innuendo. Hm, and he wasn't going to mention the word innuendo at this point either.

He stopped again, attempted to think of a witty riposte and failed. "Well, good night, then."

Ben looked around himself as if surprised to find himself outside his own garden gate. "You walked me to my door," he said in a tone that suggested he was laughing only to cover up the fact that he was moved. "How old-fashioned. Can I expect flowers in the morning?"

"You can expect to get your arse out of bed at half past five and meet us at Deeping Hall Health Club for six. We do like to get the practical exam out of the way ASAP."

"Ghostbusting?" Ben suddenly didn't look too thrilled.

"Wasn't that what you asked for?"

Ben swallowed and brushed a final scatter of brick dust out of his hair, the fear on his face gilded by streetlights. "Do I get to change my mind?"

"Too late for that now."

Chapter Thirteen

There were flowers on the doorstep. They broke Ben's stride as he came out into the hushed early-morning street, made him hop so as not to step on them. A posy of lime flowers and peach-coloured roses with their stems held together by a wrap of duct tape, standing upright in a milk bottle full of water.

"Fucking idiot!" said Ben out loud, laughing as he carried them through into the kitchen and stood them on the window ledge. The room filled with the syrup scent of lime blossom. He moved stacked dishes out of the drainer so that sunlight could throw the flowers' shadow on the floor—so he could see them from whatever corner of the room he stood in.

They must have come from Chris's garden, for no shop-bought blooms would have yellow spots on their leaves and a caterpillar dangling by a thread from one thorn. Ben smiled at them, picked up the caterpillar on the tip of his finger and, going out, deposited it on the hedge as he passed. He threw his bag into the passenger seat of the car, buckled himself in, caught sight of his grin in the driving mirror and laughed again. When had Chris had the time to do that? Stupid bastard! What a dorky thing to do. How very like him.

Half an hour later, some of the glow wore off as he turned up the exclusive drive of Deeping Hall, through electric gates that opened silently for him when he gave his name and closed as silently behind. The single-track road wound through landscape gardens and a golf course, passed a trout fishing lake still as a mirror. The gothic grey stone of the mansion was drawn in strokes of charcoal and squares of flaming orange where the sun had cleared the hedges and reflected from the many sash windows of the spa.

An early-morning freshness filled the air as he tumbled out onto the raked gravel of a car park empty of anything but the Matlock Paranormal team, standing around Chris's van, having pre-mission tea from a thermos.

"Glad you could make it." Phyllis handed him a bacon sandwich and then snatched it back with a look of alarm and substituted one with a very rubbery cold fried egg. "Should be an interesting one today—clients here have reported 'creepy feelings', feelings of being watched, things mysteriously out of place. Shadows behind doors that open onto empty rooms..."

Her own car door stood open, a wicker hamper in the passenger's seat. She opened the lid and brought out an enamel cup and plate, passed him a cup of tea. He put the egg sandwich down gingerly on the plate. "I do eat bacon, you know."

"Oh. Well, I thought it was better to be safe than sorry."

Crashing noises in the van presaged Chris emerging with an armful of folding picnic table. They shared a smile brighter for a memory of roses. "I should be doing something, shouldn't I?"

"We're just setting up." Chris folded out the table, and Stan came squirming out of the back of the van, covered every area of the table in electronic devices and linked them in a spider web of cable. "Let me get the awning up. Phil told you what we're facing?"

She sniffed disdainfully. "I'm just doing it. You get on with your job and let me do mine."

By the side of the pond, Grace stood with her head bent over her open hands, palms cupped as if she begged the

Almighty to fill them with strength. Her solitude was ominous, forbidding, and the earnestness of her prayers made him look again at the ramshackle preparations of the rest of the team and feel—as he had felt last night—that these people were really not up to the job they'd taken on. "I expected something a bit more military."

"I'm sure you did," Phyllis said, taking away the uneaten sandwich and offering him a headset in its place. This had the look of a Bluetooth headset that had been lovingly rewired by someone with a steampunk pirate fetish. It incorporated a single earphone, a small microphone on a stalk that rested just in the corner of his mouth, and a flap, like an eyepatch that folded down over the left eye. A tiny camera made an iris in the centre of one side, and a screen the size of a postage stamp showed a black-and-green image on the other side. The camera's lens shared the oily gleam of Phyllis's larger ghost filter.

"But we're only 'beyond the government' in the sense that they believe we're a bunch of quacks who are not entitled to a small-business loan. We have to make do with what we've got. But now you're making me lose my train of thought. What was I saying? Oh, yes. The ghost.

"Well, as I was saying—it amounted to nothing more than general spookiness, some unexplained shadows, etcetera, until this time last month, after which it began to escalate. Ugly things written on the mirrors. Threats and so on. A smell. Belongings moving about unaided. Guests fleeing from their bedrooms at three o'clock in the morning and demanding a full refund. You can imagine how the proprietors liked that. So, finally it became worth their while to close the place for a weekend and call someone in, and here we are."

Two throaty roars at once sent a fountain of blackbirds into the cider-coloured sky as a generator came on by the back of the van, all Stan's computers flicking into bright blue life soon after. At the same time, a metallic pink Porsche swung around the last loop of the golf links and rolled gently into the car park, coming to a practised stop outside the door.

The woman who stepped out looked like Barbie's great aunt, platinum-blonde hair swept up into a French twist, skin by sunbed and eyebrows by *ambre solaire*. Her candyfloss-pink lips were set in a hard, businesslike line as she stepped forward to take Chris's hand. "Mr. Gatrell? I'm Miss Barlow. We spoke on the phone. You can set up inside, you know."

"Thank you." He bowed slightly over the crystal-tipped nails. "But we prefer to have our own generator in a protected position outside the house. Never a wise idea to rely on the electrics of a building that may be trying to kill you."

Miss Barlow looked askance at Stan, whose bright copper fringe stood out from the hood of his Metallica sweatshirt and whose radio headset was jammed over aviator sunglasses. He had chosen that moment to open a packet of M&Ms and pour them into a bowl near the keyboard. He looked, Ben thought, following her gaze, far too young, like he should be out skateboarding or spray-painting graffiti over someone's wall.

Chris had followed their train of thought too. "Stan will be out here where it's safe, make sure we stay in contact with each other, guide us if we can't see. That sort of thing. He knows better than to put himself in any danger, don't you, son?"

"Oh aye." The monitors came on one by one. Ben moved his head and watched the picture move in echo on the rightmost screen. If he took off his headset to examine it, the screen showed his face, looking gaunter than normal, with new lines about the mouth and shadows under his eyes.

"My mates think they're something 'cause they go paintballing. Wazzocks. Okay, I've got good feeds from all of you." He picked up his own headset and tapped the microphone, watching while everyone winced. "You all heard that, yeah? Okay then, I'm ready to go when you are."

"Do we not get a briefing? A plan?" Ben asked, not finding this quite so amusing any more. "Some kind of weapon at least?"

"Grace is our weapon." Chris pressed a child's Super Soaker into Ben's hands, and he thought the man was speaking mystically, until Grace came into view, decked in chasuble and stole, carrying Bible, bell and candle. "But if all else fails a good pistol full of holy water doesn't come amiss."

The sunshine had slid from the façade of the stately-home-cum-spa now and begun to soak up the dew that had greyed the short emerald turf of the lawns. It lit up the bright yellow plastic reservoir of the gun in Ben's hands and picked out the cheerful red logo. He snorted in disbelief. "I thought we'd get proton packs."

"That's made-up TV rubbish," said Stan. "No such thing. 'Don't cross the streams?' Bollocks."

"Language, Stan." Phyllis zipped an extra lens into her camera bag and slung it on her back. She had only a small water pistol tucked in her belt, her hands occupied by the ghost camera with its oil-filled chamber gleaming opalescent as pearl.

Ben shared a half-horrified, half-disbelieving look with Miss Barlow, feeling the water slosh beneath his elbow. "You could have at least painted the guns silver."

"Oh, you're one of these marketing people, are you?" Phyllis sniffed and planted one booted foot on the lowermost step of the sweeping cascade of stone stairs that led into the entrance hall. "Image is everything? Bollocks—pardon me, Stan. If it works, it works. It doesn't need to look good at the same time."

"I'm sure it would give the client more confidence." Ben

offered Miss Barlow a sympathetic look.

"I'm not paying for confidence," she said. "Only results. You go in, do your thing. If there are no further complaints for the next month, then I'll pay you what you ask. If you make no difference, you get nowt, and I charge any breakages against you, regardless."

Chris pulled a silver chain out of his collar, raised the coinlike pendant to his lips for a second, tucked it back in again and smiled breezily. "Right. No time like the present. Shall we?"

They left her standing beside Stan's tented control centre, walked up a flight of broad sandstone steps, across a terrace ornamented by stone pine cones, farther up again and then inside. Oak doors swooshed silently shut behind him.

In the foyer, someone with no feeling for architecture had scattered postmodern chairs—great blocks of foam covered in blue baize—around a pillared Edwardian entrance hall, and parked a curvy MDF registration desk at the bottom of the marble staircase. A drowsy wasp had been circling in the centre of the hall as they entered, but the humming snapped off as the doors closed, as cleanly as if switched off at the wall.

Phyllis and Grace nodded to one another, split up and went right and left, through the doors that led to the symmetrical wings of the old house. Their feet brushed barely audible over the claret carpet, and when they were gone, the hush in the great white chamber felt like a living thing. Ben would have told himself this was all ridiculous—he did try—but after the starlings, after the photocopier, the evidence was not on his side.

"This is how it works." Chris took his elbow, a warm, reassuring touch. Chris had lowered his voice as though in church. "The name of the game is to get the entity and Grace into the same place. Somewhere approximately ten square feet is the ideal—in theory her range should be infinite, but in practice we've discovered that the effectiveness of an exorcism weakens rapidly with distance. So, we go in and look for the ghost. Once we've found it, we drive it to some point of Grace's choice."

He wiped a hand through his hair, leaving it spikier than ever, looked up at the pattern of sunshine in empty rooms. "Frankly, she doesn't actually need us. We just make the process faster and a little safer for her."

"Safer? I thought ghosts couldn't do anything to you. Not physically, I mean."

Chris laughed a humour-free version of his all-purpose chuckle. "That is what we tell children, yes. Not strictly true, however. In any case, once the entity is aware of us, it'll do one of two things—it'll either try to hide or it will attack. The holy water is, ah, dual purpose. Use it as a weapon to defend yourself. But crucially, also use it—just a sprinkling of drops— every ten paces, to close up the corridors behind you, so the ghost can't get past you and away from its date with Grace. Clear?"

Ben had a picture of them working through the old house like a slowly contracting force-field sphere, pulling in, sweeping the bewildered spirit out of its lairs and down into that white, light-washed egg of an entrance hall. "I get it."

"Stan'll be coordinating. Every fifteen minutes, he'll give you everyone's positions so we know where we all are. You get into trouble, you call for us, we come running—and vice versa. If you run out of water, go to the nearest tap, fill up with plain tap water, call for Grace and she'll come and prime it, so to speak." Chris bent his head and rubbed the back of his neck. The military tone in his voice softened. "Or you can just sit this out. Save me having to worry."

Despite a sinking feeling that he'd let himself in for something bigger than he'd bargained for, Ben turned and pulled Chris's hand from his elbow finger by finger. "I'm the least of your worries."

"Not by a long shot."

"I can handle myself."

"I'm sure you can—or I wouldn't have brought you along. But we do these all the time. It should be routine."

Why had he said that? Ben fumed as they made their way to the upper floor, separated to take a wing each. That was as bad as "it'll be a piece of cake" or "nothing can possibly go wrong".

He pushed open the set of double doors at the head of the stairs, passed a fire extinguisher and began to walk down a long corridor of closed doors. The paintwork was stark white and the stillness had the sense of a place used to bustle and cheerful chatter now emptied and in shock. He folded down the eyepatch over his eye and saw the same scene with a faint green tinge superimposed. Against the window at the end of the corridor, a wasp battered itself with a tap-tap-tapping noise. Feeling jumpy and strange and foolish, he tipped up the soaker and let a dozen drops of holy water run into his cupped palm.

He flung them at the window, and the wasp disappeared. No little yellow-and-black body any more, but the tapping remained. Tap, tap, tap, like a finger on glass. Woodworm? Deathwatch beetle? Shit! He reached up to reposition a microphone that had stuck to his suddenly dry lips. "I think I've got something."

"Like what?" Stan asked. There was a fizz and pop as he swigged Coke on the end of the line, and Ben thought rude things about young people today, though he was one of them.

"I... Um, I can hear a tapping noise—"

"It's here too." Phyllis and Chris spoke together.

"All very normal where I am," said Grace.

"All right then." The slight note of uncertainty in Chris's voice was gone now. He sounded almost cheerful, like a BBC announcer segueing into *Strictly Come Dancing*. "It's big, and it doesn't want to play with Grace. Let's change its mind, shall we? Carry on."

As Ben turned to walk back down the corridor, he thought the sun went in. The baking heat chilled as if someone had switched on the air conditioning. He looked over his shoulder and saw a cloudless sky. His shadow lay dark beneath his feet. He breathed in sharp, and the air in his mouth tasted of frost and rotting apples.

He saw something move down the corridor ahead of him—to his naked eye it was a patch of sinuous shade, swimming through the carpet like a water snake in a stream. To the screen at his right eye, it was a river of light. He followed it ten paces, spattered the corridor behind him with water, feeling braver now. The stench of overripe cider lodged in the back of his throat. Somewhere in the centre of his spine terror slipped along his nerves, chilled his skin, but his mind felt divorced from his body, calm despite his trembling.

"It's, um, retreating ahead of me," he whispered into the mic.

"Good." Chris's voice. "Gently does it. No need to make it—"

Darkness. Instant and utter, the roaring noise of his blood in his ears, all other sounds switched off like the light. Ben's separation of calm mind and terrified body snapped together, and the fear flooded into his brain like ice water. "Ah! Ah, shit!" The darkness squeezed him, crushed him, his vertebrae ground together as immense pressure pushed him down. He pumped the trigger of his gun almost involuntarily as his hands pulled into fists. An arc of silverlike lightning, a flash—he could almost hear the boom and tear of it—and the world was back. He was doubled over, forcing air into his crumpled lungs, his eyes streaming from the light.

"Ben? Ben, report."

"I'm...ah... I'm okay. It jumped me. Shit."

He thought he saw a man-shaped shadow slide across the wall, through the closed white door of one of the rooms that lined the corridor. The camera of his headset registered nothing at all, but when he flicked the eyepatch up, he saw something glisten on the primrose paint where the thing had passed. It had left a trail.

Thin, clear mucus drizzled down the wall, a band of it like the trail of an enormous slug.

"Ah, yuck, that's..."

"What?"

"What's it called? Ectoplasm. I thought they were making that stuff up."

Chris's tight little chuckle, and then the breezy voice again, as if this were all beer and skittles. "Keep it moving."

"It's gone in a room."

"Then you go after it and drive it back out." A pause for thought and a gentler tone. "Unless you want me to...?"

"I'm fine. I'm on it." Ben thought about Phyllis in her twinset and pearls, swollen knuckles and thinning silver hair. If she could do this, he'd be damned if he couldn't.

But the confidence of earlier had gone. His hand shook as he reached for the door handle, touched slime and Arctic cold and eased himself over the threshold. He'd been expecting a bedroom but this was nothing of the sort. Venetian blinds at the window striped the air black and yellow as the wasp. Tiles underfoot and strip lighting above. At least three elegant Edwardian rooms had been knocked together, lined with marble, sinks and changing rooms. White curtains hung motionless over the small cubicles.

In the centre of the room stood two ranks of what looked like sarcophagi. The place stank of pine-fresh detergent, water and the faint indelible smell of a thousand sweating bodies. Cedar racks by the door held folded white towels.

Water trickled into a drain. Ben moved through lines of light and darkness, hearing his own ragged breath, the faint caw of crows outside and a *sssssh* noise he half-felt he must be imagining, couldn't place.

Calmly. Methodically.

At the back of the room he could see where a far door opened on a gym. It was lighter in there, the windows uncurtained. The fresh morning sky reflected in a wall of mirrors. Resistance machines seemed scattered at random in the airy white space, video screens hanging above them.

Ben flicked holy water on the far wall, turned, saw himself reflected to infinity in the mirrors, and something else in there with him—something formless, pale, moving. Slipping from mirror to mirror, from reflection to reflection, as if it owned all those other worlds. His heart seemed to punch him in the throat. He didn't want to look, couldn't look away, terrified that at any moment it would shape itself into something mind-blastingly hideous.

"Chris? Everyone? You seeing anything?"

Above his head, the TV screens flicked on one by one. Cascades of white noise twisted about a blurry echo of a shape. The air filled with the sound of hissing.

"Nothing, old son. Nothing since you called last."

"Well I've bloody got something."

A scaling whirr sounded as over by the wall the cross-trainer began to move by itself. Ben bit his lip and confessed, "I'm getting a bit creeped out, to be honest."

"You're like a lightning rod for this stuff." It didn't help that Phyllis sounded fascinated, as if she wanted to catch it all on tape to analyse later. "Stan? Where is he?"

The mirrors were turning pearly around him. He thought for a moment his skin had come out in a hot, feverish flush, and then saw the steam billowing in from the room beyond in a low roiling fume.

A sound of a distant keyboard as Stan looked up the layout of the place, and Ben was going to say, *I can talk for myself, you know*, when an invisible hand squeaked down the wet glass and the words *Get out, hijra* wrote themselves in huge, shaky letters across the whole wall.

"The west-wing top floor is a gym, sauna and swimming pool." Stan's cracking voice sounded in his ear, under the prickly wave of outrage and fear. "The readings are having a party over there."

"All right." A slamming door and Chris's voice. "Everyone else, pick up the pace. Let's get everywhere else closed off and converge on Ben ASAP. Okay, Ben? We're on our way."

"Get here fast," he said, shaken by the fact that the ghost knew enough about him to use that word. All at once its malice felt very personal.

He threw a handful of water over the message—it joined the beads of steam bleeding from the letters, rolled down to splash on the floor. A distorted voice whispered from the TVs. *Get out, gaandu. Cocksucker. Get out.* The steam was around his knees now, a blanket of it, warm and clinging, making his trousers stick to his shins, rolling down his back like his sweat.

"Chris? What happens if... Does holy water get diluted?

Can it get washed away?"

Another sibilant hiss in his ear. He thought Chris had breathed in sharp, as if shocked, but the reply was in the same unruffled squadron-leader tone he'd adopted throughout. "Maybe, but Grace can't, and she's going to be with you in moments. Fall back to the corridor and wait for her."

Calm. Yes, he could be calm too. He could *pretend* to be calm, the way Chris was doing, and maybe fool himself into believing it.

The door into the steam room had closed behind him, or been closed by something. More slime glistened on the handle, minty chill. Easing it down, he anointed the lintels and uprights of the door, slid through and faced a solid wall of steam, featureless but for the diffuse stripes of light that let him guess at the windows. His indrawn breath clung to the sides of his mouth, slipped down his throat like a raw egg, and he realised with a gut roil of nausea there were droplets of ectoplasm mixed in with the steam.

As he stepped back, flung the door to the gym fully open, a force plucked it from his hand, slammed it shut again. He snatched his fingers away only just in time—wood rammed into his fingertips and pain ran shrill up his arm. When he seized the handle again it burned like liquid nitrogen, making him reel away, tuck his hand beneath his armpit and spin, doubled over, walking off the acid pain.

That was a mistake too. As soon as he could straighten up, he found he had stumbled away from the door, away from the tiger stripes of the windows. He was lost in a shifting, formless mass of steam.

"Nearly there." Grace's voice in one ear, and in the other that flat, monotone whine, whispering, *Suck my dick, refuse boy. You're not even fully human, lower than an animal.* He

Alex Beecroft

stepped forward, let it have a blast of holy water in its filthy mouth, and yes, that did lighten the steam a little, let him see something bulky, black in the grey.

Coming closer, he picked out the strange, cupboard-like shape of a steam bath—the two doors at the front, the neck hole at the top, from which a pillar of hotter steam punched its way through the water-laden air. Beyond it, he could guess at another, and another, all of them capped with towers of vapour. He followed the hot mass across the roof and down and—oh God—there. There in the corner, a shadow cast by no light, where the wet air boiled together into the shape of a man.

Reflexes he didn't know he had kicked in. The jet from his gun sliced through its forehead and down, cutting it in two. As he retreated, a blast of warmer air hit his back. He took his eyes off the steam shape for an instant, registered too many things at once. The doors of the steam bath behind him opened by themselves, the ghost disappeared and something invisible hit him in the chest, shoving him towards the dark cabinet. He pictured himself boiled alive, or worse—simply shut in with it, nowhere to run. Another blast from the gun—it felt lighter now. God, it *was* lighter! It was nearly empty! And panic gave him the strength to shrug off the massive weight and run full tilt across the room until he smacked into a wall.

He felt along it, found a door. "Come on! Come on!"

"We're right outside. You're okay."

Ben wrenched at the handle with all his strength, and it twisted with mocking ease. He set his shoulder to the door, burst through it into cooler, chlorine-scented air. His initial rush took him halfway down the side of this new room, relieved to be able to see and to breathe clearly—to be able to get away. But the relief stopped dead, and so did he, when he realised he had only exchanged the sauna for the spa's swimming pool.

188

Tendrils of steam wound through the open door behind him, drifted across the tiles and floated on the unruffled surface of uncounted gallons of still blue water.

So much water, and maybe an eggcup full of the holy stuff still in his tank. "Shit!"

"All right, we're... Fuck, what's this?"

Ben turned at the exclamation, looking back through the door into the sauna. There a rectangle of light had appeared and the fog roiled as someone came through from the corridor. He guessed at Grace—that combination of pink and dark blur above a long fall of purple cassock. Her voice was clearer, murmuring rapidly, head bent over the book in her hand. Cold broke like a tsunami with her at the epicentre. The room whitened as, around waist height, steam turned into snow.

Faintly, Ben registered lapping noises from the swimming pool. He ignored them in favour of watching Chris and Phyllis come through behind Grace. Chris took one look at the state of the room and bent to pull the plugs on the steam baths, his face illuminated by a nimbus of lightning.

Beside Ben, something splashed on the tiled floor, and then again. Recoiling, he saw the water of the pool bulging upwards. It had grown two arms, braced its runny hands on the side and was pushing itself out, like a swimmer. "Shit! Chris?"

His headset fizzed and cracked by his cheek in the moist air. "It's all right." Chris's voice sounded scratchy as an old record in his ear. "Grace has got the entity's attention—"

"Not this one, she hasn't!" The pillar of water was refining itself as he watched. As he retreated toward the far wall, it stepped forward. It had legs now and a humanlike body. It was sculpting itself from the feet up as it walked towards him, a flicker of green-gold light in its chest pulsing like a heart, and another in the still faceless head.

"There's another one in here. Chris!"

It balled its fist, for all the world like a man, but the punch, when it came, was a fire-hose blast of water in his face, knocking him off balance, driving him backwards. Heat on his cheek as the headset short-circuited, and he could see nothing but the flickering silver grey of water, his nose and mouth blocked with it, all of it pushing in, stopping his breath.

He dived for the floor, rolled, gasping, onto his hands and knees, and the creature stepped closer. Strangely beautiful now, godlike with its freshly chiselled face lit from within by that green summer sunlight glisten. Ben coughed up burning water, his nose and eyes stinging from chlorine, his chest aching as he tried to fill it, too fast, with too deep a breath of air. What to do? What the fuck to do? One shot in his tank and what good was it against a creature made entirely of water?

Two more dripping footsteps splashed on the tiles. Ben levered himself up, took aim. But it brought its left hand down, palm open, and a cable of water like an ocean tide wrenched the weapon from his grip, sent it spinning. The reservoir atop it cracked, and the holy water ran gurgling down the nearest drain.

Scrambling away, Ben found another door, wrenched it open. It was a badly packed store cupboard. He registered a swinging light bulb, boxes on shelves. A slide of brightly coloured foam shapes dislodged from their pile and scattered under his feet.

He picked them up and hurled them at the oncoming creature. It was fully shaped now, though the eyes were like two mirrors, without iris or pupil. A handsome face. A face he almost felt he'd seen before—but he had little inclination to ponder where. *Resources? What resources do I have? The imp of holy water sewn into the tennis sweatband at my wrist and...um...*

The creature had slowed, was examining him with those liquid-mercury eyes. Diamond lines of light traced a faint, uncertain frown on its transparent brow. If it had been human, he would have said it was having second thoughts about its reign of terror. If a god, it might be wondering if it should show mercy.

Ben straightened up and faced it, saw himself reflected in its gaze. It paced forwards and he retreated just as slowly away. Stalemate.

And then Chris burst through the door from the steam room, calling out, "Stand away from that man."

Both of the creature's hands came down simultaneously. A blast like a water cannon struck Ben in the face and chest, hurling him into the wall. His leather-soled shoes slipped on the wet tiles. He windmilled like a cartoon character as he fell on the base of his spine, and the shocking pain of it opened his mouth and made him gasp despite his best efforts to keep his lips pressed shut. Water scoured down his throat, hit his lungs like acid.

He had to cough. Deeper than reason or thought, his body demanded he choke out the water, breathe in again. His chest was on fire, bursting. His eyes streamed with tears that washed into the pounding thunder of liquid that still beat over his face.

He had to breathe. Had to! Had to open his mouth and breathe in air or water or *something*.

A ringing in his ears, black around the edges of his vision, he tried to crawl away. And it stopped, all at once, in a massive splash and cascade of water as a tweed-coloured blur ran straight into the creature and out the other side, putting itself between Ben and it. Ben coughed and coughed, all his starved cells tingling from the new air, wiped his eyes and streaming

191

nose on his wet sleeve, scrambled to his feet.

"Stay behind me."

Ben had got used to thinking of Chris as an eccentric and mildly amusing old codger, rapidly approaching middle age; he'd forgotten what he'd seen that first day, when he opened the door to the stranger on his threshold. It was back now, though, full force. Focussed as a duellist, brown and gold as a hunting lion, Chris almost glowed with a martial aura Ben was all too happy to hide behind. They sidled together around the spinning liquid pillar where the creature was reforming itself, retreated warily back towards the door of the sauna, where Grace formed a more permanent defence.

They made it to the floats cupboard before the creature was complete again, its back to them. It wore, bizarrely enough, what almost looked like a flying jacket—wide sheepskin collar and straps for a parachute outlined in flickering light against the smoothness of the water.

Chris hesitated, his steps slowing. Ben carried on sloshing away. "Come on! Let's get to Grace before it all starts again."

But, leaning on the storeroom door, one hand holding on to something inside, Chris stopped altogether. For a moment there was no sound but the endless trickle of the thing back into the pool, and Chris's breathing, harsh as if he had been knifed. Under the stench and chlorine and fear wound a scent of cold gun oil and tobacco.

Gracefully, inhumanly, the figure turned, aquaplaning on the layer of water that spilled out from the soles of its boots. From the swimming pool's glass roof, the sun of summer shone down and turned the thing into molten gold. It opened its mouth as if to speak, and at first Ben thought the little breath of agony and despair had come from it. And then—in the weak, watery voice of a man who's busy bleeding to death—Chris said,

"What the hell are you doing?"

"I'm not doi—"

"Not *you!*"

The creature closed its mirrored eyes, closed its mouth, opened them again and looked as though it was shouting something. No sound came out. It clutched the little breakers of its curly hair and pointed straight at Ben.

"What? What are you...?"

Its eyes thinned, its jaw hardening. It drew back its hand and let loose a volley of water like a battering ram of liquid steel, the face of it flattened by air resistance as it arced towards Ben.

"Bastard!" Chris pulled down hard on whatever it was he had been holding, darted forward, trailing some kind of cable. He stabbed the end of it straight in to the wet flank of the creature. All over the building lights flashed, burst and went out. A great white-blue jagged sphere of electricity swelled inside the watery shape. Hectic lightning flashed and reflected from its internal currents. Light built and built, blazing white.

And then the creature burst apart in a huge bubble of steam. Chris gave a shrill yell, dropped the cable on top of the pile of floats and peeled half-melted rubber gloves from burnt hands. He doubled over them, sobbing through gritted teeth.

The steam room door opened. "All right in here?" asked Phyllis, camera in one hand, water pistol in the other.

The last errant droplet plinked back into the pool and the surface smoothed. Ben realised Chris wasn't going to move; he was going to stand there forever, staring at off-white ceramic tiles, his head bent down as if by a weight, making that soft gasping noise of hurt and shock.

"Careful," Ben warned the others. "There's a live cable. Can you go and switch the power off at the mains? I'll bring Chris."

He wasn't sure what had just happened, but the situation didn't need—not right now—questions and sympathy and cups of tea. Ben came as quietly forward as he could, seized one wrist and then the other, pulling the hands into the light, revealing angry red palms and a scattering of rising blisters. Painful, certainly, but surely not enough to make Chris's teeth chatter as they were, to make him have to fight so hard against tears that it took him three tries to say, "I...I had t-to. Had to. The living come first. The living have to come first."

Ben brushed the wet hair from his forehead and the warm water away from his cheeks with careful fingers, conscious of the enormity of what must have happened to make a man so old-fashioned weep in public. "What is it? What's the matter?"

"I..." Chris shook his head, covered his eyes with his least-burnt hand.

"Never mind." Ben got an arm around his shoulders, led him back to the corridor, downstairs and out into the sunshine. Chris sat and dripped on the passenger seat of the van without raising his head once.

Chapter Fourteen

"Tell me what I can do to help," Flynn said.

Liadain leaned forward. "The boy needs to be killed."

"I beg your pardon?" This had been such a polite little chitchat, and she had such an air about her of Women's Institute tea parties, knitting competitions and cake stalls. Flynn was shaken and unprepared.

Liadain smiled. She had recovered her suave little smirk along with her daisies. He felt it was hardly appropriate in the circumstances. "I don't have an equivalent word to what I really mean. He needs...to have his spirit separated from the human form he wears. I don't really mean killed, for he—or I believe in spirit form he is a she—will simply return to its own world. No damage will be done to her, except to thwart whatever intentions she has for your friend. Killed is a rough word, simply to describe what must be done to the body."

Flynn pried bark from the oak on which he sat and tossed it into the pool they sat beside. It disappeared without making a ripple.

"I don't see how I can do that while I'm here," he said, discomforted. He was, in theory, quite prepared to kill an enemy spy, an enemy soldier on the ground. Had been trained in a number of ways to do so, armed or unarmed, but he'd never had to put that theory into practice, and he couldn't say he liked the thought.

"It is true that I cannot do it from here. But *you* can. Do you remember the dreamwalkers? Since we were forced out of it, a long time ago, your world rejects the dreams of the Sidhe, but it would recognise you as one of its own. I can help you to dream in your world, though you walk in mine."

"I'm sorry?" He thought about the shapes that had gone ahead of him into the labyrinth of the city. Something eerie and wrong about them, in essence. Ghosts, he supposed. What would it be like, being a ghost while you were still alive?

Sod that— "You mean I could visit home. Interact with my own world?"

"I do." She inclined her head gently. "To a degree."

"Quite a degree, if I could kill."

"I read revulsion in your face, Navigator. Yet I understood you were a warrior in your own world. You must have killed a thousand men. More. Does not a warrior rejoice to lay his enemy low?"

Flynn put his dirty hands in the water to clean them. He noticed nothing strange at first—that was water, all right, murky and cool—until he plunged one in to the wrist and felt his fingertips pass out of the water on the other side, into a stream of cold air. Hitching up his cuffs he felt farther down and touched the button-centre and dry petals of a daisy. He pulled back his hand, sharp, but could not make a splash on the surface.

"I sit in a heated cockpit and calculate where we are in the night sky. I've never even so much as pressed the tit to drop the bombs. Don't know whether I could, though I think so. I hope I wouldn't funk even that."

Liadain's look of disapproval sharpened her nose and chin, giving her face a faint crescent curve, like a child's painting of a witch on a broom. "Then this will be your chance to find out."

"What do I do?"

She came close enough for him to smell the green, saplike scent of her. Faint bramble and may-blossom. "Lie down."

"In the water?"

Her hand was heavy on his shoulder, with an inexorable pressure that reminded him once again this was no human woman. Just as he'd been able to fight Serpent like some sort of superman, she seemed to have an order of strength above his. A rootlike strength that could crush rocks pressed him to his knees so firmly, so smoothly, he was scarcely aware of the massive force of it.

Once he was down, he found himself lying in a hollow bowl, lined with long grass. The layer of water shimmered as a roof above him, but he lay on dry grass and a wind passed over his face. It seemed to be blowing out of the water, unlikely though that was. And as he was puzzling on that, the gravity shifted and he felt as though he stood upright in front of a vertical mirror of liquid silver.

Liadain handed him a leaf on the end of a long green stem. She set the body of the plant down on the grass, where it rooted greedily, instantly, burrowing away like a worm fleeing from sunlight. Off-put by this, Flynn tried to shove the leaf away when she pushed it towards his face.

"Navigator, I know you are a man, but do not be a child also. Take it and breathe."

Stung, he looked again at the thing. The leaf had a cuplike shape. No, not a cup, a breathing mask. It was part of the technology, like a radio headset, and she was right, he was being a scrub. Quickly, he put it over his face and breathed in.

Everything turned to silver around him, making him want to laugh, and then his reflection in the water's undersurface rippled and slithered away. The mirror became a window and he could see out. There, the shape of the pool had changed—the shadows of its edges were now straight. Trees and reeds no longer bent over him, and he saw, instead, long strips of strange tube lighting, and the moving shape of a man.

As the details came into focus, the band of water slowly descended until it was around him. He clamped the lily-pad mask more tightly over his face as grey water rushed over his eyes, and then he was weightless, swimming with the fly larvae and the little minnows, still looking out at a different world.

Getting his feet under him, he pushed up for the surface—it was lots farther now, farther than the stalk of his mask should be able to stretch. When the thought occurred, he touched his face in panic, and the mask was gone. Yet he was still breathing as he swam, taking in cool lungfuls of silver-scented air, elated and powerful. Then he broke the surface and paused, looking down at himself in disbelief.

His body was made of water. He heaved out of the pool—it was a swimming pool. God damn it, a swimming pool! He was in his own world again, at last, and yet when he set his hands on the solid reality of it, he could see right through them. Water ran from him, as if somewhere in the centre of his body he carried a spring, endlessly welling up. Oh...this was creepy. He didn't like it. They'd done a bang-up job of giving him the means to go home and stopping him from wanting to stay.

He tried to speak, and only then became aware that his mouth, his throat, his lungs were made of water too. They hadn't given him a voice.

They hadn't given him a voice.

Panic blindsided him as he felt the enormity of what had happened, what he'd become. Trapped underwater, surely he was drowning? How could he breathe? He couldn't breathe! Panic joined the water in his throat, his heart stuttered in his chest and the terror made all the particles of this strange body waver like a choppy sea.

Held down. Held down underwater! He remembered the pistol he'd bought in case of bailout, so he could shoot himself instead of falling, burning, into the sea. A clean bullet through the head instead of drowning. Yes please!

But that was in his locker back at base, he'd forgotten to take it. And wasn't that bloody typical—his last trip, the one time he actually needed it and he'd left it behind. Story of his life. Now as if fear of drowning was not enough, it occurred to him that he didn't know how to get back. Panic built on itself, in a wave of freezing and heat. How did he get back? They hadn't told him that... Bloody hell! They'd just slapped him in here and let him go. No operating instructions at all. What if they never intended to bring him back? What if he was stuck like this?

Contempt braced him. Well, if he *was* stuck, it was still no reason to act like a bloody coward! Best to do the job quickly then, find out the worst as soon as possible, and take it from there.

He straightened up and faced the man he'd come here to kill.

Flash of dark hair, dark eyes so much like Sumala's he could not restrain the feeling of betrayal. She'd been a friend, the only friend he'd had in a month, and now he found she was a spy for a foreign power. Well, this bastard wouldn't work the same trick on his skipper. Not if Flynn could do anything about it. Forget the fact that he looked about as menacing as a startled fawn.

The man had a gun—a ridiculous-looking object, bright red and yellow as a child's painted toy. He turned, aimed it at Flynn's face, and the threat of it was enough to overcome his scruples. He drew back his fist and the watery body did the same, threw a punch...and the punch went on, moment on moment. Energy moved down his arm and out with a rushing, painful heave, drawn up like vomit from the centre of him, expelled with as much force, as involuntary and as painful as vomiting.

He watched as a cable of water launched from his hand and hit the young man in the face. Not a man, remember. Some other kind of creature...some foreign kind of elf. He told himself firmly it wasn't murder, wasn't even manslaughter, he was protecting the skipper, he was only sending the creature back to wherever it came from...

The creature rolled, scrambled up from hands and knees and aimed the gun again. Another punch and Flynn took the weapon out of his hands, cracked it on the tiles of the bath. What looked like more water trickled out, as his enemy backed away, opened a cupboard, threw shapes of brightly coloured foam at him that he could not feel bouncing off.

This wasn't exactly an even match, was it?

As he stopped, the creature stopped too, collected himself and turned to face him. Flynn moved closer, looked into those dark eyes and saw fascination, curiosity, fear and puzzlement. Water snaked from black hair plastered tight to sharp, defenceless-looking bones. His nose was running and blood mixed with the water on his bottom lip, where he had bitten it through, holding his breath.

He looked human. Innocent. More than that, he looked dazed, like one of the new crews, staggering out of their kite after their first op. Blank of eye, and ever so slightly puzzled, as if they couldn't quite recognise the place they'd once called home, couldn't put their finger on what exactly was wrong.

No kind of elvish creature should look like that, should

they? Shouldn't look as if it was all a bit much for them—that they wanted to cry but would kill you if you gave them any hint that you knew.

Flynn took a deep breath and tasted another universe, the marsh-damp and methane taste of the pool in which he lay. His own hands glittered like diamonds before his eyes, deadly and strange. Maybe he was the elvish creature in this scenario? Maybe he'd been a little too quick to trust, a little hasty to believe? Liadain might have reasons of her own to want Sumala's kinsman dead, reasons that had nothing to do with wanting Skip kept safe. In fact—his thoughts clicked together with a pinch as if he had snapped a mousetrap on his finger— she had more reasons to want Skip dead.

The only truth Flynn could be certain about was that he longed for the skipper. Skip had a way with information—he'd take it all in, yes, just as Flynn did, but then he'd ignore half of it and be off, decision made, action in hand, long before Flynn had got to grips with the full ramifications of everything. And usually his instinct would be as good—better—than Flynn's careful analysis. Flynn felt he badly needed someone he trusted now beside him, telling him what to do.

As if called by his need, a voice shouted, "Stand away from that man!" He looked up and saw the skipper. He had burst through one of the room's doors and was surrounded by steam and smoke, as if he walked out of a burning aircraft. Ten years older, even his walk was changed—a hint of a limp to it. But the compressed lipped expression, he'd seen that before. He'd seen that ferocious gaze of concentration, that focussed, single-minded stare in the cockpit, coned by German spotlights.

A whole argument went through his head in a heartbeat. *Don't look at me like that! I'm not your enemy. Skipper, don't! I'm doing this for you!* And confusion burst like a bomb in the back of his mind, swept him away on a wave of anger and

201

frustration. He brought his hands down and hammered the Gandharva with everything he had. Get the bastard out of the way and maybe this hellish situation could be put right. This wasn't working, couldn't ever work, so he should do the job he'd come to do—fast as possible—go back and try something new. Something better.

A faint jolt of impact travelled up the stream of water and into the palms of his hands. The boy went flying, landed on his arse, gracelessly. Eyes pinched shut, face contorted, he scrabbled for purchase on the wet tiles, tried to push himself back up, and Flynn beat him down again, almost feeling it, almost feeling the sturdy thwack of bone and muscle against the floor, the sympathetic breathlessness.

He bit his lip exactly where the boy had bitten his, and felt nothing. But the writhe, like a grounded fish's flapping on the riverbank, that he could feel, up his arms and into the muscles of his chest. It felt like poison, like acid. *Please, please, please just die! Please just die!*

He closed his own eyes, trying not to see, but he could feel it still, the struggle, the desperation. *What kind of a warrior are you? This is your chance to find out.*

Fire behind his eyes, a flash on Hamburg, fire moving through the streets like a dragon, fire in a dome over the city, a cheery gumdrop red. His bombs. God alone knew—he certainly didn't—how many men he'd killed already. What was one more? And this one wasn't even human.

Die, damn you. Please just die! He opened his mouth to sob, drawing back his hands. No. No, he wasn't going to do it. Couldn't do it. Didn't want to do it. And as he hesitated, something smashed through his guts and backbone, tearing them out, splattering them behind him.

For a moment he was under the marsh, convulsing,

grasping at his chest to be sure it was still there. He saw the underside of the portal, grasses piercing between his fingers, things swimming above him in the grey. Then a hand replaced the mask over his face and he was back.

The skipper stood before him, looking drenched and very pissed off. He was protecting the Gandharva lad with his body, standing between him and Flynn. The creature peered at Flynn over Skip's shoulder, gasping, as they circled him and backed away together towards the distant door.

Skip doesn't recognise me. The thought was a mixed pang of bereavement and relief. *At least he didn't see me make a complete dog's breakfast of that. Did, but didn't know it was...*

The realisation hit Skip like a bullet. Flynn could see it, track its progress from the widening of those familiar hazel eyes to the whitening of Skip's face as all the blood receded. He saw the wince and the way the man hunched inwards as if sheltering a lit flame in his hands, protecting it from an icy wind. He had been upright, undaunted, that devil-may-care recklessness that Flynn admired, alight behind his eyes. Now that all snuffed out, and what was left was horror.

Flynn tried to smile. "Yes, Skipper. It's me." But he couldn't make a sound. Desolation echoed back along the path of their linked gazes. The smile felt like an abomination—he dropped it, tried again. "I've come to warn you." Water filled his throat like molasses. He couldn't even growl with frustration. "Fuck! Skipper, you've got a spy in your camp. He's not human."

Hopeless. He clutched at his hair and felt nothing there, water passed through water without touching. He was a ghost even to himself.

He tried pointing, mouthing the words, "Don't trust him," but Skip wasn't much of one for charades. His frown was narrow eyed with suspicion, his right hand clenched about something in the cupboard beside which he stood—something that pulsed to Flynn's sight like an artery of blue light. Skip had not put down his gun, and his eyes were full of betrayal and fury and grief.

The creature looked back with such a rescued look on his face, such a puppyish hero worship, like one of the new recruits shaking hands with Leonard Cheshire, and the early-morning sunshine caught the edge of his cheek, outlined the same generous mouth, the same curve of cheekbone as Sumala's. Flynn wasn't imagining it—couldn't be. There couldn't be any doubt about it.

His own desperation bubbled up like tar. *Listen to me! Help me! Don't go off with your new friend and leave me alone. Please, Skipper, you're in charge, tell me what to do!*

And then, bitter as wormwood, looking for a sign. *Stop me, if you can.*

He lunged forward, breathed up the whole ocean and sent it hurtling at the boy. Saw the look of terror with a kind of serrated edge of guilt and joy, saw Skip's determination with the same sick blend. Deliverance and misery. He trusted Skip to know what to do—the man had instincts like a wild thing and ice water for blood, and that was good. It was good. Even when he was the enemy, even when he was...

White pain. Searing, blazing white light burning through every cell, crisping everything it touched. He felt himself boil, steam away.

The electricity nosed through the water like a million sharp-toothed snakes, biting him everywhere, injecting venom. They were trying to find a way out, and he realised with a sick spasm, that they would pass straight through him and into Skip, frying every bit of his skin that touched the water, stopping his heart.

That couldn't be. Water, he was water, he could... The idea came to him in agony, like a birth. He turned the cells of his body into mirrors, reflecting the current, pulling it back in on himself, away from the skipper, away too from the Gandharva boy. Anger and jealousy aside, he trusted Skip a damn sight more than he trusted Liadain. No matter what Liadain said, the skipper didn't want the boy dead, and that being so, Flynn couldn't kill him. Not deliberately. And he'd be damned if he'd do it by accident.

He was a sun. If he opened his mouth, the world would end in fire. So he kept it closed and let the electricity cycle and cycle, build and build, whining inside his head, until agony passed into diamond calm, and even that burst, went flying, and he was back in the pool, lying on long grass, a shield of water above his face and an earwig crawling over his closed right eye.

He scrabbled to hands and knees, breached the surface. A flight of swans whirred and whistled across a sunset of milk and gold. He put his face in his hands and wept while alder leaves rustled angrily above his head.

"I'm not your assassin." Newly dry, feeling hollowed out by light and grief, Flynn sat again in the clearing, holding his cigarette case like a charm.

"Evidently not." Her dress was green now, and so were her eyes, green and gleaming as cats' eyes. She had plaited up her long hair and wound it in a coronet around her head, studded with night-blooming jasmine and ivy berries like black pearls. Either the new hairstyle, or Flynn's ineptitude, made her look tired. He guessed it was the latter. Or she was doing it for sympathy. Or...

Shut up, old son. You're just making it worse for yourself.

He couldn't decide if it was a good or a bad thing that his imaginary skipper was back, a little worse for wear about the nose, looking older, sounding exactly the same. The man had just killed him, after all. He should be at least a trifle peeved about that.

And sometimes he was. That was the damn thing about it. One moment he'd be gutted and betrayed—it hadn't been the reunion he'd dreamed of. But the next he'd just be glad the skipper was still out there, still very much the same person. Not dead, not even a stranger, still the same man to whose skill and instincts Flynn had trusted his life, night after night over Germany.

Around the edge of the clearing, moonlight reflected white from moving forms, half in and half out of sight. A gleam of eyes, quiet voices under the trees—Liadain's supporters, glimpsed as motion in twilight. Their gazes walked up his back. He felt himself move in a treacle of their expectations. It held him back, slowed him up, even as it reassured him how important a piece he was in this game.

So you're an important piece. What do you need, to make a move?

Rubbing his side, where he still felt the impact of the cable, he folded away anguish and frustration into the compartment in his head where fear went when he was on ops. There would be a chance to work all that out later, in that mythical time known as "after the war".

I need more accurate information. I need to know where I really stand, who I can trust.

Bit of a puzzle, that one. How could he get the truth from a bunch of people who were—as a matter of course, as a matter of their culture, their nature—telling him lies?

"I need cross-references," he said as the moon sailed out from behind a cloud. Light hit the stream and rippled through the clearing, silvering leaves and owl feathers, outlining Liadain's small smile.

"I thought you were about to say that all you wanted was to go home."

It made him laugh. "I do. There's a war on, out there, and I was doing a good job of fighting it. But if I have a chance of stopping the same thing happening here..."

He tripped himself up. He'd been about to say, *Then of course I will.* But what business was it of his what these creatures did? If they wanted to go to war with others of their own kind, why should he try to stop them? Did they even feel pain like people? Maybe they didn't mind, living in the squalor of the workers' camps...

What you need is a clear objective. His imaginary skipper grinned at him, lit a cigarette and lounged back on one of the rickety wooden mess chairs. *Then you can get that big brain of yours working on a route. You're just spinning wheels at the moment.*

You're not wrong. So...cross-references. Oonagh won't tell me anything. I only have Liadain's word to go on and no means of checking it. I need a second opinion.

"I want to get Sumala out of there."

Liadain's chuckle was motherly, sympathetic. "Of course you do. It is a man's nature to be helpless against the charms of an Apsara. That's why they are used, to obsess men to the point where they cannot think of anything else."

The joviality rang like a cracked bell. *You don't know how my mind works at all, do you? An obsession would be a blessed relief amid all this doubt.*

"If it's what Oonagh expects of me, I should really oblige

207

her—or she'll wonder why not. Am I right? And that will make her wonder what I've been doing instead. And that will lead her back to you."

Liadain laughed. "There's a saying in our land, 'Men are arrows, but it is women who must draw the bow.' I can see you trying to be subtle, Navigator, but it doesn't suit you." She folded her hands in her lap. "You wish to free my enemy's agent, and you cover up this wish with an excuse. It isn't necessary. I believe in the prophecy, you see. What you do— whatever you do—will lead to Oonagh's downfall. Therefore it is in my interests to allow you to do whatever you wish to do, no matter how counterproductive it seems to me. I am glad at least that you know a little more about the stakes of the game. Go. Rescue her, then. We will talk again later."

"A little help would be appreciated."

"Help to do what I advise you not to do?" She gave him a sidelong look, brimming over with amusement, and he thought how little she seemed to care that he might soon be bringing a spy into her camp. She'd given in as thoroughly and with as little resentment as a woman who didn't care one way or the other.

If she had been human, that would mean something. As she wasn't, he didn't know what to think. "If you're going to let me do it, why not help me?"

"Perhaps I'm confident that without my help you will not succeed."

"Perhaps you are, at that." He tucked the cigarette case into his top pocket, got up and offered her his hand. "Well, it's been a blast. If I get through the rescue, we'll talk again."

"You will be welcome among us, Navigator. Despite your doubts, this is where you belong. You will see it in time. Good luck."

He touched the brim of his helmet in salute and walked away. Still lost. Probably more lost than ever before.

Chapter Fifteen

Phyllis had given Ben her phone number. After the fifth time he'd called Chris with no answer, Ben called her. She picked up at once, and her hello sounded bright and breezy as usual.

"I'm sorry to bother you," he said, lining up the scarves that hung on the hooks in the hall so that the fringes all hung at the same height. "I've been trying to get through to Chris, but he's not answering. You don't know where he is, do you?"

"Trouble?" she said, with a little thud as if she'd sat down in her own hallway, bracing herself for bad news.

"Not on my part, no. In fact it's been very quiet. But after yesterday…"

They'd taken him home together, Ben pulling towels out of the airing cupboard and handing them to him, watching him drop them on his knees while he cupped both hands around the glass of whisky Phil had poured. Half-full, gone in three swallows. "Are you…?" she'd asked, and he'd closed his eyes and replied, quietly, "Bugger off, the pair of you."

"We're not going and leaving you like this," she'd said, which Ben could have told her was never going to work.

He could have told her that Chris would bound out of the chair in fury and shout, "I don't need any nursemaids, thank you. Bugger off and leave me alone."

So they had. And Ben had wondered all night if he should go back, do that listening thing his therapist did, or at the least offer comfort sex with no strings attached. But that would have been like admitting that he cared. That would have been boyfriend stuff, and he wasn't sure he was ready for that.

"He'll be fine." Phil's voice held something of the calm-under-fire breeziness with which Chris had conducted their expedition. "He's one of the old school, tough as nails. Fall apart at night, carry on as normal in the morning." Ben wasn't sure how he could hear her smile, perhaps it was the change in the tone of her voice. "In fact, he'll probably kill me for telling you this, but I'm meeting him at St. Oswald's later on today. You should come. I'm sure you could do with something to laugh about, for a change."

"I'm sorry?"

"Church summer fete at St. Oswald's, on the hill in the middle of Osweton." A metallic noise while she fiddled with a lens, her voice muffled—the phone must be tucked under her chin, leaving her hands free for the inevitable camera. "Starts at ten, goes on 'til four. I'm photographing it for *The Gazette*. Chris will be there, come hell or high water." A note of doubt. "Or if he isn't, we'll know the world is ending. Ever wanted to know about his embarrassing hobby? Now is your chance."

Outside, another uncharacteristically hot summer's day was painting the sky with indigo wash. He could hear the neighbours, one and two doors down, hanging over their front fences and commiserating with each other over their brown lawns. Even the front door smelled of crispy varnish and dust. Ben wondered if he had anything else to do, what his London friends would say to St. Oswald's summer fete. But they would think he was mad already, with this bizarre parade of Faerieland and deep-country quaintness. Sod them, it wasn't as though they ever visited.

"More embarrassing than ghost hunting?"

"Well, I'm sure you'll think so. Typical of the man, he's not embarrassed at all. No reason to be, really, when you think about it but, well, I'll let you judge for yourself."

Ben laughed. "All right, you've got me. I can't turn down an offer of seeing our glorious leader make even more of a complete cock of himself." He swallowed hard and tasted chlorine, saw gold-green light and blank eyes in a face sculpted of silver. "I didn't mean that."

Phil's chuckle was sympathetic. "I know. See you there then."

Baskets of wallflowers spumed over the grey stone walls that delineated the boundary of the church grounds. As Ben went through the gates, he caught the scent of steam engines, the sound of a miniature train and the jaunty wheeze of an accordion. Someone was playing a drum very loud, in a surprisingly complex rhythm.

Between the church and the graveyard lay a broad green hilltop, and gardens. There the worthies of the village had erected a tent village of fluttering white canvas, put up their tables and tombolas. Ben bought an ice cream from a man on a refrigerated bicycle and watched as the local primary school wound up their display of under-elevens judo.

He toured the stalls idly, thumbing through the second-hand books, buying an Agatha Christie for 20p, and for a pound at the tombola, winning a bottle of shampoo and a tub of gardeners' hand cream.

Phyllis gave him a wave from the other side of the judo display, so he wandered over and offered her the cream. "Thanks," she said, tucking it into one of her numerous pockets, bringing a bottle of Chinese beer out in return. "Can't see myself using this. Want to swap?"

"Thanks." He uncapped it and drank—the ice cream had not cooled him, but it had made him thirsty. "I don't see…"

Phyllis's head came up at the sound of bells. She gave him a bright grin and adjusted the seat of her camera strap on her shoulder, bringing the camera to her chin. Her face took on that *don't bother me, I'm thinking about composition* sternness, and Ben turned just as the accordion burst into life behind him.

With an internal roll of the eyes, he thought, *I should have known.* There were eight of them, with three musicians bringing up the rear. Eight men in white trousers, bells strapped around their calves, white shirts topped with green sashes, one over each shoulder, which met in the centre of the chest in a crest like a sunflower.

Chris was second man in on the right, wearing the same plaited straw boater as the others, the brim of it loaded with fern and flowers. They formed up in two lines, facing one another, large white handkerchiefs drooping from each hand. Ben caught Chris's double take of—something—when he saw Ben there. Widened eyes and a startled look that smoothed almost instantly into sharp concentration.

The musicians struck up a tune like the musical equivalent of a seesaw, the whistle and accordion carrying the melody, a woman on a bodhran ornamenting it with rhythm. They danced, a lumpen, ridiculous kind of dance, but one he couldn't help noticing was full of vigour and not completely without technical difficulty.

Fuck, thought Ben. *What am I doing here? I was going to have a high-tech job in a London record studio and live in an apartment made of chrome and glass. I wanted nothing to do with Folk. And these are not even my folk, as I'm sure they would be quick to tell me if I showed an interest.*

Yet the tune had a certain bucolic charm. He could see how it could be orchestrated and ornamented to make it beautiful. Looking at the musicians, he felt a keen pang of envy. How wonderful to make music for other people to dance to, no filters of CDs or downloads or even politely restrained audiences in rows of motionless seats. Music, pure and simple, that you could share with your fellow musicians in the synergy of a live gig and see at the same time expressed through the bodies of your dancers. The thought called to him on a deep level, worryingly primal.

But perhaps that was down to the fact that at least half of the group were as young as Chris or younger, and he wouldn't deny that there was something appealing about watching lithe young men leaping like stags. He'd certainly not imagined morris dancing being done with such energy. Something irreverent and gloriously stupid about it, rebelliously uncool.

The dance finished in a circle of upraised hankies. There was scattered applause, more laughter. The dancers broke into a straggle, some going to cluster about the musicians, Chris coming over to smile at them both. He was breathing heavily, looking tired, but light had come back to his eyes. "All right?"

Ben laughed. "You look ridiculous. Did you do this entirely to embarrass me, or do you enjoy cavorting around in flowers?"

"You should try it. Listen, we're here for half an hour, then we've got another set to do at half three. You don't have to hang around and watch if you don't want to."

"I'm enjoying it. As long as no one's going to object to me sullying the purity of your midsummer ritual..."

"Why would they?"

Ben shook his head and laughed, less happily this time, "Nothing... No reason. Hey, you're on again."

The next dance involved sticks. Phyllis snapped a few pictures beside him. The sound of music and the rap of wood, the quiet laughter of spectators and the drone of an aeroplane above combined into something mystical. Ben thought about *bhangra*, wondered if this was the British equivalent, and felt a very familiar isolation and resentment on realising that he didn't know. There might be other Indian folk dances closer, but if so he had lost them. His parents had left them behind, along with an entire heritage from which he might have drawn strength, if he had only had the chance. He knew why, but he couldn't help but think that he would have done it differently.

"All right then." The final dance had ended, and the youngest of the morris men gone around with a hat for donations for beer. They made arrangements for the next session and parted without fuss. Ben found himself walking next to a man in a flowery hat, every footstep accompanied by bells. "Let's go and look at the well dressing," said Chris. "They do some amazing stuff."

"Why not? I might as well get fully into the deep embarrassing quaintness of the whole thing."

Chris led the way around the flying buttress of the church into the shade of the northern wall. There a path went downhill to the graveyard, and beyond it to a stand of trees within which a shingled pavilion sheltered platforms covered with pictures made of flowers. As they walked closer, the scent of millions of blossoms filled the warm air.

Within the pavilion, they found the lips of wells. A cold air came up from them, and the water within was black and smooth as jet. Ben didn't understand how the villagers could possibly unite these passages to the underworld with the kind of prancing and ribbons and flower scenes of the fete.

"This is...old," he said, feeling it, not stopping to wonder what he meant.

"Yes," Chris agreed, leaning on the lip of the well, looking down. He tipped a penny into the shaft, and they both listened to the plunk as it hit the water. Ben stepped up beside him and saw his face broken into circles on the surface. "But then so is the dancing. The flowers may be to placate the spirits that live here—to tame them. That may be why the church is here too. But the morris dance is different."

"It's not as stupid as it looks."

Chris laughed and leaned back on his elbows, the deep drop behind him. "You have a way with a compliment. But you're right. The dance...flouts everything. Everything but itself. 'See,' it says, 'we're men. We're alive and strong and beautiful. Bollocks to everything else.' It's a kind of defiance to this sort of thing."

"Like the *haka*, but with pansies."

Chris slapped his top pocket, frowned as if he'd expected to find something there, came up empty handed. "Yes, well, the *haka*'s a bit unsubtle, isn't it? Morris is a lot more English— male-combat display, but with irony."

"Hankies and flowers instead of swords."

"Exactly." He slid a sly look in Ben's direction. "We're undercompensating."

Ben's turn to laugh. "I'd like to see what for." He thought of saying, *You seem better today,* but then lost the rest of the sentence. It should go something like, *About yesterday, do you want to talk about it?* And postmodern irony or not, he couldn't bring himself to say anything so touchy-feely. Instead he took a five-pence coin from his pocket, leaned over the long cold drop of the well. Ferns grew from the walls on the way down and held droplets that sparked like tiny lights, but the bottom was so far away that the sky looked black behind him, mirrored in a perfect circle of water where it was always night.

Chill, damp air and the scent of moss, and he found himself gazing at his own face with a feeling of dread, as though the mirrored him might blink, speak, smile at him and prove to

216

be a stranger with its own will and purposes.

"Creepy." He half drew back and stopped. There *was* something there, an unaccounted movement, a slide of grey-blue shade in front of his reflected face. A twist of mist in the long, brick-lined shaft? He caught his breath, the coin dropping from suddenly loosened fingers. "Shit!"

Chris turned fast, looked over. Ben saw again, just briefly, the face of the creature that had been in the water yesterday. A man's face, handsome, with chiselled features beneath the Biggles-like cap of an old-fashioned flying helmet. He was looking at something off-screen. Alder leaves fluttered behind his head, and there was such a look of abject defeat in his face Ben flinched away.

By the time he forced himself to look back, the five pence hit the bottom, and the picture broke up into static and then nothing, like a TV when the aerial has been blown down.

Next to Ben, Chris made a tiny sound, like someone swallowing a pill of anguish. He walked away, stumbled over the sinking of the *Titanic* depicted in dahlias, righted himself with a curse and carried on walking, all the way down the hill, to the pine hedge and dry stone wall that cut off the end of the churchyard. There was no gate in it, no gap big enough to squeeze through, so he stopped and stood, facing the dense thicket of needles, a slender white shape with flowers on his hat, covering his eyes with his hand.

He didn't move away when Ben came up beside him, wasn't weeping, was just standing there, staring at the root of the wall as if he were timing the grass as it grew.

How to start? "I've seen him before," Ben said, quizzically, as if this was all that troubled him. "Where have I seen him?"

Chris's head lifted an inch. "The pool." He had closed up so utterly Ben couldn't tell if he was grieving or just thinking hard.

"No, before that. I thought I recognised him at the pool too. I couldn't think that if I hadn't seen him before."

The sunflower in the middle of Chris's back seemed to pulse in the sunshine as he sighed. He turned around slowly in a glissade of bells, took off the hat and wrung its ribbon in one fist. "You're thinking of Errol Flynn?"

"Oh." Ben exhaled on a smile. "No. Maybe I was, but no. I've just remembered. When I slept over. The photo on your bedside table." Seven young men in RAF battledress, lined up in front of a Lancaster bomber. All of them grinning like this was a big *Boys' Own* adventure. A skinny one with jug ears, one with acne on his cheeks and another with a monobrow. A curly-haired lad with the moustache of a man twenty years older. A coloured face. Native American? One that looked like a movie star, and one that might have been a younger version of Chris. "He was there with someone who looked like you. Your father? He flew with your father?"

"I ca—" Chris tried to walk away again, collided with a branch, sending needles flying. "Ow! Fuck. Bloody trees." He dropped the hat, returned to glaring at the ground, fists clenched.

"I'm not the only one in trouble, am I?" Ben picked up the discarded boater. Flower petals felt fragile against his fingers, inappropriately celebratory. "Come on. Let's go sit in the church or something. I'll buy you a cup of tea."

Ben juggled two paper plates of coconut macaroons and two polystyrene cups of tea. Conveniently, there'd been a cake-and-coffee stall just inside the west door of the church, and he'd queued, leaving Chris to get himself together in peace. Tea threatening to scald his fingers, he pushed through the crowd and out into the dimness of the main aisle where voices were lowered and—embarrassingly enough—the occasional person knelt in prayer amid the cold pillars and splashes of coloured light.

He was just in time to catch Chris opening a door marked *No entry* and slipping inside. Following—getting his foot in the jamb before it closed, levering it open with a knee—he found a staircase, a room full of decaying books above his head and, beyond that, a door he had to bend half-double to get through. Sweat stood out on his forehead as he squeezed in—too tight and the room too close, the air too stuffy to breathe and his mouth prickling as if it was numb. But beyond it stretched another stair, Chris sitting on the topmost tread, and above him in the cool darkness, the machinery of bells.

Ben's claustrophobia vanished in a breath. Slatted windows on all four sides of the tower poured pencil-thin lines of light into the emptiness. The stairs clung to the wall and so did he, watching the white strokes of the ropes against the dim shadow of the long fall. The smell was of warm dust and metal polish. And tea.

"Here." He passed cup and plate to Chris, sat on the step beside him in the kind of silence that made his ears ring.

They sat for what seemed a long while, Ben sipping his tea and watching the shadows of clouds strobe through the sunlight, picking out wheels above him and the domes of the bells, their mouths turned up towards the spire. Politeness vied with hurt—it was none of his business, but Chris should want to tell him anyway—and built up enough pressure for him to ask, "So what was that all about, then?"

Chapter Sixteen

Chris sighed, looked down and found a coconut biscuit with a large splodge of jam in the centre of it balanced on a paper plate precariously on his knee. When he looked up again, it was to see Ben's face striped with blue light, as if coned in miniature searchlights. He had beautiful eyes, dark as treacle, and for once empty of any kind of defensiveness. The team weren't sure whether to trust him or not, but Chris went with his instinct and said, "Let me tell you a story. It's a fairy story, so we've got to start with 'Once upon a time'."

He sipped the tea and the taste of it was a reassurance. Tea meant the crisis was over, at least for a night. Tea meant you had another twelve hours before they would try to kill you again. "So, once upon a time—about seventy years ago, in fact—there was a young man. Let's call him Christopher. He was young and loved to fly, so when his country went to war and called for volunteers to fly their fighter planes, Chris signed up like a shot.

"They put him through various training camps and, although the epitome of his desires was to fly a Mosquito, they declared he would have to prove himself first as a pilot on the heavy bombers. He was shipped off to one more camp where he was dumped in a room with a lot of other bewildered-looking aircrew and told to find a team to work with. They thought, you see, that it was better seven chaps who were to go to hell together should at least begin by being friends."

Chris laughed, remembering it. It had been a winter

afternoon when they'd all arrived, been turned into the mess for the first time together, expected to pick a crew by some kind of alchemy or sixth sense. Hard on the shy ones. The sound of rain on high glass windows always took him back there, to the fug of cigarette smoke and the smell of wet greatcoats and heater oil.

"They didn't expect it to happen at once," he explained. "They gave us a week or so of hanging about with nothing else to do but play cards and chat and size each other up." He'd slipped out of the storyteller mode and felt too revealed, too naked that way. A mouthful of macaroon and a sip of tea, and he carried on, back to the fairy tale.

"Well, our hero had no idea what he was looking for. Lucky for him, then, that he'd barely got through the door, was hanging his wet coat on one of the ranks and ranks of hooks, when he saw a vision. I should have mentioned that our hero was a died-in-the-wool poofter, who'd never believed in anything so soppy as love.

"Evidently it believed in him, though. Because there stood this…" He shook his head, tipped it back against the rough stone of the wall and looked up to where a sparrow stood on the lip of the smallest bell, its peeping call echoing in the bowl of iron. He didn't have the words for this. "This vision. It was one of those ground-open-up-and-swallow-me moments. Should have had a heavenly voice and choirs of angels and all that, but if the heavenly choir had tried to come in, our sergeant would have shown them the door. Anyway, picture Errol Flynn in his youth, doing the clean-cut our-brave-boys-in-blue act for the Ministry of Propaganda—only with a puzzled look on his face and rain dripping from his wet hair—and you'll have the idea.

"This was Geoff. Geoff Baxendale. Ace navigator, chess player, a fine hand on the piano and altogether at sea in the company of human beings. He liked numbers. You see, they

221

don't lie, they don't cheat, they don't suffer a failure of nerve in the middle of the night, or tell you things they don't mean, or mean three different things at once. Poor lad, he had a great big brain but very little in the way of instincts."

Geoff wouldn't thank him for this recap, he thought, letting a seedling of hope put out a leaf in his chest. As a message from the afterlife, the picture in the well had been a washout. That was not how ghosts communicated at all. So perhaps he really wasn't dead? Suppose they had simply been keeping him prisoner all this time—*and I abandoned him for over seventy years*—somehow unaltered, eternally youthful, and alive. Alive!

But no, that made no sense. Geoff was not the sort who would attack a stranger at random, the way the creature had gone for Ben. And God knew, during the short and terrifying time he had been in their world, the elves were capable of anything. Wasn't it more likely that, now he had drawn their attention once more, they were doing this—playing with his most sacred memories—just because they could?

"Anyway." He frowned, got up and found the nearest window, from which he could look down at the bright colours of the fete where a troupe down from Derby were dancing *dandiya raas* in the centre of the meadow, swirling silks and glitter of gold. He thought of the creature trying to tell him something. Pointing at Ben and clutching its hair in frustration when he didn't get the message. Under his heart, his flesh chilled, his breath came short with suspicion. And he threw the feeling off, stubbornly. Having decided to trust Ben, he wasn't about to shilly-shally over it. Not at the word of something that might not have been Geoff at all.

"I decided I would have him. I had fewer scruples in those days, and besides, there was a war on. You could leave regrets to tomorrow and be half-sure you'd be gone by the time they caught up with you.

"At any rate, the poor lad didn't stand a chance—I knew what I wanted, he didn't—bit of a disadvantage for him. To cut a long story short, we...became the best of friends.

"We had a full tour of operations with various crews—acting as stand-ins. Then, when I got my chance to fly on Mosquitoes, I took him with me. Forty ops there and we were old men when we volunteered together for a second tour on the Lancs, on the understanding that this time we'd get a plane and a crew of our own.

"And we did. We added Arnold Keynes—known as Occe—mid-upper gunner. Hank Brownbear, flight engineer. Always called him the Yank because he was Canadian and it pissed him off. Reliably got a laugh, that one. Archie Mountford, bomb aimer. He was our golden boy. His family used to hold the most amazing house parties, to which I was invited providing I let him wear my jacket. He'd told his mother he'd made pilot, you see.

"Mark Barlow was our rear gunner, red as a traffic light—his hair, I mean—and lived up to all the stereotypes. We called him Red, of course. And the final crew member was Tolly Green, wireless operator. A bugger who was never out of the doctor's office, boils and runs and constipation and ulcers and whatnot. Ate like a horse and ran himself ragged on his nerves."

If Chris closed his eyes, he could see them all, their faces as sharp in his mind as they had been ten years ago. Sharper than the memories of anyone else in his life, mother, sister, other lovers. They were haloed and hallowed by terror and death, but he always remembered them smiling, larking about in the mess, or on brief days of leave, travelling into town and watching the weepies together at the cinema, scoffing cakes in whatever corner shop they could find and basking in the admiration of the waitresses for their wings.

"To cut a long story short—I realise it's too late for that already—they were the best men who ever lived, all of them. We flew twenty-three ops together. Enough to get the only-seven-more-to-go-and-we're-free jitters. There's a story on every raid, but I won't bore you with them."

He looked aside at Ben and saw no signs of boredom. Ben's tea was turning to tar, the teabag left steeping, and Chris could see the dust, sifting through bars of sunlight, descending onto his plate where it was shoved into the corner of the step. Ben's beauty was nothing at all like Geoff's, and he was glad of that.

"So, raid twenty-three, we've been sent to bomb an oil refinery. That's all done and dusted, bombs away and the kite is flying light and happy through a clear, cold sky. Mark's fingers and toes are about to drop off, back there in the rear turret with no heating and ice on his eyelashes, but apart from that we're all feeling golden with relief. Going home."

The ends of his fingers had begun to tremble. He tucked them between his legs and hunched forwards over them. But that only added to the memory. He was seated now as he would have been in the cockpit of the Lancaster, crouched over the throttles, and he could almost feel their moulded smoothness in the palm of his left hand, the ridged grip of the steering yoke in his right. Light on his face. Light in the corner of his eye, and no sound of any other craft. Base roar of propellers. Stars above like falling needles. And light in the corner of his eye.

It was all going to happen again. He could feel it, rushing towards him, foreknown, a nightmare he'd lived too many times already. Only a light against the peaceful night sky, but he could already smell the burning flesh, hear the bacon-fat sizzle.

Someone pried his grip off the wheel, and a distant voice said, "It's all right. You don't have to..."

He breathed in deep, expecting the smell of rubber, tinned

oxygen, kerosene and sweat, but the hand around his wrist held him down, pinned him to a different time. Dusty oak stairs and darkness, an echo that whispered around the walls. He breathed in sharp again, and a wave of shuddering travelled up his back and stirred the hair on his head. *Oh, thank God. Not today.*

Sweat on his upper lip to be brushed away clumsily. His shirt clung to the small of his back, icy and wet. He'd been pulled that far into memory, but someone had held him, stopped the nightmare in its tracks. Ben, of course, who was looking at him now without a shred of contempt because he knew what it was like.

Chris decided to make this fast and short. They deserved a book of memoirs—to sit as he'd seen some of his comrades sit, signing autographs at air shows. But since he couldn't give them that, they'd have to settle for the unvarnished truth, spat out as quick as possible.

"We thought it was flak at first—a perfect sphere of red light coming up from below, but when I ducked out of its way, it followed us. Two or three minutes of weaving and it matched our speed, hanging over us, locked on as if it was studying us. We're thoroughly spooked by now. I call 'corkscrew to port' and shove *Victor* into a screaming dive and roll, and just at the bottom, just when I've got to pull the stick hard back and hold on for dear life, it's there, full ahead, looking at us. And there's a light like pepper snorted up the nose. Everything in the cockpit is outlined in fire, and I see Hank going up in flames, a burst of sooty smoke from the front turret—that's Archie, burning like a candle. The upper gun turret's gone black, and all *Victor*'s engines have shut down, and in the silence I can hear a kind of humming, like swan wings in flight.

"The light gets stronger. I can't feel my body, I can't see my hands, and I'm wondering if this is what it's like, being burned alive and still, *still* thinking *if Hank doesn't get those engines restarted we're going to hit the ground nose first.*"

Chris gulped a mouthful of cold tea, and another, feeling his dried throat moisten, washing away the remembered taste— the taste that meant he'd never eat roast pork again. Wiping his sweating hands over his face, he tried to wash that clean too, scrub away the thick coat of ash.

"There's this flash of pure, visceral, bowel-loosening terror. Dreams—God, the dreams! And then I wake up in military hospital in 1995."

He chewed a mouthful of macaroon, reminding himself of reality—nothing more real than the shape of a thing, felt by the lips and tongue. "Top brass want to know what I'm doing, picked up in a field, unconscious, in the shattered cockpit of a World War Two Lancaster, surrounded by bodies."

It gave him the creeps, even now, revisiting that part of his life, the doubt and confusion, the sense that everything was askew. "I thought at first I must have come down in Germany, fallen into the hands of some intelligence unit that was trying to screw with my head..."

He looked up at the bells, which had been hanging here for two hundred years, the bell tower, which had undoubtedly been exactly the same in his day. If he'd sat here on the stairs with Geoff, he'd have seen the identical things, smelled this very complex of dust and stone and warm metal. Probably a better bunker against the Good People could not be found than here, right underneath the long-term resonance of a full peal of church bells.

"The uniforms had changed, you see. The way people spoke had changed. I thought they were Germans, doing a good job of pretending to be our chaps, just not quite good enough. The puzzler was—why was I worth so much effort? I knew nothing they couldn't have got out of me easier with torture.

"Took me as long to accept their word that this was 1995 as it took them to accept that I was who I said. It must have been some feat of detective work on their parts, but what was left of *Victor* matched the records of a plane that went missing over the Channel in 1944. They tracked down some living relatives of the boys, DNA matched them to the corpses. Tracked down my sister—"

"You have a sister?" Ben sounded startled, as if it was impossible that Chris should have an actual blood relation. As a matter of fact, he wasn't wrong.

"My baby sister. She died last year, aged eighty-five. I didn't try to get in contact, after. Water under the bridge, you know? And she looked...fragile, in the photographs."

There was an old ache sealed tight in the basement of his psyche. A whole world, lost. Every so often it felt as though the residue of whatever rotted in there trickled beneath the door. He carefully mopped it away every time, but he didn't think the stones would ever be clean again.

As if the thought had prompted it, Ben edged forward, tightened his grip on Chris's wrist and said, "You are seeing a therapist, right?"

That was what came of opening yourself like this—people stuck their fingers in and tugged. Chris wedged a few more sandbags around the mental door and moved away quickly. "I had enough of that at Wingham. Is he mad? Is he an unusually imaginative murderer? Is he who he says he is?"

Chris brought his other hand up and covered Ben's fingers, and even that had too many factors to process, too many undertones for him to know exactly what he felt—resentful, guilty, comforted.

"They told me they were all dead. All the crew but me. They

showed me a room, six shapes under green rubber covers."
They'd peeled back the blanket on the first one, and he'd known
from the gold canine, the missing left-hand ring finger that had
frozen off on their third run, had to be amputated at base, that
it was Mark. After he'd puked for two days solid, he didn't ask
to see the others.

"So, when we saw Geoff at the pool, I thought it was a
ghost. It was the one explanation that fitted the facts."

"That's what you meant." Ben gave a little sigh of
revelation. "When you said 'I had to choose the living.'" The look
of revelation dissolved into a frown. He wiped his free hand
through his hair, looking down. "Shit! You killed... What was he
to you? The love of your life?"

It lifted his spirits, strangely, to hear from the tone of Ben's
voice that he wasn't the only one messed up in a tangle of
complications. "I don't know. It felt like it at the time, but then
things were different, in the war."

What would have happened, after all, if they'd survived
until peace came? They'd have married wives, probably. Raised
families. You did that sort of thing in those days, regardless of
personal preferences. He'd have grandchildren by now. Would
he and Geoff have been able to stay together, after the war? Or
would that have been it? Separation, distances, letters, frequent
at first and then tailing off as they each grew into different lives.
First love, like the cherry blossom beloved of the Japanese, no
less beautiful for falling in the wind.

"We never expected to live through it, that was the thing."
Some of its sweetness, its power, had been borrowed from the
knowledge that tomorrow or the next night or the one after that,
they would die in a fireball together, falling out of the sky like a
comet. A funeral worthy of warriors, brief and blazing and gone.

"We never thought about what might happen on the other

side. That would have been tempting fate." *And I think I hoped that peace would never come.*

He pulled himself together. From the glassless windows came the sound of a fairground organ and distant laughter. The beribboned ends of his baldrics were the same marigold colour as the flowers around the well, and seeing it, remembering, felt as though someone had struck a match and rekindled a votive light in his heart. "But the thing is, I didn't kill him, did I? Last night, yes, that was a rough one and I spent it with my old friends, whisky and regret. But today, back he is again. Now either he's already dead—in which case I at least didn't do any harm—or he's not a ghost at all.

"When we saw him in the well, I thought at first it was another dig at me—twisting the knife, you know? But what if whatever it was they did to me, they did to him too? Wherever I spent that fifty years, maybe that's where he is now? Alive and well and able to come back. If that's so, then my first priority has got to be to bring him home."

Ben pulled his hand away. His mouth hardened. "Whatever he is now, he tried to kill me."

Chris tried for humour. "It's a mistake anyone could make." The attempt failed in prickly silence, and he fumbled for words to rescue the tranquillity, the comfort of the last half hour. "I'm sorry. My joint top priority, along with keeping you safe."

Ben grimaced. "Don't do me any favours."

Chapter Seventeen

The door to the dungeon of the sleepers would not open for Flynn. He had watched, closely, as Serpent laid head and both palms against the solid crystal, presumably willing the door to open with all the authority in him. When Flynn tried it, after waiting for Serpent to go off-duty, all that happened was that he left a smear on the transparent surface, and the guards laughed at him.

He returned to what he grandly called "his room". The loremasters' quarter—a short street lined with bookshops and booths where advice or writing could be had for gold—contained many shops with countertops extending from the windows. Flynn had co-opted a number of unused tables and hammered them into place beneath one of these counters to make himself a wooden box a little larger than a coffin.

Throwing open the hatch-like door to let the light in, he dug out pen, ink stick and paper from beneath his pillow and sketched a map of the city from memory. It wasn't hard to do—there was only one long street, spiralling through the market, the public baths, the parks and concert houses, smithies and workshops of mages, the fields of grain and the libraries, artisans' houses and the mansions of the rich until it finally wound into Oonagh's lair at the centre.

At apparently random intervals, the single street was blocked by a gate. Seven gates, altogether, each with their guards. He looked down at his map and marked the gates, thinking that he'd never yet seen the queen come in or out.

Either she never left, or she had passages and roads of her own on another level. And then there was the watercourse beneath the road. He hadn't had more than a glimpse of where he'd come out before the swift-flowing river swept him away, but at the end there had been a stench which had surely been the stench of sewers.

He tucked the map into his jacket pocket, rolled the blankets into a corner and emerged once more into the quiet of the street. Displacing wandering scholars and paper sellers, he made his way into the large central library. There, lanterns like yellow stars hung from wrought-bronze sconces.

Flynn tested his invulnerability, took a brass candlestick from its place on the table and used it to prize open the claw of a lantern. Snaffling a piece of paper a forgetful scholar had left beneath a book of poetry, Flynn put the paper in his pocket, tucked the lantern under his arm and departed.

He lay on top of the hill of the city all night, watching the strange stars spin. Recognising groupings and giving them names. The Brillo-pad and the Cup of Tea revolved around an empty spot in the sky where at home there would have been Polaris. It felt strangely bereaving to have an absence where a star should be, but he spat on the ink stick, mixed the liquid in until he had made treacly ink, and wrote down *Pole Void*, with a little circle on the map of the sky he was making.

Now he knew where north was. He watched and waited, dew falling on him, and the curious wild ponies of the meadow coming close enough to nose him, until the sun rose, and he could mark east on his city map.

Full east, facing the rising sun, a great river split meadow and forest. It spumed over a series of weirs close to the side of the hill and then, with a waterfall roar, descended almost vertically into a round millpond-like hole. Water vapour cooled the air, and he could see, if he leaned over, mill wheels and fish traps set into the side of the shaft. Doors too, where the dwellers in the depths of the city, under his feet, could lean out into the punch of falling water and pull in fish and water fowl and reed that had come too close to escape the abyss.

In Flynn's emergency escape kit was a magnetized needle. He scooped up a handful of water in his tin cup and floated the needle atop it. It spun in circles three times before settling in a SSW direction, and when he nudged it to set it spinning again, it came back to the same alignment.

What a world. It seemed symptomatic of many things, to Flynn, that they had a pole which didn't point north. Still, he marked that on the map too, and crossing the river on the white marble bridge, he carried on around the outside of the mound.

The stench of the river outlet met his nose as he was halfway around the curve, treading through heather and picking his way through flowering yellow gorse bushes, garlanded with thorns. It was a peculiarly complex smell, with elements of perfume from the bathhouses and spilled wine from the cellars mixed into the sharp citrus and hay scent of animal dung, the disturbing, metallic scent of something unknown that his hind brain told him was a threat.

The entrance from which the boat had emerged proved to be a sizeable cave, with a small and slimy footpath on either side. He brought the lantern out of his coat, hefted the candlestick in his other hand and picked his way slowly into the belly of the city.

Good to know you're going up in the world.

Shut up, Skip.

But the imaginary friend was a comfort as he slithered, face pressed to the tunnel wall, along a ledge the span of his hand, through increasingly absolute darkness. The roof of the tunnel above him showed long slots and boards over them, and when he got past these, he left the smell behind. He also left the tiny pinprick of daylight.

Having counted his strides as he circumnavigated the city, he'd been able to calculate its overall diameter. Now, trying to pace as evenly as possible while going sideways with his heels out over the racing stream, it was harder to judge, but he thought he was about a mile in when the path widened and wooden jetties began to thrust out into the stream.

Spiral stairs wound up out of sight, and in the chill dampness, boxes glittered with moisture. Bags of grain, forgotten in a corner, had begun to grow colourless sprouts. Light filtered down from a grill above and showed him a trading post and boats moored, empty of everything but oars.

Praising his luck, Flynn untied a small skiff and got in, it was a lot easier to row up the stream than to carry on with his crablike walk. Setting the lantern in the prow, he put his back into the stroke and watched entrances and exits go by like black wormholes on either side. A snatch of music, the full-voiced sweetness of an unearthly choir, floated down from a street grating above, and then gave way to the sound of distant hammering. But as he rowed on towards the centre of the city, the grates above his head grew farther away, and then disappeared entirely. The only glimpses of life became the occasional furtive reflection of his passing lantern on the shore, and once a snick and metallic stirring of huge feathers as he gazed through a grill to his left and saw a massive steel eye and pinions made of aluminium, something that flinched out of the circle of his light even as he passed.

After another five miles or so, another landing caught his notice. This one was bare of piled detritus, but it gave back his yellow light with a faint dour grey tinge. At some point, the carvings and the vaultings said, this was an important place. At

233

some point it was an honour to use these stairs. The curve and depth of them seemed familiar, and he could see the trace of footsteps down the treads. A small bare foot and a booted one.

This must be the place. Tying up his boat to an ornamental ring held in the mouth of a carved unicorn, he stepped out. Even the tunnel had been ornamented here, sheathed in white stone and pocked with designs of steel that reflected his lantern light in long grey waves. He wondered if this was where they once had brought their dead, shuttling them out of the city in secret to maintain the illusion that they lived forever.

Enough speculation, old son. Get on with the job.

Even though the phantom memory of his side felt marked with a white burn scar from being stabbed with an electric cable, he still smiled at the often-repeated rebuke. The electrical thing had not been Skip's fault. If anything, it was a reassurance that one thing in Flynn's life had not become strange—because of course Skip would defend his team with all the strength in him. Of course he would. And if some watery creature with Skip's face had attacked Sumala, Flynn would have done the same, or at least tried. The hurt he'd felt at first was a purely physical thing, unconsidered, unsubstantiated, and now he welcomed back the voice in his head with all the slight overzealousnous appropriate to a reconciliation.

Smiling, he climbed up twist after twist of stair until he came to a trap door that lay sealed and smooth over his head. More of the steel and crystal decorations pitted it in apparently random scatterings of blobs. But Flynn had spent the night looking up at the same patterns, memorizing them.

He knew enough now to recognise the area of the night sky in full view at midnight. But there should have been a greenish planet somewhere between the wiggle of the Snake and the handle of the Cup of Tea.

Curious, he reached out and rubbed the place where it should be, dislodging a layer of dust. Invisible beneath the dust lay a faint, thumb-sized depression, and when he pushed at it, a glimmer of green light raced across the surface of the stone, tracing the joins of a door. Setting his back to the stone, he pushed with a feeling of triumph. Sometimes, after all, it paid to pause and think instead of just reacting.

The stone swung open and he was in the room of the Sleepers. Without Serpent and Willow there with him, breathing and moving alongside him, the stillness was eerie. The voice of the river beneath him, dim though it was, felt shattering loud. He thought he could hear the spiders weaving cobwebs in the corners, and then realised there were no spiders. Nothing moved in that void except him.

He tiptoed past the thing that looked so much like a captive demon and made his way to the stone table where Sumala lay. Now that he had orientated himself, the decoration on the walls and vault of the room meant something to him. This room too had stopped at midnight. The crystal lines which Serpent had used to call for help radiated out from the room's grim stars to polar north and magnetic SSW, as though they anchored it, prevented the world from turning and time from passing. They squirmed up the side of each mortuary slab and intersected with lines of silver steel to form a twisted, vinelike swastika.

The sight gave Flynn pause, made him wonder, for a sickening instant, whether he was somehow dreaming all of this. In a hospital bed somewhere, perhaps, conjuring up this world out of fragments of *Le Morte d'Arthur* and the war. Except he knew the swastika was an older thing than the Nazis. They had perverted rather than created it.

Still, might it be evidence that Liadain had spoken the truth when she had drawn such comparisons between Oonagh's Elfland and Nazi Germany? Or might it be a mere innocent device, like the Hindu sun cross? Like... He hunkered down and examined the side of the table on which Sumala lay. Might it be a version of the compass rose? If so...

The flat surface of the stone had been pitted all over with small holes. In some, gems twinkled, and in others shone the baleful glint of grey stars. But the majority gaped open, black as the night sky. He felt something shift inside his head as he looked at it, and—like the way an optical illusion of a candlestick suddenly becomes two faces—it transformed itself in his understanding into a clock face. The position of the gems and metal disks described a time.

He worked it out, knew instinctively that it must be the time she had been laid down here, the time the bubble in which she lay was activated, beginning to siphon off her seconds and hours. He could almost see them, flowing like electricity down the interconnecting silver and crystal paths, out through the walls. They would go to some sort of storage system, like electricity to a battery.

When he straightened up and looked at the miles of sleepers, the jewellery of conduits, he understood better what Liadain had said about the elves using time as their greatest resource. Time was being harvested from each of these prisoners, used to fuel who knew what?

"Bloody hell."

Kneeling beside the plinth, he pried the jewels from their settings, began to slot them back in in a new alignment, his fingers working sure and fast without his conscious will. He knew what to do. But gradually it occurred to him that he didn't know how he knew. His hands seemed to work without him, leaving him to watch them and feel a creeping horror. True, it would have been a shame to come all this way and be stumped now, not knowing how to revive the sleeper. But that would not have made him feel a prisoner in his own body, fear that it would never answer to his command again.

A new star alignment took shape under his swift movements. It must be, to the second, the time it was now, outside. Five grey stars in a wheel, and then a symbol like a bolt of lightning through a hoop, and with a muffled pop of equalizing air pressure the dome of dust that arced over the plinth popped. Motes began to drift down and to spiral back up from over Sumala's open mouth as she breathed again. Her bells gave off a faint glissade as her chest rose and fell. Even in this light her skin was the colour of caramel, and he had a fancy that the right thing to do in a situation like this was to wake the sleeping princess with a kiss.

But that didn't seem exactly sporting when the girl wasn't awake to say yes or no, so instead he leaned over and shook her gently by the shoulder. The pliant, warm flesh and faint honeysuckle smell of her, the way the movement made her breasts stir and her hair slide over her throat was bad enough. A kiss would definitely have been a terrible idea.

"Nnnnnn," she mumbled. "Go away." And then, faster than he could feel hurt, "Oh, it's you! Thank you. Aren't you clever?" She swung her feet off the stone and roused with a sound like cymbals. "We should go. Quick!"

Flynn stopped her as she turned for the stairs. "This way." He passed her the lantern and hefted the candlestick more comfortably in his right hand. "We don't want to go through the city."

"Of course we don't." She flowed down before him like a candle flame, a poised and cheerful glitter and tingle in the pressing dark. "You seem changed. Did you talk to your friend? You're a man with a purpose now, I see it. And the purpose is to help me? That's a good thing!"

It should have been annoying, but Flynn was no chatterbox himself and he found it restful, like going home and being fussed over by his ever-nattering mother, to have company who did not require him to fill the silence with speech.

"I met the leader of the resistance." He handed her into the boat, casting off and jumping in himself. "She said I have a role to play, but I don't know what it is."

"It's to get me home." Sumala hung the lantern on the prow, put her hands together and leaned her pointed chin into the hollow. Her cheeks dimpled. "And to do that we have to get you home first."

"How so?"

"I had forgotten," she said as the current whisked the boat back down the corridors he had so laboriously rowed up. "I can't get a message to my father from here. That's why the spell showed me my brother instead. He is in the human world."

"I'm not following."

"Think of it like, um, bubbles. Each of our worlds is an individual bubble, and your world is the skin between them. I can't get out of this world and into my own without passing through yours. My father cannot come here against Oonagh's will—the kingdoms are sacrosanct. But he can find me in the human world, and he can thwart whatever she wishes to do there."

She smiled, rather too brightly, he thought, for someone who had been in a dungeon for the past week. How could she be picking up the conversation as though it had never been interrupted? Shouldn't she be more dazed from having been unconscious all this time?

"I closed my eyes," she said, "and then I opened them. That's how long I was there. For me, the time you have lived through simply didn't happen."

"How did you..." *...know what I was thinking?*

Innocent smile. She looked down and picked a tangle of silver wire out of a clump of reed as they sailed past it, wrinkled her nose at the smell and threw it back.

Flynn thought about his own hands, moving as by someone else's will. His chest filled with a stinging smoke of suspicion. "What did you do to me?"

She tilted her cheek into one open palm and raised an eyebrow.

"That thing. When you looked at me and everything went strange. Liadain says you cast a spell on me, that I rescued you because you have made a slave of me."

Sumala frowned. The corners of her well-shaped mouth turned down. "They always think it's got something to do with sex." She sighed and rubbed sulkily at the edge of the plank seat. "Doesn't that make you annoyed? The way they think men can be led about like that by the *linga*."

"By the what? No. Don't change the subject. What did you do to me?"

Sumala laughed and pulled a lock of her hair over her shoulder, inserting the end of it into one of her bells, like a bee in a foxglove. "I put a part of my soul in you," she said, looking at it, rather than at him.

"You did what?" The world around Flynn gave a lurch as though something huge had moved through the stream beneath them, slopping the boat against the walls. He rethought his words and actions of the past week, trying to trace any difference that might lead back to an alien soul lodged behind his eyes. "What did you do that for?"

"Because you were cross with me." She looked up from beneath her long lashes with wide brown eyes, innocent, vulnerable. "And I didn't know a better way of making you less

239

cross than to help you see things, just a little, with my eyes."

"Damn you all." Flynn held on to the rudder for dear life while he tried to fight down the wish to throw something at her—to push her hard in the throat and tip her overboard. And as he did, he found a part of himself arguing that what she had done was only reasonable. He was bigger and stronger and an unknown quantity. She didn't know she didn't need to be afraid. A man might have shoved him away, but she couldn't do that...

"Is that me or you?" he asked, sickened but intrigued. Now there was a mapping problem worthy of the name—find out where the invader began and ended, where the contours of his own mind were buried beneath the graft.

"Some bit of both," she said. "But don't be angry. If I hadn't done it, you couldn't have known how to free me. You couldn't have known the right alignment of the stars. More to the point, I couldn't have known what I know now. I have been seeing your experiences. The ones you didn't understand yourself. I know how to get us both home."

Flynn clapped a hand over his nose as they burst into the final stretch of the river, and then over the lip and out into a world that seemed carved entirely of pearl. Fog capped the water and shrouded the banks, concealing even the distant sun. He and Sumala were the only two coloured things in a world gone entirely white. "How?"

Sumala got to her feet. Standing with a dancer's balance in the prow of the speeding skiff, she looked out at the banks with a disapproving eye. "They took you to a portal, but because you are so stupid you didn't know what it was."

"Stupid, eh? You know, this is not the fairytale rescue I was promised in my impressionable youth. What happened to 'my hand in marriage and half my father's kingdom'?"

Sumala's face resumed the sulky look. "Was that why you rescued me? Because you think I have to marry you now? I can't marry a human. That would be disgusting. I am a princess of the Gandharvas, and I will marry a prince of my own people. So you can forget any notions like that."

"I was joking." Flynn rubbed the bridge of his nose and tried to cordon off the part of himself that agreed with her, along with the part that was hurt. "I don't want you—I have someone waiting for me at home. So you'd better tell me how to get there fast, and let's have this over with. Then you can take your soul back and we'll be rid of each other for good."

Looking at her expression, a mixture of insult and relief, Flynn found it all but impossible to believe that Liadain spoke the truth. Sumala, alone out of all the people he had met here, seemed as transparent as clear water. How could she be a spy for anyone? Yet...was that his own opinion or was it hers, transferred to him by some process of spiritual osmosis through the part of herself she had left embedded in him?

Alternatively, he supposed it was just as possible that if he had a part of her spirit in him he should be able to feel what she was feeling? Surely if she was lying to him, and she knew it, then the taste of the lie would bleed through?

You know what I always say.

When in doubt, go with the gut feeling? Yes, Skipper, and I know how many bar fights, charges, arrests and broken hearts that policy left scattered after it.

It wasn't the old skipper who grinned at him at this thought, but the sandy-haired thin, scrappy boy he'd first met, back when recklessness had seemed the very defining note of what to look for in a pilot. *But it never led me permanently astray, old son. You want to try it some time. Live a little.*

And who's going to rein me in? You?

But this voice was unfamiliar, older, shadowed with too much grief. *Yes. I'll be here, a team like the old days, with our places swapped.*

He wanted to ask about the extra years, what had added that weariness to the mental voice, but he knew too well that he only spoke to a construct his loneliness had created. Better save that one until he could ask it in person. And at that thought his gut feelings rolled out of his belly and up his spine like hot tar, spread across his ribs and sucked all the air out of his lungs with loss and yearning to go home.

Let the elves fight their own battles. He had his own country to think of, his own world, his own loves. "Let's not quarrel," he said and freed a hand from the tiller to pat her arm. "Let's just go home, both of us."

Her eyes had filled with tears. They glistened as she nodded, like the myriad of fog droplets beading on her cheeks, turning her black hair grey and silvering her bells. "My father always told us, all of us, that this sort of thing would happen. We'd be taken hostage to force him to act one way or another. He said that we should understand that he would never acquiesce to demands from hostage takers, and we should be prepared to find our own way back as we could."

She rubbed her fingertips over her eyes, smudging kohl, rubbed again and looked at once ten years younger with un-made-up eyes and streaks of dirt on her cheeks. "But I think he would have made more effort to find me if I'd been a son. I don't think it would all be down to me if I were a son."

Flynn looked at the banks hurrying by in order to avoid her gaze. So it did go both ways, after all. She felt his grief and echoed it with her own, both exiles together. He'd have said something to make it better, but he couldn't think of what. Fortunately he was saved by spotting the shallow shelving beach of stones, all white and bone and chill in this featureless world, with a grey water whispering down the edge of it. A hollow full of disturbed silt and tumbled rocks told where Liadain normally stood, but she was not there now. That was fortunate. It would make things a lot easier.

Flynn ran the boat up on the shore and together they pulled it out of the water. "Righty-ho." He brushed his hands together, gave a tug on the straps of his parachute harness. It was a bugger, frankly, wearing this all the time, but he didn't see a safe alternative. Even if he buried it, someone would be bound to dig it up.

"Tell me where this portal is that I failed to spot."

Sumala stood at the top of the bank. As always she looked as if she had just been caught in the middle of a complex dance, as if—rather than simply stand there—she posed in a carefully orchestrated position. This one, legs bent, front foot turned out, weight on the back, her arms raised in an arch that was a mix of protection and denial, spoke of a wild thing startled, readying itself to flee. The fog eddied around her like veils of gossamer, and even her bells sounded dim and far away in the moisture-laden air.

She turned her head, tracked the movement of the air. "Something is here with us. Something is watching."

He saw only the shapes of fog, white blankness and a roil of paler and darker shapes where the wind stirred the cloud. Water trickled and ticked from the reeds around his feet. The distant sound of trees came like the sea, but he noticed how much the sound resembled a crowd of whispering voices. "I don't..."

"There!" She pointed as the breeze opened the mist and let through a brief impression of darkness.

"There's nothing there," he said, but when he moved over to

the place he could feel no breeze. The air hung flat and heavy as in a tomb. Something else must have moved it. And then there came a buzz like an angry wasp and Sumala was pirouetting, a dart with black feathers caught in the whipping material of her skirt.

"Quick." She grabbed him by the wrist and hauled him up onto the causeway. "Let's get there and get out."

Flynn unstrapped the candlestick from his webbing. After Serpent, he had very little fear of this world's warriors. "No point trying to open it and get through with these chaps on our tail. Let's see them off first."

"No." She pulled again. She had a stronger grip than he had expected, and he found himself swayed by the urgency in her face. "You can't fight what you can't see. Come on!"

He'd guessed himself where they were going now—back to the pool where he had dreamed himself into the real world. Crouched down against the threat of more of those darts, he ran the mazelike paths through the marsh with sure feet, hearing only his own footsteps and Sumala's bells shrilling. A dart hit the water two feet ahead of him. One tangled in his jacket, and fell out, leaving a smouldering hole. He dodged right, rolled and dived off the boardwalk and through the waterlike surface of the grey mere. It parted under him like fog and he fell, jarringly and broke his fall with painful wrists at the bottom of the grassy hollow whose surface was a silver meniscus of water.

"What the...? I still can't see where they're coming from." Flynn levered himself up, tried to stand but could not find his balance. The surface of the pool should have been "up" but it felt "out" instead. The turf pressed into his back as if he were attracted to it by a magnet, but if he reached out and let a blade of grass fall, it fell towards the surface of the water, not towards his feet. The mismatch made him feel sick, jumpy, and the nausea was not helped by Sumala pulling at his clothes in panic.

"What are you up to now?"

"The dust," she said. "We need the dust, to make a physical breach between the worlds. You sent thoughts before, but we can't send bodies without it. Where is it? Quickly."

The pool stood shimmering and vertical in front of him like a wavering wall of glass. Elongated black shadows skimmed over its surface like swallows. With a splash and a thud, a polished black dart hit the long grass by Flynn's elbow. He wriggled himself away from it and fished the hag's magic dust out of his inner breast pocket, uncomfortably exposed and waiting for the next dart to fall.

"I should get out and fight them. We're sitting ducks here."

Something silver flashed above—outside, on the other side of—the water. Dark shapes stretched and elongated and sound came through like a bad record, scratchy and booming, magnified by the lake's surface. A shout, a snap of something that flapped like wet leather. Sumala grabbed the pouch from his hand and hurled a handful of dust at the silver mirror of the lake. Like a drop of washing-up liquid in a bowl of oily water, the dust made a single circular ripple, a pushing back. The light from beyond changed, greying, growing tired and dispiriting, pewter rather than silver.

Then Sumala pushed her other hand through the inch-thick layer of water. It made a hole, which slowly widened, like a pinhole in a balloon, forced apart by internal pressure. Outside was scrubland and a standing stone. A distant building, ugly and rectangular as a prefab bulked against a sunset smeared with orange light. The wind fluttered the surface of the lake, but could not get in.

Flynn couldn't swallow, scarcely dared move, but he drew his feet up under him to spring through. Home.

And then his doubtful, hateful, unwelcome intelligence tossed up a thought. He'd read fairy tales in his youth—who hadn't? They came back to him now, as though the radio-play soundtrack of his life had modulated into a minor key, brought in the little dissonances that telegraphed terror. He wanted badly to ignore it, but didn't dare. "You go," he said, and struggled out of his parachute harness.

"I'm not leaving you. You helped me, so I owe you. We'll go together."

More arrows punctured the pond, missed them by sheer luck. Flynn bit his tongue and swung, let the silk, rope and metal pass through the hole and fall with an audible clank onto the exotic and wondrous grass of the world of Man.

"Come *on*! They'll close it. What are you waiting for?"

Hard to tell in the tricky twilight light, but as he watched, with hope choking him and despair coupled on behind it, it seemed to Flynn that the ropes of his harness rotted into the ground, the buckles flaked into red clots of rust. He watched until he couldn't take it any more, had to put his face in both hands and dig his fingernails into the roots of his hair.

Sumala had a foot through now, balanced halfway between one world and the next, but she'd turned her head and was watching him as he clawed his braced fingers down his forehead, drawing blood.

"Don't do that! Come on!"

The water wavered, a horizontal rainfall mingled with the gore on his face. Blue flashes coruscated across it like distant lightning, and Sumala took a second pinch of the powder, poured it into one of her bells and pinched the lip closed. She yanked it off her bracelet and threw it out onto the heather.

"There. If Father comes looking, he will find that and he'll open it from the other side." She ran back in, took Flynn's hands and began to pull him towards the portal. "That is if you won't come. But come. Quickly, before it…"

Two steps was all it would take, and the struggling would be over. He took the first, numbly. So this was what it felt like, walking out to a firing squad? Sick with anguish, lightheaded, determined to carry on gouging until the blood veiled his face.

Before he could take the second step, there was a little watery smacking sound, like a kiss, and the glasslike lake reformed behind Sumala. The portal to earth was closed and it was too late after all. The story of his life.

Unaware that she'd lost her chance, Sumala backed into the water and through. On autopilot, too destroyed to make any more choices, Geoff followed, emerged into Elfland teetering off balance on the edge of the marsh, with a dozen gleaming arrow tips aimed at his face.

Queen Oonagh, today black as jet and crowned in diamonds, awaited them, seated on the back of a black dragon. Even the dragon seemed to be laughing at him, diamond smoke curling up from its open jaws.

"Congratulations," she said, nodding to the guards, who bound their hands with thin, cutting cords. "You have found the one thing I cannot allow you to do."

Chapter Eighteen

As the door swung closed behind him and the bank's air-conditioned chill began to work its way through his shirt, Ben suddenly remembered the photocopier: the music and the exploding lights. Yes, he had told Chris, though it seemed such a long time ago now. And then this business with Chris's own tragedy had intervened, and he couldn't really blame either of them for concentrating on that and letting a harmless bit of rogue weirdness slip his mind.

Besides, the photocopier incident happened before he knocked down part of his newly built extension. Now that he'd done so, there was always the possibility that he'd paid his dues, he'd placated them, and this weekend's fun stuff had been directed at Chris rather than him. *Yeah, and a Nigerian businessman really does want to send me a million dollars because he thinks I'm such a great guy.*

Putting his suit jacket on, Ben hesitated before the door into the office spaces in the back of the bank. The door opened, and Paul gave him an unctuous look. "In you come, Mr. Chaudhry. Unless you were thinking of skiving off today too?"

And there were some of his colleagues it wouldn't bother him greatly to see tangle with the otherworld. Paul could do with some shaking up, either to make him a better man, or just because it would be fun to watch. "I don't..." he began, *think I should come in, because if I do, you will be in danger from elvish assassins.*

Okay, it really wasn't something he could say.

"Cat got your tongue?"

It seemed it had. Replaying the past forty-eight hours gave him nothing on which he could hang a reasonable reluctance. "Have you got the wiring fixed in the basement?"

"Pretty much." Paul smirked and leaned on his elbow against the doorframe, blocking Ben's way in. He'd begun to put on a senior executive's beer belly, and his shirt parted at the waist, pulling out to give a glimpse of pink skin and peach-fuzz hair. "Why, are you spooked?"

"You have no idea." Ben straightened his tie. Chances were, even if he didn't come in, the creatures would continue to interfere here until he did. It was bait, or a trap, or an inevitability. "But currently I'm not coming in because you're standing in my way."

Paul sneered as he stepped aside. "I've put a couple of files on your desk. I want them summarized before the bank opens. Then there's some data entry I need done on the Ashcroft account. It'll only take a half hour or so. I expect you can do it over lunch."

Ben looked at the clock. It was an old friend, the big plastic numbers a perennial source of fascination. Half past eight. "I can come and do it now. If I do it from your terminal, the system will log it to you."

And hopefully if I'm sitting in your room, they'll come after me there. That way it's just you and me caught in the crossfire. He had a twinge of conscience but decided that it was better that than inviting fire on the other cashiers. Paul had built up a certain amount of negative karma over the years. This would help pay it off.

"All right. If you have something to do at lunch." Paul managed to make the idea of using the lunch break for eating sound like slacking off. "I'll be in the managers' tea room, if you need me to explain how anything works."

Even better. Ben walked almost jauntily up the carpeted stairs to the managerial section, pushed open Paul's office door with a movement copied from *The Professionals*—a quick shove and then a dive to the other side of the door, so he could take in the whole room at once. It might have been better if he'd carried a gun—at least he wouldn't have felt so damn stupid when there was nothing at all there.

He switched on the computer, sorted through the files and read the note explaining which entries had to go on which spreadsheet. It could have gone to Paul's secretary, instead of to one of the cashiers. Should have done. Make work, entirely designed to show Ben his time was not his own.

He sighed, looked at the phone. He should phone Chris, see if there was anything the MPA could do. But he was pretty certain outbound calls were logged. That was a conversation he didn't want to have. So he sat down in the leather upholstered chair, dragged over the first file and got to work.

A half hour later with nothing more to do, he reluctantly closed everything down again and left the office. Nothing spooky had happened yet. Maybe it never would—or at least, not today. Could he hope for that?

"All right, Ben?" Enid was taking off her sun hat and diving into her bag for the cardigan she'd brought, adapted as he was to the vagaries of the air conditioning. Her hair had turned blonde over the weekend, was now cut in a feathery bob around her face.

It didn't suit her at all, but he was wise enough to the ways of women to say, "You've had your hair done. It's very stylish." Which had the benefit of being true while omitting the part about it making her look like mutton dressed as lamb.

"Thought I deserved a treat after that photocopier thing,"

she said cheerfully. "I tell you what, I'm not going down there today. Not for any money."

"They say it's fixed." At Ben's appearance, the early-morning routine of the cashiers kicked in, with Don coming over to put the percolator on and Laura providing the box of girding-our-loins-for-the-day Danish pastries. Don filled up the percolator with water, slapped a coffee bag into its slot and continued. "They had the electricians in over the weekend, so I heard. Lots of overtime. I can't see that going down well with the boss."

"How d'you know all this?" Laura kept her thumb on the crinkly paper case of the chocolate éclair she'd marked as her own, held the box out to Don.

"Oh, I was in early this morning. There's a big tournament happening in a fortnight at my club, so I thought I'd get the overtime in today so I could take time off to compete. Anyway." He smoothed his receding hair. "They hadn't finished by eight. Said it was a scandal to find such old wiring in a modern building. Right back to the Victorians it went, according to them. With us plugging the copier into it, the only wonder was that it hadn't gone before."

Laura looked a little disgruntled. "I didn't expect them to move so fast. Was kind of looking forward to a fight over it, to be straight with you. It's not like them to put employee welfare so high up their priorities."

"Well, it was a room full of inflammable old files, right at the bottom of an inflammable old building," Don's bowtie had recently come back into fashion since the advent of the eleventh Dr. Who. He had responded by buying a couple of even louder versions than his usual. Today's was one of these, bright blue with large yellow dots. He adjusted it proudly.

"I suppose. We've had a narrow escape then." Laura

accepted the box back and smiled at the discovery that she'd been left the éclair. "Could have been nasty." The clock now stood at quarter past nine, and the sound of feet from the marble foyer indicated a sudden influx of customers. "Oh well, to work, I suppose."

As they slipped in to their counter spots, Enid paused and looked at Ben with a frown. "All sounds so...normal when they put it like that, doesn't it? We did, you did...see something?"

"I did." Ben smiled, in an attempt to be reassuring, though he could see from her reaction that it failed. "I think you're right. I don't think we should go down there, fixed or not. At least... If you need something, tell me and I'll get it. I don't want you going into the basement alone."

"Oh, and what about you?" She pursed her lips and her face hardened. "It's not like the days when it was all 'I will defend you, fair maiden' and all that. What makes you think you'd do any better down there than me?"

Ben watched as Mrs. Dwivedi from the library queued in front of Laura rather than have her money handled by him. Another part of the regular Monday-morning routine. He said, "I spoke to someone who deals in this kind of stuff. I've got a...a sort of charm."

"Oh, great minds!" Enid dealt with a student withdrawing money from their savings account while Ben paid in a couple of cheques and a hundred pounds in cash for a window cleaner who had left his bucket of water outside and kept glancing away as if afraid that someone would pinch it.

In the next lull, Enid opened her bag and pulled out a complicated sculpture of different-coloured wires and gems. "I was telling my neighbour about it. Turns out she's a white witch—I'd never have guessed—and she made me this."

That was *Torchwood* again, Ben thought, conscious that

he'd begun to regard himself as part of some sort of specially prepared task force. Ridiculous though that was. It made you imagine you were the only one in the world with a functioning brain. He laughed. "All right, I'll do less of the fair-maidening, if you like. I don't know why it hadn't occurred to me you'd think of it too."

"It's my girlish good looks," she sniggered. "Brings out your protective streak."

"Yes, that must be it."

The rest of the morning passed without incident. He spent the lunch hour in the pub, trying to get through to the MPA by phone, and failing. Grace had left a voice mail to say she was taking a funeral in one of her attached parishes. Chris's mobile was off, and the other numbers just rang and rang. It looked like he was alone with this today. Whatever "this" turned out to be.

The afternoon slid sleepily in off the street as Ben returned to work. He checked the clock: half past one.

Paul straightened up from putting down a stack of files by his chair. "Just put these away for me, would you?" Ben looked at the pile and thought about the filing cabinets. They too were downstairs. Rack upon rack of brown wallets, on long metal shelves, stretching away into gloom. The shelves rolled on tracks built into the floor and squealed like stuck pigs as they did so.

It would be a good place to invite an attack—a place he'd be alone. There wouldn't be any danger to the others. If anything, he should be pleased.

He looked around the foyer, but the morning's rush had tailed off, and there was only one customer, sitting by the desk the bank used when a customer wanted to talk about their mortgage. An old man, whose gold-rimmed spectacles framed eyes milky with creeping cataracts. He wore polyester trousers and a cardigan with leather patches at the elbows, and held his documents, in a supermarket carrier bag, on his lap as though they were a sleeping child.

"Is someone looking after you, Mr. Uh...?" Ben asked, and received a bemused look in return that slowly melted into a smile.

"Oh. Smith, Sidney Smith. Yes. I mean yes, thank you. She's just..." A waved hand meant that the advisor had ducked out for a moment to talk to Paul or the branch manager. So Ben returned the smile and punched in the combination to open the door, go through into the heavy presence of the old building. He didn't really want to file at all. Didn't want to go down there on his own.

He stopped by his desk, picked up the phone again, rang Chris's mobile and an artificial voice advised him to leave a message. Laura was watching, so he ducked out the back and whispered, "I'm at work. What if they try and get to me through someone else?"

He thumbed the phone off and took a deep breath. If that was their plan, then the only way to counter it was to keep to himself as much as possible. Maybe hang out with Enid, protected as she was by her charm. That wouldn't look odd, they were well known for getting on like a house on fire. And then...what? Carry on, wash and redo every day for the rest of his life?

No. There was no sense worrying about that. Just get through today, get hold of Chris this evening and make him think of something. Make *them* leave him alone. He'd faced up to enough bullies in his life to know you could only run so far before you had to turn and show them you were not going to take it. If only he knew what the elvish equivalent of smacking your tormentors with a cricket bat was.

He picked up the files, edged guiltily around Enid's accusing look as he headed for the stairs to the basement. Quiet fell like the dust as he tiptoed down the white treads. The ink came off on his hands, and the bundles of papers smelled accusingly damp. A paper clip fell with a ting that made him jump, and it didn't seem possible to step off the last riser into a well-lit, white-painted room with a smell of cheap new carpet. The photocopier had all the menace of a cardboard box, but he edged by it nevertheless and dived into the older, vaulted space where the files stretched out to brown infinities.

A subterranean window opened onto a hole in the pavement, capped with a grill. Crisp packets, chewing gum and old cigarettes had piled up against the glass, so that the light came in as a pattern of grey dots. He stood with his hand on shelf A-1 and waited for something uncanny to happen. Water gurgled down the outside drainpipe from a sink upstairs. For a heart-stopping moment he thought he heard music, but as it grew louder then went past, he realised it was an open-topped car in which someone with no sense of irony was playing Enya loud.

Giving himself a mental shake, he rolled the shelves open and walked down the row of paper, looking for Atkins and Armitage. Maybe the demolition job and the milk and honey had really done the trick, and the creatures had moved on to tormenting Chris? Maybe it was actually over? False alarm, the tumour turned out to be benign and the operation was a complete success?

By the time he'd found Zumaya, he was humming softly, and embarrassingly enough it was the Dambusters theme. That was bad taste but it didn't stop him smiling as he passed the photocopier again, bounded up the stairs and looked at the clock.

Half past one.

Three steps passed on autopilot before that kicked in and he turned and looked again. Half past one. Then his breath stopped. He grabbed onto a chair as the spike of horror rammed into him, shattering his backbone, making his skin crawl and chill. *The clock's just stopped. Don't overreact. The batteries are dead, that's all.*

He gulped in air as though it were tar, choked on it and fixed his gaze on the clock. Tick, tick, tick. The second hand moved gently around the dial, the minute hand stood perfectly still. Half past one.

And where was everyone? All of the cashiers' positions were empty. Outside the toughened glass, only the old man still sat in the same chair, his hands in the same position on his cup, the tea untouched. Something else was wrong. What? Ah, Ben couldn't make his brain work. It was as though he'd been turned to stone.

My mind is darting around like a fly in a jam jar. The thought came with a snap of self-disgust as bracing as a face full of cold water. Phyllis wouldn't panic like this. Grace wouldn't. All right. So *they* were here. What did he do?

Get out and run for the nearest cover. That's the pub.

He picked up one of Don's golf clubs as he passed the cubbyhole where they stood, unlatched the door to the foyer, dived through, club raised to shoulder height, ready to smash down on the first silver-limbed shape he saw. Despite the air conditioning, it was hot as a greenhouse out here, smelled like one too. The thick, acrid smell of hot-house plants filled the air. As he burst through, the old man seemed to come back to life. His expression of bemusement was closer to panic now.

"They all went," he said. "I've been sitting here for three quarters of an hour waiting for that lady to come back. And when I tried to get out, the door..."

The door! It revolved, as it always did a great, glass-and-chrome fan with four panels in a great glass-and-chrome cylinder. Outside the windows, he could see the movement and sunshine and the normal workday bustle of Bakewell on a summer afternoon. Through the glass of the door, only a glimpse of dark foliage and a smoke of pollen. The brushes on the bottom of each panel swept through moisture, and the glass was clouding over with steam.

"Bloody hell." Ben grabbed a phone from the nearest desk, raised it to his ear. A humming vibration began along the surface of the desk. The tea slopped over the edge of the cup. Silence on the end of the phone.

He slammed it down just as the computer screen flickered into life. The sound of its hard drive whirring up to speed was echoed from all the other desks in the foyer.

"What's happening?" The old man put down his plastic bag of documents, hauled himself upright. He was beige from head to toe, saggy as his cardigan, and Ben thought, *Why couldn't I have a damsel in distress at least*, as one by one the computer boxes began to shudder beneath the desks. With a tinny little ping, the first light bulb shattered above his head and shards of glass came raining down.

White light through the monitors filled his head with jagged edges. The whine of the tortured machines scaled up until the veins burst in his nose and blood poured over the back of his hand. The old man began to hobble to the door, and Ben grabbed him, leaving a red handprint. "Sir! Don't go out there. Please. I don't think you can get out that way."

"I fought in Singapore, you know."

"Yeah, but you've never faced these things."

The first computer monitor cracked with a shower of

257

sparks. Wire and circuit boards came spewing out on to the desk. The thick glass of the screen lay like daggers on the floor, and a hot, thick wind skirled in under the door and lifted them into a whirlwind around his feet. "Please, sir. Just...um..." There wasn't anywhere safe in the damn room!

He ran to the door back into the old building, punched in the combination. If he could shove the guy through there, back into the fortunate bubble of real time wherever the rest of the staff were, then—

But it didn't budge. The same whining, gnat-wing vibration shivered through each tiny silver button, made his hand hurt with tingling, drove needles through the heel of his palm as he tried to force it open. Cracks had begun to form in the bulletproof glass of the windows.

Mr. Smith looked at him, hopefully.

"Don't look at me! I don't know what to do!"

From beneath the nearest desk came a bang and clatter as the metal sheets fell off the servers of each computer, rattled along the ground. Green jagged edges of exploded motherboard glinted with solder and chips as it burst into fragments and joined the whirlpool in the centre of the room.

Ben circled the thing, looking for something to hit.

"What is it?" Mr. Smith was fumbling with his glasses, peering at the frenetic shape. A wind tugged them out of his hand, and the thick lenses and wire frames were sucked into the pillar of metal and glass. "Those cost nearly one hundred pounds!"

"Just stay away from it!" Ben raised the golf club, took a swing at the whirlwind entity, and a sucking magnetic force wrenched his weapon out of his hand, sent it spinning. "Fuck! You just stay back, all right? I think...I don't think it's you it wants."

"It wants something?" Mr. Smith took a firmer hold on his walking stick, propped himself carefully upright with the other hand on the back of a swivel chair. In a moment of terrified irrelevance, Ben thought, *This is what Chris would have been like, if they hadn't taken him. Shit.* And he felt a strange wash of gratitude towards them, even as the spinning pillar of metal and glass began to speed, and to compact, shrinking inwards with pinging noises and giving off sparks and showers of debris.

There was a shape in there. The components scrunched together as though a great hand was assembling a man out of clay. Ben thought about cartoons, the grotesque violence of them, and shivered. He grabbed a chair, but it was padded, swivelling on castors, badly balanced and too heavy for a weapon. What else? *Come on, there must be something in here I can use!*

Beneath his cuff, he could feel the sweatband pull on the material of his shirt, feel the padded dimple that was a glass imp of holy water, tucked into the folded stretchy material. His whole defence and a weapon only of last resort. If he used it once, nothing would stand between him and their next attempt.

The thing had developed arms and legs now. The sound of metal crumpling added to the disturbing tick of the crack in the windows spreading. Darkness spread slowly out from the door. Ferns were nodding in a thick undergrowth a foot into the right-hand window. The dappled radiance of a green sun dazzled on the flagstones of Bakewell high street to the right.

With a thud, a thrown dictionary bounced off the coalescing creature. Ben looked beside him, found Mr. Smith holding his wrist and breathing hard, hurt and too proud to show it. The spirit was willing, but the body was weak. Taking courage from the example, Ben opened the nearest desk, threw files, Miss Cartwright's spare shoes, the wad of unopened printer paper.

They bounced off. But the whirlwind in the centre of the room slowed, stopped, and there stood a creature seven feet tall, its face formed out of broken glass, its body armour-plated with computer systems. Its metal hands held an axe of glass. Around its head, the torn-off cover of an office chair was wrapped like a red scarf. The little book of fairies turned up unbidden in Ben's mind at the sight. Red Cap, he thought, remembering tales of dread, not remembering that there'd been any advice at all on how to deal with them, other than "run away".

A smile made out of copper wire, and the creature's diode eyes fixed on him. It raised the axe and swung, turning. Ben had barely time to launch himself straight at Mr. Smith and push him out of the path of the blade. It whiffled down just beyond Ben's snatched-back fingertips. He felt the faint breeze of it, and then a cold, tingling rush of adrenaline and fear, and he grabbed the handle of the axe as the creature raised it, trying to pull it out of its hand.

All the mad strength of fear and fury did was to let him hold on as the Red Cap lifted the axe again, took him with it. It drew back its hand. He flapped from its wrist like a medieval dagged sleeve. To the thing, he might have weighed as little as a length of cloth as it tried to shake him off, and—failing—struck at the old man, Ben tugged helplessly through the air behind it.

Mr. Smith threw himself to one side with a soldierlike movement, but hit the ground like an invalid, crying out in pain. The wrist he'd cradled before he now pressed into his stomach, bowed over it, hunched over something broken. Ben got his feet under himself and lurched up, smacking his shoulder into the gnarled elbow of green plastic and grey metal. The pain was excruciating, it was like having his arm hacked off at the shoulder. He heaved in air to breathe around the zinging white agony of it. Pain spread like infection from shoulder to spine and thence throughout his whole body.

And the creature's arm didn't move a centimetre. It was like punching a steel door. It picked him up again. He got his feet under the armpit, reached one foot up and over to smash into the glass face, astounded at himself. But that too was as effective as kicking bulletproof glass. All it did was drive the edges deep into the rubber of his sole, make him wince and cry out as a knife-sharp shard pierced his instep.

Mr. Smith was fumbling with a dropped file, his broken wrist cradled against his chest, his other hand too weak to pick up the heavy bundle of papers on its own. The axe swung back with a crackling sound of thin metal and thick green plastic. The old man managed to raise the papers in an inadequate shield in front of his face, his mouth tight with Dunkirk spirit. The swing forward began, accurate and deadly, and Ben unlocked one hand from around the creature's arm, fumbled with his own wrist, and smashed the vial directly in the grinning glacial face.

It fizzled for an instant, like the fuse of a TV cartoon bomb, and then the face caved in around it. There was a little hole in the masklike purity of the glass, and it dragged the face into itself. The head followed, and the arm, sucked into nothingness just before the blow fell. The rest of the body followed, folding in, imploding into darkness, and from darkness into a pinprick of white light.

As fast as it had imploded, the light shattered apart, and shredded office equipment tumbled down on Ben and on the huddled form of Mr. Smith. A rush of cool, dry air flooded from the doorway, where Bakewell's innocent human sun shone on oblivious passersby.

"Mr. Smith?" He scrambled over to the customer, touched his shoulder gently, rounded fat flesh under cable-knit cardigan. "Are you all right?"

"All due respect, son." The milky eyes were gleaming, like an old warhorse that hears battle at a distance and remembers what it was once like. "I think I'll take my business to the Halifax instead."

"I have to…" After days of its presence under the dip where his pulse ran beneath the skin, the emptiness where the imp had been felt like a wound. "I have to go. It'll come back for me." He checked the phone on the desk, heard the dialling tone without surprise and handed it to the old man. "You phone for an ambulance. I've got to go."

He didn't wait to go back into the office for his jacket, just pushed his way out of the doors and down to the car park without thinking. Paused with his hand on the door of the car, the keys in his fingers. Drive or walk? The pub was only down the road, shrouded in its field of the mundane, but if he walked it would take longer, expose him and the crowd around him to whatever might be coming next.

And—remembered lines from the books he'd read—wouldn't he be safer in the car? They didn't like iron, did they? Like salt and church bells, he'd be safer inside a metal shell than he would walking unprotected down the high street. Yes. Car it was then.

He unlocked the door, started it up, eased out into the haze of summer sunlight, dust and smog that clung around the overused high street. The bank was on FitzGerald Street, so he should turn left, drive up Donan Avenue and park as close to the Red Lion as the midday crowd allowed. Cars beeped at him as he swung out into the traffic and the high sun poured glitter through the windscreen, illuminating the dust on the dashboard, making the inside of the car smell of upholstery and panic, sweat and aftershave. Where *was* the turnoff anyway? He thought he *had* turned left, but this was not the faded red brick grandeur of Donan Avenue with its big houses and their mock Tudor chimneys.

Maybe he was still on the high street? How could he even be wondering about that? He knew the high street better than he knew his own face. He walked or drove down it every working day of his life. There should be the new sweet shop with its bold cartoon adverts in the window, prime colours, ironic, Batman-style logos, and shelves piled high with humbugs and bull's eyes. It shouldn't be hard to spot. He shouldn't be asking himself whether that multicoloured blur out of the corner of his eye could have been it or not.

The street drew itself out to the distant horizon, full of a golden haze that blurred the contours of the buildings. He spotted the turnoff with a lurch of gratitude mixed with terror. That *was* the house with the blue blinds, wasn't it? Opposite the pillar box and next to the hedge where climbing roses grew amongst ivy and crackly brown dead firs. It must be. Yes, it was.

So that meant the pub was only five hundred yards farther up the road, just after the bus stop and the... But where was the chippy? Where had the *We Will Wok You* Chinese takeaway gone? Was this not Donan Avenue after all?

Ben bit the inside of his lip, slowed down. Behind him the dark and glittering blur that he thought was a Montego, following, gave an indignant blast on the horn. He couldn't stop—just stop in the middle of the road—could he? And if he did, if he got out, would that make everything okay? Would that mean he could suddenly see clearly, suddenly recognise where he was?

His breath speeding up, his heart hammering under his breastbone, he put his foot down again and drove past more houses, their front gardens nodding cheerfully bright, full of flowers and stripy green grass. No one was on the pavements now, no one walked the streets. Ahead of him, the traffic had thinned and only a single light-blue Volkswagen scurried over the tarmac like a scarab beetle.

He rooted in his pocket for his phone, and as he was about to thumb it on saw, again, a fleeting glimpse of something he recognised. But that was the entrance to the crematorium, unmistakeable between its archway of stone pillars, hanging lantern suspended between them on a trellis of wrought iron. The crematorium! No, he *really* didn't want to go there! But that meant...

A U-turn at the bottom of the hill, back up the road which led into the centre of town—how could he have come this far already? A soft sob of panic escaped him as he looked out of the back window and saw nothing but fog behind. Tendrils of the stuff began to spill into the narrow lane in front of him. The road cut through high banks of trees here, their broad limbs stretching from one side of the road to the other, making a tunnel of leaves. He thought he could hear the whispering as they tossed above him in a breeze that he couldn't feel.

He couldn't get out here. It was miles from town. Miles to walk, away from any other living person, beneath the shade of ancient trees. No. Even though he hated the car with a growing monstrous resentment, the thought of stepping out of it into the wilderness, alone, was worse than going on.

Up the hill and a little to the right, there would be a right turn which would take him past the church. He tried to moisten his dry mouth, tried to stop his racing breath from turning into sobs, and put his foot down. Mist rushed up the grill of the car and tore in ribbons across the windscreen, and he knew he would miss the turn—knew it for every one of the ten minutes it took to get there, for every one of the twenty minutes afterwards he spent turning, driving back, trying to spot it.

The ground levelled beneath him. The fog had come up all around, and the light dimmed to the point he could no longer pretend to be able to see. He stopped, waited for the crunch of traffic into his bumper, waited again, while the sound of bird song, or maybe pipes, came dimly through the shut windows.

His fingers shook so much he could scarcely punch in the number for Chris's phone. When the assured, cheerful voice answered him, terror almost stopped his throat, left him as dumb as the water effigy of Geoff Baxendale—the warning of what he might become. "The person you have called is not available. Please leave a message after the tone."

"Fuck you!" So that was why poltergeists began with cursing? Because the cry of distress was the only human language left to them.

"Fuck you! Damn you to hell, Chris. What the fuck are you doing? Oh please!"

The stationary car trembled as something moved outside, invisible in the fog. So white were the windows that he felt the whole world had been destroyed—the universe had been destroyed—and only he remained, trapped and alone, something monstrous moving out there like a shark beneath still water. He'd thought he'd been coping well until he opened his mouth again and what came out was a high-pitched whimper, and then a sob. "I'm lost.

"There was a thing at the office. It was going for a... It was going for a customer. I had to use the vial—the water—to get rid of it. I thought I'd run to the Red Lion, but now I don't know where I am. There's nothing outside the car. It's all just white. I'm s-scared, Chris. I don't know what to do."

The car trembled beneath Ben, and then with a squeal and shriek of tortured metal, a set of five claw marks opened on the car's bonnet, furrows of shiny silver turning over, the scores beneath them running up the polished surface like wounds, red paint flaking off and falling like blood. "Shit! There's something out there. Am I safe in here, Chris? It's iron, isn't it? They can't get me in here?"

But if they couldn't touch the car, then where the hell had those claw marks come from? It was probably nothing of the sort—probably fucking aluminium, about as protective as a layer of tinfoil. And he'd cleaned it—he'd damn well cleaned it inside only a week ago, leaving nothing on the seats or in the footwells he could use as a weapon.

A second row of claw marks joined the first. It ran up the bonnet, past the deepest point of the first and carried on. Something hooked itself beneath the windscreen and tugged. The car bounced, the windscreen shattered with a boom into millions of tiny squares, and Ben gasped as if he had been punched, grabbed the door handle. "Chris! Chris, where the fucking hell are you? You promised not to let this happen to me. You promised!"

Yes, but making Chris feel like shit when he finally picked up was not going to help him right now. Whatever it was out there, it could take the car apart to get at him, so long as he was still in here. But what if he could lose it out in the fog?

It was a shit plan, he knew that, but he flung open his door and bolted out into the milky-white nothingness nevertheless, the phone held like a dagger in his hand.

Grass underfoot, heavy with dew. There was a sound of water, and the sweet, piping music that never grew stronger, that fell away eternally half-grasped, poisonous with yearning. Something darker ahead, a shape in the fog, swelled up like the prow of a ship. The mist was cold on his cheek, and as he stepped forward, he smelled again that stench of the deep earth, the choking, wet, inorganic stench that had dogged him ever since the bomb.

He recoiled, ancient panic adding to his present terror, and saw standing stones to the side and behind him. Ahead, they marched half fallen, half drunkenly leaning, covered in lichen up the slope of a green hill. He stood at its base, and just before his feet a hole had begun to crumble open in the side of it, letting out that chthonic reek, that outflowing of the eternal dark.

He knew he was meant to go in. Under the earth again. And just at the thought of it, he could almost feel soil falling on his face, on his open eyes, filling up his mouth. "No!"

He turned and ran, and a hand made up entirely of knives seized his ankles as in a vise, pulling his feet out from under him. Hitting the ground hard, he scrabbled for purchase. "No. Chris. Help me! Help me. No!"

But even when he dropped the phone and dug both hands into the turf until they bled, he couldn't stop it dragging him inexorably under the hill.

About the Author

Alex Beecroft was born in Northern Ireland during the Troubles and grew up in the wild countryside of the Peak District. She studied English and Philosophy before accepting employment with the Crown Court where she worked for a number of years. Now a stay-at-home mum and full-time author, Alex lives with her husband and two children in a little village near Cambridge and tries to avoid being mistaken for a tourist.

Alex is only intermittently present in the real world. She has lead a Saxon shield wall into battle, toiled as a Georgian kitchen maid, and recently taken up an 800-year-old form of English folk dance, but she still hasn't learned to operate a mobile phone.

You can find me in many places, but chiefly at my website http://alexbeecroft.com.

Fight a fire-breathing dragon with a wooden airplane?
It'll take a madman...

Dogfighters

© 2012 Alex Beecroft

Under the Hill, Part 2

Kidnapped by the faerie queen, Ben is confronted with his own supernatural heritage, a royal family and a lover he doesn't remember. His first instinct is to turn his back on them all and get back to Earth. Compared to this, Chris and his wacky cohorts seem almost...normal.

Back on Earth, Chris Gatrell is having trouble convincing the police that he didn't do away with Ben and hide the body. Determined not to lose another sweetheart to the elves' treachery, he presses his motley crew of ghost hunters to steal a Mosquito bomber...and prays the ghosts of his WWII crew will carry them through the portal to Ben's rescue.

Meanwhile, Chris's elf-trapped WWII love, Geoff, has a dragon and he's not afraid to use it. If only he could be entirely sure which of the elf queens is the real enemy—the one whose army is poised to take back planet Earth for elf-kind.

In the cataclysmic battle to come, more than one lover—human and elf alike—may be forced to make the ultimate sacrifice.

Warning: Dragons dogfighting with fighter planes, time travellers and reincarnated celestial beings are all very exciting, but have your hankies ready for a bittersweet ending.

Available now in ebook and print from Samhain Publishing.

Always have an ace up your sleeve.

Coyote's Creed
© *2011 Vaughn R. Demont*
Broken Mirrors, Book 1

If con games were taught in high school, Spencer Crain would be on the honor roll. As it is, he'll be riding the edge of failure to graduation next month. Then Spence gets the news that his long-gone father is not only dead, but was a Coyote, one of three clans of tricksters in the City.

With a near-catatonic mother on his hands, Spence couldn't care less about the Coyotes' ongoing feud with the Phouka and the Kitsune—until it lands on his doorstep. Suddenly he's thrown headfirst into a dangerous world he knows next-to-nothing about. His only guide is Rourke, dashing King of the Phouka, plus a growing pack of half-siblings, a god, and Fate herself.

As Spence embarks on a journey to learn the Coyote's creed, the truth about his heritage, and how to handle his growing attraction to Rourke, he wonders when his life turned from TV sitcom to real-life danger zone. And what price must he pay to survive the next roll of the dice...

Warning: Contains PG-13 rated violence, R-rated language and X-rated hotel scenes. Meta-humor, pop-culture humor, utter disregard for the 4th wall abound.

Available now in ebook and print from Samhain Publishing.

www.samhainpublishing.com

Green for the planet.
Great for your wallet.

It's all about the story...

Romance

HORROR

www.samhainpublishing.com

CPSIA information can be obtained at www.ICGtesting.com
Printed in the USA
BVOW021425270313

316627BV00002B/114/P